Pages From an Immigrant's Diary

are ... kindnesses. All the best. Sudhir Jan. 24, 2013.

Sudhir Jain

outskirtspress
DENVER, COLORADO

Pages From An Immigrant's Diary
All Rights Reserved.
Copyright © 2013 Sudhir Jain
v2.0

Outskirts Press, Inc.
http://www.outskirtspress.com

ISBN: 978-1-4327-9810-9

Outskirts Press and the "OP" logo are trademarks belonging to Outskirts Press, Inc.

PRINTED IN THE UNITED STATES OF AMERICA

This is a work of creative non-fiction. The writer of the diary is not an individual but a composite of many of the author's acquaintances. Person and place names have been altered and actual events modified to protect their privacy.

The book is dedicated to Evelyn who has been a guiding light for most of my life.

Contents

* The first of this set of stories was published in The Story that Brought Me Here, Linda Goyette, Editor.

** A slightly abbreviated version was published in Calgary Herald.

*** First two essays were published in the Globe and Mail, Facts column after some abbreviation.

Acculturation

~ 1 ~

It was a farewell dinner for me. I was leaving Dehradun in the Himalayan Foothills for England on a two-year scholarship to learn how to explore for oil. The fact that England had no oil production and nowhere to explore and the University I was going to join had no experienced staff or equipment was beside the point. What mattered was that it was a First World country and we from Third World could always learn something from them. My mother was so upset at the thought of my departure that she had taken to her bed. I suggested to her that I had lived a thousand miles from her for the last six years. But it was not across the seven seas she argued. And it did not take three weeks on boat and cost several years' salary to travel. I had no answer but the die was cast. The boat was to depart from Bombay the next day and to get there I had to catch a train late that evening. Bhabiji, my sister-in-law, had cooked a super supper with all my favourite dishes and ordered all the sweets I loved from the best bakery in town. The table was croaking under the load of dishes heaped with food.

What with all the final touches to the packing, the continuous stream of visitors saying goodbye, nervousness about the first boat trip with not an acquaintance in sight, I was in no mood to have a big dinner. Still, it was Bhabiji's responsibility to make sure that I was fed enough to last at least the first half of my three week journey because it would take that long to get used to foreign food served on the boat.

In good times or bad, Bhabiji was always a persistent host; she insisted you had more helpings till you couldn't count. She couldn't bear the thought of not being to able to feed her kid brother-in-law for two years and as if to make up for it she was infused with a new determination. Apart from that, there was another consideration. There was no refrigerator in the house. It was still summer. The left over food would not last even for a day. She had worked much too hard to give it to the beggars; they won't appreciate it anyway. It had to be eaten and I had to eat it. No sooner did I make a dent on the mound on my plate, it was replenished with a new not-so-mouthwatering-now dish. This went on for two hours till the horse cart arrived to take me and my luggage to the station. She filled a cotton bag with sweets for me to eat on the long journey on the train. I had no choice. With as many bags in my two hands as I could carry, a heavy tin suitcase and a sleeping bag there was barely enough room for me on the cart. I had to pity the poor horse; I doubted it had ever pulled along so much weight before. On arrival at the station I gave extra tip to the driver with instructions to buy special feed for the horse. He accepted the tip graciously but I got the feeling that the words of a budding sahib were not taken seriously.

In due course, the boat arrived in Liverpool. My first order of priority was to find a place to stay. My landlady was a kindly middle-aged woman with a dour husband and four rambunctious children. She told me when showing me the room that she served her students, three in all, breakfast at eight and dinner at six. She expected that we were dressed decently for dinner to set a good example to her children.

What she meant by decently is not clear to me to this day. The University was within a walking distance. After locating my department, I hastily returned to my new home without seeing anybody there fearing the consequences of being not dressed decently. Or worse, being late.

The meal was superb, an improvement on that served on the boat. It could be that by now I was developing a taste for meat, having been a strict vegetarian all my life. Due to my inborn respect for my religious edicts, I am still a strict vegetarian but only when I am in India. The edicts were not intended for foreign consumption, I console myself. The chicken broth was followed by shepherds' pie with carrots. Then came the piece d'resistance of the landlady – chocolate cake baked the same afternoon.

She carefully cut a good size wedge for each person around the table and every one enjoyed it with appropriate expressions of enjoyment. I was greedily eyeing about a quarter of the cake still left on the serving dish when the generous host asked if any one would like the second helping. The dinners with Bhabhiji flashed before my eyes and I graciously declined fully expecting her to insist that I had some more and serving some on my plate over my vehement protests. Alas! This was not to be. She whisked the dish away. Unlike my dear Bhabhiji, she had a refrigerator to keep it fresh for ever.

I learnt my lesson. Now I ask for a second helping whether I need it or not.

~ 2 ~

During the summer holidays I got a job as an assistant helper in the city's utility department. I was one of a crew of four; supervisor, operator, helper and an assistant helper. I was told that there was no formal training involved, I would learn on the job. It was fine with me; learning is what I was in that great country for.

The shift started at 9:00. I was at the workshop at 8:45. The helper arrived at nine, the operator a few minutes later and supervisor at 9:29. He got a work order from the "boss", herded us in a truck and drove to our first job of the day. A street lamp had died and our crew was ordered to change the bulb. The supervisor drove well within the speed limit, waved pleasantly to other drivers, slowed down as we approached a traffic light to make sure it turned red before he got there and took his time before starting again when the light turned green. He smoked an unfiltered Pall Mall all the way and blew the smoke in the truck with relaxed air that justified his station as the supervisor. Others got the enjoyment of smoke without wasting their cigarettes. Being the only nonsmoker in the crew I breathed as little as possible without choking to death.

We got to our destination in about half an hour. Considering we were only a kilometer away from the workshop, it was a compliment to the driver's ability to stay within the union rules for driving a city vehicle. When we got there I jumped out of the truck and took several deep breaths before starting to get the equipment out. But my rush upset the supervisor. "Why are you in such a hurry? Get the tea going first," he shouted.

I went back into the truck and found a camp stove, a kettle, a water can, milk, sugar and tea. I got the stove going, filled the kettle with water and put it on the stove. Other crew members stood in a circle smoking their Pall Malls and discussing the football match of previous Saturday. The women who happened to come within the earshot got complimentary remarks on their comeliness with only a few responding to them. In due course the tea was ready. I went back into truck and found the mugs. We leisurely sipped our tea, my colleagues still discussing the finer points of the game which were beyond my comprehension. It can take a while to finish a mug of tea, particularly when you have to dissect something more important than many a surgical operations being done in the hospital across the street. At last, the tea was drunk just as the consensus was reached on the game. Now the operator asked, nay ordered, me to get the ladder and set it up. He checked it, grunted satisfaction and climbed up while the helper held it firmly in place. He unscrewed the lamp shade and brought it down. He gave it to the helper who placed it carefully in the truck. In the meantime the operator lighted his cigarette and we stood around watching the passers by hurrying to attend to whatever business was at hand till the operator took the last puff and nonchalantly threw the stub on the road. Once again he climbed up, unscrewed the bulb and came down gingerly holding the bulb in one hand. He had a chat with a passer-by about the lousy weather we were having. Once every one had agreed that it indeed had been an awful summer, he asked the helper to get a new bulb from the truck. It took a while to find the right bulb. When he returned, the operator took the bulb, thought for a moment whether he should light another cigarette, decided against it, climbed up, screwed it in and came down. The tough part of the job done at last, he lit another Pall Mall and opened the discussion on next Saturday's game. The supervisor ordered me to make more tea. The debate on the relative strengths of the two teams continued as long as the tea lasted. Then I was ordered to wash the mugs while the helper got the lamp shade and passed it to the operator. The operator climbed on the ladder and screwed it in place. He came down, ordered the helper to put the ladder in the truck and asked the boss what was next. Supervisor looked at his watch and exclaimed, "Blimey, time sure goes fast when you are working hard. We will barely make it back to workshop in time for lunch. Hurry up Paki, put your things in the truck. We got to get going."

The union rules were forgotten on the way back. The supervisor rushed across when the lights turned orange and fidgeted when they were red. His puffs were hurried and comments on slow drivers in front rather rude. We made it back to the workshop in barely five minutes. Bells in the clock tower were announcing noon as we got out of the truck feeling content with a job well done. The "boss" welcomed us as long lost friends and asked the supervisor how the new assistant was. "This Paki is a quick learner, will soon be supervising a crew of his own, he will," replied the supervisor. They both shared a loud laughter which still resounds in this Paki's ears after more than forty years.

~ 3 ~

In my second year I moved to an international students' residence with sixty students from all over the world, including a few from the nearby towns. A pretty English girl barely out of her teens had recently moved into the residence and we had exchanged polite greetings a couple of times. This intimacy flattered me no end. To impress her with my importance, I invited my research supervisor Dr. Block, an internationally renowned geologist and his wife for dinner at the residence and asked her to join us. The dinner was a simple affair you would expect where you paid four pounds a week for room and three full meals a day. However, the guests seemed to enjoy it. The revered Dr. Block was in a voluble mood, telling us tales of his upbringing in Persia as the only son of an executive of the Anglo Iranian Oil Company and of his struggles to adjust to the British customs when he returned to his parents' roots. I was quite pleased with myself, not having learnt how good the upper classes in Britain were at pretending. In any event, the focus of my existence in those days was impressed. What more could I wish for?

A month later, an engraved card arrived in the mail inviting me and my 'friend' to a dinner at the Block residence. She was impressed by the address and agreed to be my friend for the evening. We dressed carefully, she in a tight mini dress as was the style of the day and I in my only suit which was quite snug around the waist. We planned to be fashionably late by fifteen minutes but thanks to the vagaries of the bus service, it was almost an hour after due time when we crossed the well-tended grounds and rang the door bell of the Georgian home. We were ushered into a large room where ten of my fellow graduate students and their partners, for the evening at least, were sitting cross-legged on a large oriental carpet around huge trays of Persian delicacies. Indian and Persian culinary arts have developed in tandem and the dishes were familiar to me. There were mouth watering samosas, pakoras of three different kinds, meat balls, chutneys galore and a jug of mango sherbet; A feast for the eyes as well as for the palate. Guests huddled closer to make room for us. We wondered whether our waist bands would stand sitting on the floor but not much could be done. After all, the others had managed it. My friend hitched her dress up as much as it would go and slid down. I silently prayed the buttons of my suit would hold for the evening. However, dress and pants were soon forgotten as the delicacies were loaded on the plates and then transferred past our delighted taste buds to the constricted spaces. We met strange looks when we expressed our admiration for the dinner as the dishes were taken away. We soon found out why.

After a few minutes of literate discussion about the poetry of Omar Khayyam and the Sufi philosophy, the host disappeared into the kitchen and his wife regaled us with the excuses invented by Persian nobles to visit them for a taste of his curries. I was about to ask when will we be honored with these wonderful dishes when Dr. Block entered the room followed by the maid pushing a trolley. A couple of students tried to get up but he imperially waved them to stay where they were. He placed a huge brass dish of chicken biryani in the middle and four big copper bowls of steaming curries around it. There was enough food for fifty starving teenage boys, leave alone twenty weight conscious adults already stuffed with what was clearly intended as the appetizers. My mouth fell wide open in amazement even though my waist band was digging deep in my belly. It wasn't long before the mound of food on my plate was touching the ceiling.

It was a short hour before every one belched in true Persian style and the food was cleared away. The discussion now moved to the eating habits of different classes; how upper classes tasted delicately and lower classes shoveled hurriedly as if there was no tomorrow. Every one looked at me when the later point was made. I was much too happy to mind this slight. My friend was looking more and more inviting in her revealing dress that crept higher every time I looked at her.

No sooner had the conversation flagged a little, baklava and espresso magically appeared. Dainty china cups and the elegantly crafted silver coffee jug sat in the middle while a tray of six varieties of baklava loaded with honey and pistachio powder was passed around. It became clear, to me at least, that I was the only one there who had a full appreciation for the heavenly blend of these super sweet cakes and the bitter coffee when I observed that no one else took more than one piece while I took a couple of each kind. Again, the guests looked at me curiously but doing justice to the offering was more important than the good manners of upper classes.

The conversation over coffee turned to opera and the classical music. It was a world I had never visited. Being in the state of soporific stupor induced by my indulgence, I found it hard to go there now and notwithstanding several cups of the strongest coffee I had ever tasted, with or without the dessert of the gods, I dropped into the dream world instead. This had an unfortunate consequence.

When charming Mrs. Block shook me awake late in the evening, every other guest was gone, including my friend. I rubbed my eyes, thanked the hostess, probably in my mother tongue, and staggered to the bus stop. My friend never forgave me the transgression of the etiquette of her culture and I have lived my life regretting that evening.

~ 4 ~

I completed my doctorate, found a job in the oil industry and married Monica, a fine young lady. The company decided to send us to Libya for a long foreign assignment. We left London on a cold wet day in February and arrived in sunny Rome to pick up our work visa from the Libyan Embassy there. The company had engaged an agent, Guido, to secure the visa and to look after us when we were in Rome. His fee included a percentage of costs incurred by him in securing the papers and on our hotel and meals. Therefore he made sure that we were booked in the most elegant hotel in Rome. If I remember it right, the hotel was called Excelsior where the glitterati stayed when The Grand was full. However, Rome is not an attractive destination in winter and the hotel was practically empty. We had a room large enough for the entourage of a star and a bed that could accommodate several couples if they were that way inclined.

The dining room of the hotel was designed for several hundred diners. When we went down there for breakfast on our first morning, every table was beautifully set but there were no takers. The absence of clientele did not seem to bother the imperturbable maitre d'hotel who led us to a table by the window with a view of Via Veneto. Another elegantly dressed waiter arrived to serve us coffee and yet another to take our order. Just to be safe, we ordered "English Breakfast" consisting of fried eggs, bacon and toast. Looking at the smartly dressed staff, we felt a little embarrassed, dressed as we were rather humbly as suited our limited means. The waiters were not concerned, however, safe in the knowledge that a hefty service charge was added to the bill before they presented it to us. The Italian chef did a good job with eggs and bacon and we were quite content to have all our meals in the hotel. This also conserved our limited cash reserves.

Although we were supposedly on business, we really had nothing to do except wait for Guido to appear with the visa. Guido was a short round man with a big bald head and short legs. His walk reminded me of a huge rolling ball. He spoke good English with a unique way of accentuating the vowels. He was a pleasant man who liked to talk and told us funny stories about American tourists. He had coffee with us every morning at ten sharp to tell us about all the people he was going to see in the embassy to push our applications forward. He gave directions to the tourist sights for us to visit during the day and the best means of transportation. He confided that Cannelloni served in the hotel was almost as good as his mother used to make and he ordered it whenever he ate there. But he was most emphatic on another dish – Crepes Suzette. He said that although it was a French dessert, our hotel excelled in it and we would regret for ever if we didn't try it at least once.

At lunch time we found Crepes Suzette listed in the pride of place in the dessert menu. It had to be ordered for two and was by far the most expensive item on the whole menu. We felt that a dish costing one thousand and seventy five Liras had to be substantial and to do it justice we should have it in place of the main course. The waiter tried to persuade us to supplement it with some pasta. But we stuck to our guns. The undiluted enjoyment of the famous crepes and our determination to do justice to Madame Suzette demanded no less.

The waiters were also intent on enhancing our enjoyment by taking their time. I had already consumed three glasses of dry sherry when a waiter in bright white overalls arrived pushing a trolley with a small camp stove in the centre, several containers of various exotic ingredients, presumably needed for the crepes, and a dozen liquor bottles balanced precariously at the edge. The waiter greeted us, lighted the gas stove and under our watchful eyes proceeded to prepare the crepes. While they were cooking, he poured carefully measured amounts of liquors in a certain order on the crepes. The colors of flames from the burning alcohol were something to behold. When the crepes had acquired the desired hue, he turned off the gas and placed one crepe on each of the two large plates and then drenched it with a liberal quantity of orange liquor. What with the heat from the stove and all the hard work in cooking, the chef cum waiter was sweating by now. He took out a shiny white handkerchief whose tip was projecting from the breast pocket of his overall and wiped his brow with great delicacy. This was the last act of the performance and deserved an ovation it didn't get. The tough job over, he smiled as he placed his creation in front of Monica and me. We saw the plates and almost died. Not having gone to Heaven we looked at each other in consternation. Great minds think alike and for a moment our minds were great. "This small crepe floating in liquor may get us drunk, it is never going to save us from starvation" we both thought. We managed to thank the waiter before making short work of his long labor. Monica was much too circumspect but I managed to surreptitiously lick the plate clean of all the wonderful liquor.

After signing the bill, we agreed that our best course was to cross the street to a stall selling hamburgers to American tourists on a tight budget. When greedily biting into my bun I noticed the waiter trying not to look at me from the dining room window. He must have succeeded in his attempt because he showed no sign of contempt when he served dinner in the evening.

~ 5 ~

Our visa eventually arrived and we settled comfortably in the routine of the expatriate life of Libya. Among sixty people working under my charge ten were expatriates, mostly from England. These ten did more work than the other fifty and caused more problems too. In fact, just one of them shouldered the latter burden with the greatest ease.

Charles was a tall, wiry, handsome man in his thirties. He had left England in haste, having promised several ladies to marry them and a number of publicans to pay their due by the end of the month. I do not know which of the two problems was bigger. Neither had been resolved but from that distance it didn't bother him unduly. There was too much fun to be had in this Mediterranean paradise. He was a great hit with the wives of other expatriates. He made full use of this popularity. The husbands were away in the desert for two weeks out of three and he could carry on three clandestine affairs at any time without facing a husband. The bar owners were never a bother; there weren't any. However, there was no shortage of booze, the homemade variety. Charles was too lazy to ferment his own but he chose his amours from among the better brewers. He could enjoy the wives while getting drunk in the process. Life couldn't be better. Not for Charles, not for the pining wives of my desert crew.

One day it came to an end. All good things do. Not that it was too good to last. Nothing ever was too good for Charles, not in his opinion any way. The end was completely unforeseen and amusing to many who envied his success with the fair ladies. No, a husband did not return unexpected. There was no way one could. Charles was in charge of flight operations and he knew who was taking off and who was landing. He was at the airport to make sure his victims left and arrived according to their wives' convenience. It was a lamp post, yes a lamp post, that was his undoing.

Charles was driving home drunk one early morning. I don't blame him. It was the season to be jolly and his mate for the evening was rather frisky. It took longer than usual to calm her down and in the process more hooch was consumed than normal. He had to leave before it was advisable to get behind the wheel because he had to be at the airport at an ungodly hour. His satiated partner reminded him to be careful as she turned over in her sleep. He drove slowly along the coast road watching for stray dogs that like to sleep on the warm tarmac on cold nights. When he saw an oncoming vehicle, he got off to the sand embankment rather than play chicken as he would have done if he were sober.

The defensive driving contributed to his downfall. A truck was hurtling towards him with its headlights aimed at his eyes. Very sensibly he got off the road. No sooner had he hit the sand he saw a dog walking lazily towards just where he was headed. All he could do was to steer to the right. His car struck a barrier and came to a halt. He had hit a lamp post.

It was not his lucky day. Any other time, he would have backed down and driven off and nobody would be any wiser. But not this time. As he put the car in reverse, the screaming horn from behind made the heart jump out of his mouth. It was a police car with two burly Arab officers. They came out of their cruiser and ordered him to produce his papers. The papers were all in order but his breath was not. They took out the hand cuffs. Charles was alarmed, nay shocked.

"Look, all I did was I hit a lamp post. It is not as if I killed a man or something," he said with an expatriate's bravado.

"You kill a man, thousands of men. You hit a lamp post, only one lamp post," officers replied in unison.

Charles had no answer. He spent a week in jail. I managed to get him out of the country before the trial and sent him home to face his women and barmen. Which I am sure he did with typical aplomb.

~ 6 ~

After five years in Libya, we moved to Dallas, Texas. We now had two daughters who were four and two years old. It was a hot morning on Sunday before Christmas, mercury touching the levels not seen since the hottest day in the summer. We packed the lunch – peanut butter sandwiches and apple juice for the girls and cold turkey salad with a flask of tea for ourselves, bundled the kids on the back seat and hopped into our newly acquired ancient model of tiny Ford Pinto to go for a picnic. Monica was soon singing seasonal songs like "I'm dreaming of a white Christmas," "It's a season to be jolly" and some hymns extolling the virtue of sharing with others less fortunate than us. The girls were joining with gusto in the fun. I had to watch the road but one could judge the tempo of the songs from the speed of the car. Suddenly, everything came to a halt with a bang.

Yes, a big bang that made the driver of the car in front jump out, rush to the back, look at the dented trunk of his Cadillac while paying no attention to the folded hood of my humble Pinto and start screaming obscenities to no one in particular. He was a Texas-sized man, dressed in his Sunday best with a ten gallon hat firmly on his head, no doubt on his way to the church for the Christmas service. I turned the engine off and got out of the car sheepishly while the other three members sat quietly like mice hiding from a cat. The other driver was completely out of control. He was yelling to the gathering crowd, "This stupid idiot has crashed into my new Caddy when I was innocently driving to church to pray for world peace and prosperity for all. Not only will I be late for the service, I will not have transportation till the car is fixed. I will have to take a cab to all the parties till New Year's." If it occurred to him that he could now imbibe countless number of glasses of his favorite bourbon at hosts' expense he did not show it. His wife, who was giving final touches to her make up when she felt the jolt, finished it to her satisfaction before joining her husband. She started competing with him in the loudness of her own complaints. I had never been in an accident in my new country and didn't know what to do. Traffic was building up behind us. Horns were blaring and the crowd was getting bigger to such an extent that the attendance in the neighborhood churches must have shrunk on the very morning they could be certain to attract the largest crowds of the year. For most people the fun of watching a two-meter Christian in his full regalia squaring off with a tiny Hindu dressed to play in the sandbox with his kids was too much to pass up for the vicar's harangue about the Christmas spirit. I was standing their helplessly staring at the point where the two cars had tried to unite and absorbing the litany of accusations being hurled at me. My attempts to make them aware of my ignorance on what was to be done were to no avail. I was becoming scared of the Texan family; their three teenage children had now joined them as well. My family, on the other hand, tactfully stayed in the car.

After a while the people started drifting away rather disappointed by the one-sided battle. Then out of the blue, the frustrated lady in the full make up, not able to stand my silence any longer, grabbed me by the collar and shook me vigorously to instill some sense in me. Her long beautifully trimmed and perfectly polished nails drew blood, only a trickle though. Just then a police van came by with sirens bellowing even louder than the aggrieved family. The policeman saw my white collar turning red as a result of the Texan treatment being meted out by the matriarch and firmly advised her to take her hands off me. He then asked the drivers what had happened. The loudmouth had nothing to say other than a fool had bumped him from behind when he was slowing down to turn left to go to the church. I had nothing more to say than I was listening to the chorus of "O Come all ye, faithful" from the back seat. However, the crowd was not entirely with their fellow countryman and there must have been some pity for the bleeding foreigner in his tiny jalopy. A voice in the crowd pointed out the 'NO LEFT TURN' sign to the cop to the utter dismay of the mad driver. He stammered something like "Bbb But he.. should..have..seen..me." The policeman was not impressed. The widening red patch on white shirt coupled with attempted left turn when it was not allowed had won him over to the side of the dumbstruck little man. He demanded the driving license from the Texan, took his pad out and issued a ticket for reckless driving. He told me to be more careful in future and gave me the necessary paper to get the car fixed.

No one was hurt in either car and the damage was not as bad as it looked. God is kind after all, especially when you are singing his virtue at the time misfortune strikes. I got the car fixed at my own cost because it was important to build a no-claim record. It made a dent in our saving and delayed our buying a home, not to mention my feeling that I looked foolish in the eyes of the family members. Good wife was forgiving as always. Now grown up kids, on the other hand, still remind me of it when I complain about speeding tickets they collect with total equanimity.

~ 7 ~

The major opera houses on this continent rarely present late 20th century works. There are several advantages in only doing the established works the audience is familiar with. They can attract the top stars of the opera firmament, minimal publicity fills the hall and the audience does not need to be educated about the work to be performed. Calgary Opera has taken a different tack. The General Manager believes that if the current works are not presented to the audience the art form will die. Therefore, every season the Calgary audiences are presented a new work not seen before. Calgary Opera does an excellent job of bringing such operas on stage, particularly considering the limited resources of an organization that presents only three operas in a year. In view of Calgary's reputation as a cow town and grudging support among the citizenry for cultural events, success of the opera has been nothing short of astounding. The credit for this goes to the events opera organizes to generate interest in the performance as well as to inform the public. They really pull out all stops when staging North American operas.

La Fanciulla del West, one of the operas last season, was related to the settling of the Wild West in the nineteenth century. In addition to a series of seminars spread over a week, the opera advertised an evening of 'spaghetti western.' Monica had felt for a while that we had not been very social of late and she decided that this would be a great event to invite some friends. We could all enjoy spaghetti dinner and the entertainment that goes with it. The tickets were cheap and if we car pooled the whole evening would not cost more than a hundred dollars for three couples. You could not ask for better value if you enjoyed Italian food and romantic singing by the members of a professional cast.

After some discussion we invited Rosa and Tom Green and Flo and Al Noseworthy to join us for the evening. Our guests lived on the same street and we suggested that they rode together because the parking at the auditorium can be tight, not to mention expensive. The function started at seven and we decided to meet in the lobby half an hour earlier to give us time to exchange notes on recent events in our lives – in other words brag about the great things our kids were doing and how our grandchildren were doing calculus at the age many kids can't count or were reading Shakespeare when their class mates could barely read at all. Just as well we all have smart families. May be that is why we are still friends after what feels like eons.

We dressed smartly; after all it was an opera event. Monica wore a long black skirt with white blouse and I put on my dark suit with pale blue shirt and a red tie. We got there soon after six to make sure that the guests did not have to wait. As most couples who have been married for two score and ten years we did not have much to say to each other. So the half hour till the arrival of the guests felt like a whole evening. However, our friends were in great form and we were laughing our hearts out while sipping the drink which was included in the ticket price. We must have been really enjoying the company because none of us noticed that there were no tables set where spaghetti could be served. By seven o'clock the lobby was quite crowded and the six of us were stepping on each other's toes. Ushers now started to hustle the crowd towards the auditorium. Once inside we saw a huge screen on the stage but nothing which could remotely relate to spaghetti or any other dinner. We were all rather hungry and looking forward to our spaghetti. Our guests were, of course, circumspect and followed us closely. Monica now decided to take charge and asked an usher when and how the spaghetti dinner was to be served. He looked at her blankly and we knew that something was wrong. Monica is a quick thinker, especially when she is on her feet. She instructed us to make our way back to the lobby where she wanted to talk to us.

Our conversation was short and to the point. If there was to be a dinner it would be after the show and we could not enjoy the performance with our stomachs protesting as loudly as they were. Monica is also a decision maker and she told us what we were going to do. We were going to an Italian restaurant a few blocks away which regularly made the illustrious 'Where to eat in Canada' list. She checked on her cell to make sure they had a table for six, gave Al detailed instructions on how to get there and in fifteen minutes we were ordering drinks and examining the extensive menu.

We had an excellent dinner. No one had spaghetti because there were so many more delectable options available. Wine flowed freely and conversation matched the dinner in quality and quantity. It was after ten when we finished our liqueurs and no one was in a mood to return to the auditorium. I signed my visa bill without daring to look at it, apologized to the guests for the confusion and we headed home.

I called the General Manager of the opera next morning to clarify the confusion. His laughter will ring in my ears for next hundred years. In between the guffaws he told me that spaghetti western is a movie on a cowboy theme made in Italy in fifties and sixties with cheap actors on miniscule budgets. Clint Eastwood got his start in these movies and after he became famous his early Italian films revived the whole genre on this continent. Spaghetti western at the opera was the screening of one of these movies. He did tell me the name but my mind had switched off by then.

When I got home I told Monica the reason of our confusion. We had a good laugh and did not think of it again till I opened the visa statement a few weeks later.

~ 8 ~

After our youngest daughter flew the coop, Monica and I felt rather lonely, particularly at the weekends. This problem never arose for our parents in our home country; there were any number of cousins, nephews, nieces who would visit at all hours of the day with their problems, sometimes job related at other times romantic which they could not discuss with their parents. But we were here in Canada where no one visits unless invited with great ceremony weeks in advance. One Saturday I was feeling particularly downhearted. I asked my mate of a quarter century, "Do you know what the locals in our situation do to keep depression at bay?" It was indeed a sixty four thousand dollar question because that is what the answer cost us. Monica, whom my mother called Saraswati after Hindu goddess of wisdom, had already looked into the matter and had the answer ready, "Younger ones go to the mall, older ones go to the cabin. They have plenty of odd jobs to occupy them there and they don't miss the company. If we don't want to die of boredom before our time, a cabin is what we need."

Well, I did not want to die then any more than I do now. May be of old age a hundred years from now, but not of boredom; not then, not ever. So the hunt began. We wanted our cabin to be within easy driving distance, as different in character as possible from our comfortable home in the heart of the city and with minimum maintenance requirement in money, if not effort. Our search took us to the lakes, mountains, prairies and creeks. It is not that we did not find any decent cabin; it is just that it would have cost all our savings and then some to acquire any of them. We were ready to give up and look for something else to occupy ourselves when a sign, "For sale, one acre of forest, price reduced" popped up on our way back from a yet another fruitless search for the elusive cabin. We followed the directions and came to the sign "Summer Village of Wayforus, No Facilities." We turned right on a narrow road and arrived at what was indeed a forest of spruce and aspen that had been divided into one acre lots. The lot on sale sloped to the west and from the eastern end one could glimpse the mountains through the trees. A creek could be heard if you cupped your ears. There were several stacks of wood which were probably too old to give much heat indicating that the place had not been used for a while. Several dead trees of both varieties were leaning dangerously waiting for a strong wind to uproot them. There was a clearing in the centre of the lot. In the clearing stood what I said was a log house. "Log cabin, not log house" corrected Monica. It was about 25 feet across and 20 feet deep and seemed to be in a reasonable condition.

A call to the phone number on the sale sign set the time for the second visit. The realtor was a short, stout man with black hair and carried a search light. "I am Sam Yokomoto. It is my great pleasure to meet such a fine couple," he introduced himself in the hearty voice of a successful realtor while vigorously shaking our hands. We told him our names which he noted down in a diary. "You know that there is no electricity, water, gas or telephone line here," he told us nonchalantly as if it was an irrelevant detail. He opened the door, not much bigger than most windows, switched on the search light and stooped to enter the cabin. We followed him in to what felt like a dark dungeon. Our host opened three wooden windows, one on each side in front of us and we saw a room about twice the length and width of a normal room. We had to walk carefully, the supporting beams were the height of our forehead and we soon discovered that bumping into them was not a pleasant experience. There was nothing in the cabin except the dust accumulated over a long period on every surface. Sam told us that the owner was an old lady who had built it with her own hands fifty years ago for her use. She was short, barely five feet in her high heels, and saw no advantage in incurring the cost of placing beams a little higher to allow the clearance of more than a fraction of an inch over her hair. That also explained the shortness of the makeshift door. She was now living in a retirement home and needed to sell the property to pay her upkeep.

It did not take long to negotiate the final price and we were the owners of the cabin and a thousand alive and dead spruce trees before the month was over. We hired a young man to install a woodstove, do some essential repairs, build an outdoor fire pit and fix the outdoor toilets and the clearing for the car to the cabin. I took over the responsibility to clear the dead trees. It needed just one failed attempt to cut off a branch with a hand saw for me to realize that the job needed a chain saw. All I knew about chain saws was that they were dangerous and needed great care in handling. I undertook a careful search on the internet, noted recommendations of the bloggers, inspected several models and grilled the salesmen about their safety and maintenance needs. By the end of the week the most expensive chain saw ever built was in the trunk of the car along with safety gloves, apron, goggles and the right fuel. As soon as we got to the lot, I poured the gasoline in the tank, donned the safety gear, found a tree needing to be chopped and started the chain saw. The noise from the machine bothered Monica and scared the birds for several miles. But it did not worry me. I steadied my feet and put the metal to the wood. Sparks flew as the chain saw bounced a little out of control. As luck would have it Monica was watching my progress, or the lack of it. The bouncing saw and the sparks scared her out of her wits. "Stop, stop" she screamed. I followed her orders as any novice trying to learn a dangerous trade would. But a few seconds of observing her husband was enough for my good wife to make up her mind. She ordered me to put the saw away and never touch it again. Like any loving husband, I took her words to my heart and never thought of using it even in my wildest dream.

We spent many afternoons and a few odd nights in the cabin before the winter arrived. My friend from school days and his wife insisted on spending a week there. They fixed two water barrels, hung two hammocks outside and suspended hummingbird feeders from the lower branches of Aspen trees. We became more daring with each visit. So much so that on our last night of the year there, we dragged our bed out and watched the stars twinkle in a dark blue sky from a comfortable horizontal position till exhaustion won over excitement. The swarm of mosquitoes did not bother us but

SUDHIR JAIN

our sleep was interrupted nonetheless. A downpour had us
rushing inside the dark cabin. How we managed it in pitch
dark without getting drenched and our heads still in one piece
will always remain a mystery.

In spite of the ever-present fear of banging her head,
Monica enjoyed the cabin and furnished it such that it was
comfortable without being cluttered. I could not suppress the
urge to show it off and persuaded my better three-quarter to
invite some friends for a winter barbecue to inaugurate the fire
pit. For once Dame Fortune smiled on us and on the appointed
day, sky was blue, sun bright, gentle breeze not unpleasant and
temperature not high enough to melt the three inch thick layer
of snow on the ground. It turned out to be a fun afternoon
even though some cars skidded into the ditch and had to be
pushed out by younger and muscular members of the party.
The success of the event reached our daughters' ears and
prompted them to visit the cabin on the New Year's Day for
a picnic lunch. It was a miserable cold day, made worse when
they looked at the thermometer on the wall – the level of
mercury below heavy zero Fahrenheit line sent shivers down
their young and sturdy spines. The wood stove was lighted
and fortunately the fire was roaring within a few minutes.
However, the frozen heart of mercury was not moved by all
the shivering around it. After an hour of cursing the cold and
sipping tea or coffee from the flasks they noted that it was
indeed warmer - by five degrees. Young people these days are
not as patient as our generation, nor as hardy. They decided to
call it a day and had their picnic in the car on the way home. I
know their hands were not all that steady; cleaning the crumbs

from the seats of my car the next day was a tough job.

Monica met a young man in her Yoga class who had just moved to our city from a small village in the foothills and was feeling homesick. She told him about the cabin and invited him to use it if he wanted to. He jumped at the chance and visited it regularly. Although six feet tall, he did not seem to mind the low beams but he did look after the fallen trees, improved the toilets, fixed the fence and vastly improved the appearance of the property. Then he met a young lady who also loved rustic outdoors. They took to visiting the cabin and did whatever young people of different genders do these days when they are together. Before long they married; bought a property nearby and settled down to a life of pastoral bliss. We have our eyes open for another homesick young man from the boonies; there are several trees that need attention.

Other than the low beams, dusty floor was another problem, particularly because I banged my head harder when sweeping the floor. But it turned out to have an easy solution – two generous coats of paint carefully applied by Monica with a thick brush. Not only did the floor become dust free, it was easier to clean and the cabin became a little brighter. One improvement led to others. An architect friend devised a way to raise the beams. He also put two skylights on the roof, added a porch and replaced the old door by a new one of standard height. The cabin still kept it old charm but it became so much more inviting. Porch became our living room, with cooking facility, i.e. a propane camp stove, along the wall and a large table with comfortable chairs around it. We are so pleased with our cabin in the forest that we plan to spend next New Year's Day there. I somehow doubt that our daughters will join us even if we bribed them.

It took us ten years to get our cabin in shape. Not only did it help us in overcoming the separation from our daughters, it was an enjoyable journey towards integration with the host culture for this immigrant couple.

Down the Memory Lane

~ 1 ~

A lot happened to me during the first six years of nineteen sixties. I left India on a slow boat for England, got a post-graduate degree in geology, secured my first job, married a cute English girl and moved to North Africa with her. Monica and I spent five prime years of our lives in the Mediterranean port of Tripoli in the Kingdom, later the Arab Republic of Libya. It is a picturesque city sandwiched between the beautiful blue sea in the north and barren boundless Sahara desert to the south. My work in the Exploration department of a large American oil company was not strenuous and it was quite well paid. For the first time in our lives we felt affluent because what we could not afford did not stare at us from the store windows. The pace of life was slow and after the hectic time in England we felt an aura of peace had surrounded us. Still, all was not a smooth sailing. The reverie was interrupted, albeit for brief periods, on two occasions by world shattering events. Births of our daughters may have played a part in triggering both of them. One week before the due date of the first daughter, Israel attacked the Arab countries on its borders and caused a panic in our expatriate community. My employer ordered the evacuation of all spouses and children, pregnant Monica included. As a result, Geeta was born in far from ideal conditions in England and her father had an interminable wait to cuddle her till she arrived in Libya at the ripe old age of six weeks. Two and a half years later, a month before our second daughter Yamuna was due, junior officers in the fledgling

Libyan army replaced the King with the "Revolutionary Command Council" consisting of themselves. The result was a curfew which lasted several months. Fortunately, the baby was born by induction and the hospital visits and the birth could be arranged in permitted hours. In spite of these upheavals, and some minor inconveniences like having to move house a few times by government order and living through the wind storms that dumped on Tripoli all the sand the desert could spare, life there was relaxed and pleasant. The sun, sand and the sea provided excellent environment for Geeta and Yamuna and our international social circle and frequent vacations to exciting tourist destinations provided plenty of recreation. However, like all good things do, the happy expatriate life came to an end. Politics brought petroleum exploration to a halt and with heavy heart and some nervousness we decided to move.

We couldn't return to Monica's England or my India for several practical reasons. Therefore, we applied for visas to the United States and Canada with the intention of going to the country that granted us the papers first. I mailed the Canadian application to the nearest embassy in France and visited the US consulate in Tripoli. A friendly officer asked me to fill up some forms. He examined them in private and then interviewed me. I don't remember the details but do remember the consul as a kindly man not much older than me. His last words were, "You are a person of special merit, we need the people like you and the necessary papers would be in the mail within a few weeks."

The Green Card, permission for the family to live and work

in the Promised Land of America, duly arrived in a couple of months. About the same time, Canadian consulate invited the whole family, including three year old Geeta and one year old Yamuna, to an interview in Marseilles, France which the letter emphasized was no guarantee that the application would be approved. The divergent responses from the two countries left us only one option, America. Our American friends considered the decision to leave a good job and move to the New World with no job to go to daring in our presence and utterly foolish behind our backs. They knew that the oil industry back home was in a slump and the job prospects were dim. But I was young and brash and felt in my bones that my special skills would land me a job in no time. Monica was nervous but supportive. My employer and a number of other major oil companies had their exploration departments in Dallas, Texas. Both of us had spent some time there. We booked flights to that city with a three day stopover in Philadelphia to visit Monica's two uncles.

The uncles greeted us at the airport. The older brother was a widower in his sixties. His home was in a rundown part of Philadelphia which was fashionable when he had acquired the property thirty years before. The younger sibling was a bachelor in his fifties who lived in an apartment a few miles away in New Jersey. We stayed in Philadelphia because it was convenient for sight seeing. The uncles were gracious hosts. They treated us kindly. They escorted us to the Liberty Bell with its prominent crack, nation's founder Ben Franklin's home, Bertram's garden supposedly the first garden in America and the home of Betsy Ross who stitched the first flag and shared the family name with Monica. In the evening they regaled us with the family history Monica was not familiar with.

The largest company in aerial surveying was located in this 'City of Brotherly Love'. My postgraduate studies were vaguely related to this line of business although the work experience was in a different area. Monica suggested calling them to see if there was a job opening. The receptionist put me in touch with Ron Hartman, the Chief Surveyor. He was impressed by my qualifications and offered to interview me for a position in Algeria. I was dumbstruck. When my senses returned I pointed out that returning to the country next door to the one we had left only three days earlier was not an appealing proposition. He did not understand my viewpoint but invited me to see their facilities any way. I accepted thinking that there might be some need for their services if I joined an oil company and it would be useful to know the extent of their abilities.

The company was located in a residential area which was suffering like the rest of the city from the recent mass movement of middle class to the suburbs. Ron Hartman showed me round and introduced me to his colleagues. When we were reviewing some maps, an elderly gentleman shuffled in leaning on a stick and squinting as if the light was hurting his eyes.

"Who is he?" asked the old man.

"Dr. Hermann Ackerman, let me introduce you to Dr. Rakesh Lodha, he has just come from Libya," said Ron.

"Rakesh Lodha, of Roy and Lodha fame?" Hermann looked questioningly at me while referring to an obscure paper I had coauthored ten years earlier.

"Yes sir, Ackerman of Ackerman and Dix, I presume," I replied referring to a celebrated paper of thirty years ago. This must have pleased the old master although he did not show it. He turned to Ron, "What is he doing here?"

"Looking for a job", Ron replied.

"What are you waiting for? Hire him. He will solve all your problems." With these fateful words Hermann disappeared into a cubbyhole nearby.

Ron offered me a job which included a significant component of research and development. That suited me to a T. An hour later, I was boasting to Monica that I had secured a job on the first working day after arriving in a country in the middle of a recession. She was relieved although not happy with the salary.

We settled down in a rented home in suburban Bucks County. After a year, we bought a palatial home nearby in a Sheriff's auction which we could afford only because it needed a thorough renovation. With the help of my kind colleagues and a lot of hard work by Monica we completed the job within our tight time frame and limited budget. There were still things to be done on the outside and we proceeded with them after moving in as the time permitted. It was three months to the day when Monica put the brushes away after painting the outside. The same evening, a call came from Calgary, "Will you be interested in managing research for a small company with big ambitions?" I looked up Calgary in the map and casual enquiries revealed that it was the oil capital of Canada. Thinking that there was no harm in interviewing the company

I took the first Friday in November off on a phony pretext and flew to meet my next employer.

The view from the plane was interesting. It changed from gold colors of autumn to the brown of early winter as the plane crossed into Ontario. The scenery became somewhat monotonous west of Ontario; small hamlets dotted here and there in the bald prairie under a thick blanket of snow. The plane circled over the downtown Calgary before landing. Bright lights of the city were impressive in view of brownouts common in the American cities but the downtown area had only a handful of tall buildings other than a tower. The small size of the city was confirmed by the tiny airport. Yet, the cab managed to get lost while taking me to the home of Mahoney's, our friends from Libya who had come to Canada about the time we had moved to the U.S. They told me how much they enjoyed living in what looked to me a godforsaken city in the frozen Tundra. They assured me that it was hardly ever this cold; I had the misfortune of arriving there on the coldest November day on record. They showed me the equipment for winter recreation, downhill and cross-country skis, skates and snow shoes and the necessities for survival like thick parkas which kept them warm when it was forty degrees below. Next morning, the problems of living in Calgary were brought home. The engine froze and Mahoneys' car refused to budge. I called a cab and got to the interview an hour late. The prospective employer was most understanding. He showed me round, checked my credentials and offered me the job. Saying the taxes and the cost of living were high in Canada, he set the salary at a significantly higher level than I had suggested.

Pleased as punch I flew home the next day. It was middle of the night when I slipped into bed. Monica opened one eye and asked. "How did it go?" "Calgary is a very clean city," I replied.

Calgary called to confirm our understanding and advised me to visit Canadian consulate in New York the following Monday. After waiting for an appropriate duration, we were ushered in the elegant office of the consul decorated with the pictures of old men not known to us. The interview was short and to the point. "Will you learn French?" the esteemed official asked in heavily French accented English.

"I am going to Calgary, Alberta. Every one speaks English there," I replied.

"Canada is a bilingual country, you know." The consul enlightened me.

"I already speak three languages, learning another is not my top priority," I said honestly but, as it turned out, foolishly. Strange though it may seem, the two often go together.

"It will take five years or more for your turn to arrive. Hopefully they will keep the job open for you." The counsel got up to escort us to the door.

Monica was secretly pleased at this rebuff. It had taken her two years of hard work to break down the doors of social fortress common in established Eastern cities and she was feeling settled at last. She had agreed to move with great reluctance when I went down on my knees and told her with folded hands how important the promotion was to me. The gods were on her side for once but she did not gloat. Like a good wife of ten years standing, she consoled me and pointed out the possibility of a promotion in my current company.

I called Calgary to inform them of the consul's final words. "Don't worry we will look after it," played on my ear drums after two thousand mile journey over telephone lines. A week later, the Minister's permit arrived. Two months later, we were in the driveway of Mahoney residence in Calgary. It was a cold day, the coldest February day on record, if you believe such pronouncements. We got out of the cab in total darkness at four in the afternoon. Our daughters disappeared into the snow bank as they hopped out of the cab but expert shoveling by the driver got them out in the nick of time. This experience must have made a lasting impression, both of them moved to warmer climes as soon as they became adults. As for Monica and me, I must have exceeded the level of my competence. No company offered another job and we settled down to a sedentary life in a self-proclaimed cow town. I never learnt to skate or ski, but being a masochist, learnt to enjoy freezing in the dark while counting my blessings on my shivering fingers.

~ 2 ~

Calgary was a small city of 250,000 when I moved here. It didn't take long for me to find out how small the place was and what I could expect in a small city. A month after settling in the new job, I had lunch in the restaurant of a luxury hotel with a lady who was a postgraduate student with me fifteen years earlier in Liverpool, England. When I got back to the office, a pink message slip was waiting for me – call home immediately. I promptly did, worried if somebody was sick or the house was on fire. Thank goodness my fears were groundless. But a new fear took their place. "Who were you having lunch with?" Monica asked without any formalities when she picked the phone. Thankfully, she remembered my mention of this fellow student and gracefully accepted the good intentions behind my lunch date, if it could be called that. But it became clear that I will have to mend my ways; there could be no philandering in the cow town called Calgary.

I stuck to lunch with male clients for several years. If client was a female, or a female colleague wanted a bite together, I cleared with Monica in advance, often to her annoyance at being made to feel petty. Couple of decades went by. I went past the male menopause and became bald, fat and even more unattractive. Now there was even less danger that any desirable woman would look twice at this almost repulsive character.

SUDHIR JAIN

My business went down too. Now I only had one person, Darlene, working with me – a happily married mother of two who looked after the administrative affairs of my office as well as those of Monica's medical practice. The city grew like weeds in the garden and the population now approached one million. You would think that Darlene and I could be in public without Monica being told about it. Alas, no such luck.

There were occasions, shareholder meetings of companies we had invested in, brokers' parties and lunch on special occasions when Darlene and I were out together. When we met an acquaintance, Darlene was duly introduced and pleasantries exchanged. But this frankness did not allow me an open road. There were tough corners to negotiate, often completely out of the blue. A colleague of Monica invited us for brunch at their home which she shared with her father-in-law in ancient Indian tradition. This elderly gentleman, about the same age as myself, was a very traditional Indian; very polite and very firm. When Monica was introduced to him, he insisted that they had met a week ago at the broker's reception. With my luck, this was one outing I hadn't got round to clearing in advance. Cat was out of the bag and it took a lot of persuasion to put it back in when we got home.

Then there was the occasion Darlene and I were having a drink while waiting for arrival of our spouses (spice?) for birthday lunch for her. A lady on the next table kept giving us strange looks which we tried to disregard. Her discomfort was very obvious and if I had a medical background I would have offered help. But she did not have long to endure. Monica soon arrived and the relief in lady's countenance was palpable. The situation became clear when she greeted Monica. She was worried to death wondering why the husband of a friend twice removed was becoming familiar with a young good looking gregarious blonde. Amazing how anxious some friends are to maintain marital harmony among those dear, though not near, to them.

A client was having a Bridge evening and he was a pair short. He invited me to find a partner and help him out. Monica does not play Bridge and suggested I asked Darlene. Darlene and I are Leos, we play to win. We had never played together, so there were misunderstandings. We exchanged harsh words very much like married couples commonly do at the Bridge table. After a bitter argument towards the end of the evening, a kindly old lady asked us how long we had been married. We looked at each other in a state of shock. I gently asked, "What makes you think we are married?" She replied with some annoyance, "You call her 'darling' and she calls you 'dear'; what else is one to think?" After this answer Darlene and I silently vowed to pronounce each other's name more clearly from then on.

Only a couple of weeks ago, Darlene and I were having a quick bite in between meetings at a restaurant with most tables occupied by Christmas revelers. Alana, my neighbor and a patient of Monica, was one of them. She came over to check us out. I introduced her to Darlene and wished her family a Merry Christmas even though I am a Hindu and she a Jew. When she left our table, I felt that she was not a little perturbed. It so happened that we ran into her at a New Year open house. I gently took her aside and whispered in her ear, loud enough for other curious ears, to keep my date to herself and not mention it to Monica. A wide grin of a cat that had just made dinner of a canary spread over her pleasant face and she promised, totally unconvincingly, to keep her mouth shut.

I could go on boring you with similar tales but I think I have proven the point: It is good for marital harmony when a wife is certain that no one is going to fall for husband's non-existent charms, particularly when his financial means are too limited to attract gold diggers. With all these busy body well wishers around, a husband needs all the help he can get from his lady luck for his happy marriage to stay the course.

~ 3 ~

Monica and I moved into our new home in the middle of winter. We didn't get any chance to really know our neighbors till the spring arrived in late May, earlier than usual. It was a beautiful spring morning, the snow from our south facing back yard was almost gone and poplars were beginning to sprout leaves. I was gaily whistling Rides of Valkyrie tune while attending to the fence which separated our two children and a cat from three children and two raucous dogs of Babette next door. Babette and I had exchanged pleasantries a couple of times on our driveways when getting out of our cars. If the rumor mill was to be believed, Babette was in the middle of a messy divorce from her wealthy doctor husband who had moved to Carolina with his nurse Caroline. Babette saw me through her living room window; our eyes met and she came out to greet me dressed in a substantial dressing gown over her equally substantial nightdress and house slippers. She was in a chatty mood and complimented me on my whistling of a difficult tune. When I asked her how life was treating her, she took my quarry seriously and told me all about her problems with the lawyers who were costing the earth but not working hard enough to get her a reasonable settlement. I patiently listened and nodded, although, being gender prejudiced, my sympathies were with the eloped doctor who was only trying to protect the means to maintain the standard of living Babette had set for him as his wife. I was looking for an escape from her monologue when she suddenly looked up and down at herself and exclaimed, "Oh God, you are in your outdoor clothes and I still have my night clothes on. Don't go away. I will be back in a jiffy." She rushed off to change into her "outdoor clothes".

I put the missing bolt back in its place and hammered it in along with a small part of my thumb. Just as I looked up, there was Babette returning to carry on her monologue. Her "outdoor clothes" were two pieces of skimpiest bikini of just the right shade to enhance her tan from her Mexican holiday. The thought struck me that the bikini suit contained less material than the belt of her dressing gown, yet probably cost several times more than the whole suit of night clothes. I had just finished my examination of her charms and was beginning to wonder what the old doctor found in Caroline over Babette, when I heard Monica's call from the kitchen window, "Dear, come quick, I need you here." I apologized to Babette and rushed inside. Boy, did I have a fire to put down! I only wish I knew how I was responsible for it.

Monica and Babette became good friends over the summer. They went for regular walks in the nearby park. For some strange reason, Monica always made sure that I got my fresh air on my own. Babette's well-cut shorts and tight-fitting shirts may have been a consideration.

~ 4 ~

Plus Fifteens in downtown of Calgary are wonderful. The second floors of office towers are connected together by bridges at least 15 feet above the busy roads. Pedestrians love them because they save walking in the snow, being splashed by passing vehicles, waiting at the lights, chasing the hat blown off by northern winds and most of all freezing on the dark streets nine months of the year. Most buildings have converted plus fifteen floors into shopping plazas which provide plenty of opportunity to drop in the store to pick up a suit to raise the morale, 'forgive me' gift for the angry spouse, coffee and donut to soothe the nerves, you name it. Attractive shop windows do their best to lure those rushing by and to make them late for their meeting. There are models of sex-starved females males can't keep the eyes off and testosterone-plus males females can't help but desire. Strangely, they are touting the merchandise for their gender and attracting the other. No wonder stores are as quiet as the ghost infested caverns.

It is 9:30, time to leave for the meeting at ten with a prospective client. I have eight blocks to walk, most of it on plus fifteens. I pack my demo reports and other marketing paraphernalia, slurp the remnants of coffee in the mug and leisurely walk to the elevator. I press the down button and hop in as the door opens. It goes up all the way to the top stopping at most floors. It does the same on the way down. Why do I always forget that 9 to 11 is the rush hour for elevator traffic?

I am on the street. It is 9:37. Plenty of time for eight blocks, there is no need to hurry. I look both ways to check the traffic and cross the street to take the stairs to plus fifteen. As I step on the pavement, a uniformed lady with a pen poised on a notebook stops me, "You have been jaywalking, sir. It is hazardous for you; it is unsafe for traffic and sets a bad example to kids waiting patiently for the light over there. I will have to write you a ticket, sir." I give her my name, address, phone number, show her my driving license and she gives me a traffic violation slip in return. Slip informs me that I have been fined $50 for jaywalking on a busy street, gives me directions on how to pay and informs me of the penalties for delinquency - six months in jail and/or maximum of ten thousand dollars in fines. I wish the lady a good day and look at the watch. It is 9:45. Still enough time for eight blocks.

I climb the stairs and enter the make believe world of constant temperature, soft music, bright light and a mix of happy shoppers and people rushing to their meetings. I haven't gone a block when I feel a tap on my shoulder. It is an ex-client wanting to catch up on how I have been, what I am working on, how the company is doing, what my plans are? I give hurried answers and, being an owner of a service company obliged to be courteous to all past, present and future clients, ask him the same questions. He seems to have plenty of time at his disposal. He gives the details of the projects he is supervising, how well my major competitor is doing for him and how future work has already been contracted out to that company. My patience is wearing thin with so much praise for people trying to eat my lunch. As he stops to breathe, I jump in with "I got to run, I will call you to set a lunch date and exchange more notes about your great contractor." I hear something like "Please do" as I rush off. It is 9:55 and six blocks still to go.

I see my destination through the windows on the plus fifteen on Seventh Avenue. Two minutes to get there, one minute on the elevator, I calculate. Five minutes late is not bad. The prospect is a fine lady, she won't mind, I console myself. I turn the corner. "Hey Rakesh, so glad I ran into you. You have to smarten up your billing department. There are major errors in your last invoice. I am sending it back." It is Joe, my major client. The invoice he is talking about is large. I am depending on its payment to meet the payroll and pay the office rent. I stop dead in my tracks, greet Joe with politeness due to his position, and discuss each item in the invoice as I remember it. He points out the errors as he remembers them. I explain our reasons. He disagrees as is his wont and we agree to meet in his office the next day. As he turns to leave, I look at my watch; 10:25, a disaster.

As I rush towards my destination, I see another client. He waves to me and I wave back and shout, perhaps a little too loudly, "Got to run, will call you later." I get to the elevator, press the button, jump in as the doors open and exclaim as the doors shut, "Damn, the floor number?" It is my lucky moment, the elevator hasn't moved. I bang the open door button. Doors take their time to open. I rush out, check the tenant registry for the floor number, jump back into elevator, and get off on the right floor. 10:29 on the client clock.

I give my card to the receptionist. He calls the prospective client. Sorry, she has another meeting at 10:30. She will call you to set up another meeting. As I turn to leave, the competitor after my lunch walks in.

~ 5 ~

It was a busy morning at the office with a number of phone calls to attend to, some urgent papers to read and sign and many volatile stocks to track. Still, I had promised my friend Sammy to pick him up from the hotel at 9 AM. Sammy was visiting Calgary to attend a wedding and was returning to Charlottetown by the noon flight. The plan was to pick him up from the hotel and bring him to the office. He planned to attend to his own business till 11 when I would take him to the airport. Hotel was no more than ten minutes from my office. No place is farther than ten minutes from another in Calgary. At least that is the common perception.

I left my office to pick him up at nine sharp. As I approached the railway crossing, the red lights flashed and the gate dropped down missing the car by an inch, if that. A long line of cars and trucks soon formed behind me, all contributing to Global warming as they waited with their engines running. It didn't take long for the train to arrive but it sure took a long time for it to get past. It was the longest train I have ever seen and more heavily loaded than usual. The engine struggled along breathing hard just like a new marathon trainee on his first run but unlike him bravely pulling hundreds of cars behind him. At long last, the train passed, the gates opened, cars behind me hooted with impatience as I started the engine, shifted into gear and set off. A few road works along the way slowed me further including a ticket from the traffic cop for exceeding the speed limit in a construction zone. To make a long story short, I was half an hour late when I got to the hotel. It must have been overdone poached eggs; Sammy was grumpy when I held out my hand to greet him.

When we got in the car I noticed the red light on the dial that indicated an empty gas tank. I headed for the gas station attached to the grocery store because I had a discount coupon which would save a couple of after-tax bucks. When I got to the store, I remembered that we were running out of milk at home. When I was getting skim milk for my breakfast cereal, 1% fat for the tea, homo for the granddaughters, half-and-half for the daughter-in-law I noticed that toilet rolls were on sale. After filling the cart with 96 rolls to last the rest of the month, it struck me that my toothpaste tube was on its last squeeze. As I rushed towards the cashier from the toothpaste shelf I passed mangoes with their irresistible aroma. I had to have some. Their was a line up at the counter and it was ten by the time I got back to a hot car with a rather agitated Sammy talking to himself on the passenger seat. Fortunately, filling the gas did not take long. Then I had the irresistible urge to get the car washed. As I swung towards the wash lane, Sammy gave me a look that made the urge disappear instantly and we were on our way. Normally it would be ten minutes to the office. But we were passing close to the hospital where a mutual friend was recuperating from surgery. We stopped to see him for a short visit. However, a whole brigade of doctors and residents was examining him as we arrived. A plume of smoke was coming out of Sammy's nostrils when we left half an hour later.

We got to my office a few minutes before eleven. There was enough time to sign my life away in return for leasing the office for another year and to learn that all the stocks I had bought to sell on the rebound had dropped further and ones I had sold to pick up on "correction" had kept moving on upward trajectory. Sammy talked to his folks in Charlottetown and learnt that his company had won the big contract they had expected to lose. On this note of mixed news, we left for the airport, he talking on his cell in a jolly frame of mind and I staring at the road in front somewhat grumpily. A parking ticket at the airport when I was helping Sammy with his suitcase loaded with contract documents may have caused my sour mood for rest of the day but no one in the office made allowances. They had their own problems.

On her way home, my secretary peeked into my office to remind me that it was my turn to cook the dinner. Baked beans on burnt toast, albeit with pork sausages, did not go well with the family. Not surprisingly, no one offered me a shoulder to cry on. After doing the dishes and cleaning the messy kitchen, I dropped into my easy chair with the newspaper. It fell open on the Comment page. There it was, tucked in the bottom right hand corner; a heavily edited and almost unrecognizable version of the letter I had sent to the Editor. The kindness of the far-off Editor made me forget the events of the day and imparted a new burst of energy. I got up whistling a merry tune and headed for the lawn mower in the garden shed.

~ 6 ~

A combination of silent auction and noisy dinner is hard to beat when raising money for a good cause. To this Calgary Opera adds an interesting twist. A sumptuous four course dinner is served on stage of the opera being performed in the spring. The event is very popular with city's cultural elite. To some, the attraction of this dinner is to hob-nob with the stars. To others, like my humble self, it is the silent auction.

At the dinner held on the set of Don Giovanni a couple of years ago, I succeeded in outbidding all star wannabes and won an as yet undefined supernumerary role in the main offering next winter. I gambled more than I could afford because the conductor is a world-renowned musician who had shown me some kindness on his visits to Calgary. He occasionally accepted my invitations to meet for lunch after the morning rehearsal. We chatted a little about Canadian art scene but his main interest was stock market. I did most of the talking because he wished to rest his sore throat, I suspect from screaming at hapless orchestra members. He sat in the restaurant enjoying the view of the hills across the lake and a medium-rare Alberta steak while I ranted against the Tech fever and how every one was about to lose their shirts in the first wave of panic and pants in the next.

In my ignorance of procedure for casting an opera I hoped

that it might be possible to persuade the maestro to cast me as the African king in upcoming Aida because I am brown and my baritone is not altogether unpleasant. I started taking private lessons in Italian and singing lessons from a former star of Metropolitan Opera. When the maestro was in town a few months later to conduct the symphony orchestra, I invited him for a drive to Banff for morning coffee and then to Lake Louise for leisurely lunch. He accepted and set a day when he did not expect rehearsals.

The maestro was much impressed by the beauty of the snow-capped Canadian Rockies and two hour drive to Banff seemed short in the pleasantly warm car. There we had a stroll and a cappuccino. However, thanks to the slush thrown off by passing cars our pants and shoes got quite dirty. The maestro did not like dirt on his clothes and injury to his aesthetic sensibilities was conveyed to me by a frown which had turned many a burly tenor into jelly.

We drove to Lake Louise and had lunch in a restaurant overlooking the magnificent lake, a jewel of the Canadian Rockies and a destination of half of Japan during the summer. The impeccable service and excellent wines to go with superb Mushroom Forestiere followed by London Broil soothed maestro's sensitivities somewhat. Genuine Sherry Trifle and excellent Espresso was followed by 28 year old Port. I felt that the maestro was enjoying the spirit of the Rockies when his fingers started tapping the music of 'Song of Death' which was on his concert program.

On our way back along a picturesque but slow side road, the maestro had a little snooze. An hour away from Calgary he woke up with a start, looked at his watch and shouted: "Hurry, hurry, rehearsal starts in thirty minutes." I pressed the pedal to the floor and D300 engine roared into action. But not for long. A police car waited for me a few miles down the road. I accepted the $200 speeding ticket without wasting time in protest because the car clock was ticking hurriedly towards the rehearsal time.

We got to the rehearsal hall late but well within the limit allowed to someone of maestro's reputation. We said goodbye at the stage door. Then he suddenly turned around and said, "I must thank you not only for today but also for your warnings on Techs. I got out in time with all my profit intact." This unexpected remark delivered with a smile that induces great divas to surrender unconditionally, bolstered my courage. "About my role in opera…" I began. The maestro cut me off with the wave of his conducting arm, "Discuss with the General Manager, I have nothing to do with casting" and disappeared into the cavernous hall.

A month later I got a call from the General Manager. "We can not accommodate you in winter's opera. Will you mind switching to the spring one? It is being done in English and you don't have to sing." Imagine my disappointment! All those Italian and singing lessons to no avail. "Talk to my agent" I replied in a huff and passed him on to my assistant. She agreed on my behalf, much too readily I thought.

We wore our costumes for the first time for Dress Rehearsal

and the deathly routine of the previous seventeen occasions suddenly came to life. Actors lived their roles and the tense director breathed a sigh of relief. Clothes may or may not make a man, they surely make an actor. Three performances went like a charm and standing ovations went to the head of at least one supernumerary. At the next opera function I tracked the General Manager down and the following dialogue ensued:

I, with some humility, "Bob, did I do anything wrong in the rehearsals?"

GM patronisingly, "No, you were just fine."

I, with more humility, "Did I not do well in the performance?"

GM, with some exasperation, "You did just fine, actually you were splendid."

I, with some insistence, "Did the Director think so too?"

GM, looking for an escape, "Yes, he thought every one was great."

I, with impatience, "How come then, I haven't been invited again."

I don't know why but GM has not invited me to the opera functions since.

~ 7 ~

Several years had gone by since Louisa and I had said more than a rushed hello to each other. She had been busy with her teen age kids and the activities of medical wives' club and I with my growing grandchildren and the bridge league. Then one fine spring evening in May I ran into her at a birthday party for a mutual friend. I suggested lunch and got an enthusiastic response, "What a wonderful idea. Call me tomorrow between 10:47 and 10:59 to set up time."

I called her number at 10:53. The phone was engaged and I did the gentlemanly thing - left a detailed message suggesting next Friday as the day and a restaurant near her place. Couple of days went by and I gave up the hope of a pleasant hour or two in the company of a beautiful young lady. I was not particularly disappointed. This had happened to me hundreds of time before and no doubt would happen over and over again.

Then the phone rang. "Louisa here. Sorry I didn't get back to you sooner. Been running around like a chicken without a head. How is June 25 at 11:49? We can meet at Sam's." Sam's is a restaurant known for elegance but the choice surprised me because it is a long drive for both of us. I looked at my diary. That was one day in next thirty three where I had something marked. This something was not to be taken lightly either. Monica's kid brother had a stopover at local airport on one of his many business trips and wanted to meet us in between flights. "Sorry, that is one day in five weeks I can't be free." This response did not go well. "Trouble with you men is that you play so hard to get even when you are working from home. Next date on my calendar is July 13. Wait, that is Sally's birthday. How is July 29?" My diary was blank for the whole of July. Now it lost that distinction as I duly recorded the engagement.

I spent intervening ten weeks enjoying the grandchildren when I was not playing bridge at the club or doing odd volunteering jobs. Usually I had lunch alone or with doddering old men like myself sharing the mishaps of our families and reminiscing about good old days when the wishes of parents were paramount. On the morning of July 29 I called Louisa to confirm that she was still game for lunch. Her line was engaged but there was a detailed message. "If it is you Rakesh, I have booked a table at Sam's for 12:17. I may be a little late. You won't mind waiting a little, will you dear? Go ahead and order the drinks. I will have sherry. Tio Pepe; they are sure to have it."

I got to Sam's at 12:01 and reported to the reception desk. A tall elegant lady ushered me to a window table at 12:17 sharp. Other than me and another couple, the dining room was empty but a number of waiters in tuxedos were rushing around looking busy. When I ordered a glass of hot skim milk for myself the waiter looked at the ceiling in dismay. He cheered a little on the order of sherry for the absent lady. 15% of sherry would make up a little for skimpy milk.

I drank the milk so slowly that it was merely lukewarm for the last sip. Restaurant now had a few more customers but not Louisa. "Lucky, I don't have anything planned for the afternoon" I thought. I opened the menu once again, this time to while the time. Just when I was wondering whether I should replace my earlier selection of Beef Wellington with Chicken Maryland I heard the clicking of high heels approaching me. I looked up. Indeed it was Louisa, dressed to kill and with a smile Paris Hilton would be proud of, rushing towards her sherry. "Oh dear, I am so sorry. Roads are terrible; every traffic light was against me. Then it was so hard to find a parking place. Any way, we are both here now. Let us order a fine meal. I am free till 1:24," she said holding both my hands in hers. I could not help being envious of her dainty diamond studded watch which showed that it was a little before one.

I drew the attention of the waiter who was acting busy as a good waiter should. Louisa gave him a thorough grilling about daily specials and fancy dishes on the menu. She satisfied herself on the culinary merits of each item before ordering chicken broth and fish and chips under fancy French names and I ordered plain salad and noodles under equally incomprehensible entries in the menu. We did not have time to do justice to a bottle of Deinhard Goldtropfchen so we ordered wine by the glass. As soon as the waiter was gone Louisa launched into all the troubles of driving in this town. "When we came here thirty years ago, the population was a hundred thousand. It took less than ten minutes to get anywhere. Now the population is approaching a million. Everybody still thinks it takes ten minutes and drives like a maniac." On and on she lectured me about the drivers, young and old, who made lives of other drivers miserable. "And cell phones. If they are not speeding through red lights, they are crawling in the fast lane with the cell phone stuck to the ear and talking with all the seriousness of the US President finding excuses to start a new war." Now the lecture shifted to a new topic – cell phones; how every one has to have it whether they can afford it or not. "Imagine, I have tenants who don't pay rent on time. Each of them has cell phones, even their ten year old kid." Now the lecture shifted to how poorly kids are brought up. She kept it going with fast changing topics and I was reminded of her debating prowess at school where I mentored her more than twenty years ago. She displayed full mastery of the art of talking while eating and I have no trouble listening whether I am eating or not. As soon as the last bite had slipped past the full stop of her last sentence she got up. "Thanks for inviting me for lunch. It was most interesting to hear how your family is doing. Call me between 10:12 and 10:24 next Thursday and we will do it again." She picked up her hand bag and was gone but not before an almost royal wave of her right hand as she disappeared round the corner.

I had a leisurely cup of coffee to recover my bearings. I paid the bloated bill with 15% tip already included and strolled to the car. While crossing the street I heard Louisa's ringing voice. She was chewing some ear on her cell phone as her car crept towards the green light with a long line of patient drivers behind her.

~ 8 ~

What with the premature baby, then the breast cancer of the daughter followed by heart murmurs in Monica, our social life had been in limbo for several years. Our daughter and her family had been living with us for last three years in our little bungalow. By the end of the summer, the cancer treatment was pronounced a success, Monica had reasonably recovered and the granddaughter was in a good shape. Time was ripe for daughter and her family to return to their home in New Orleans. After a two week spell of hectic packing, they left with little one in her car seat and U-haul with belongings in tow. Grandparents shed a few tears and then resumed their life as well as any grandparents can with the precious little one thousands of miles away.

After spending a couple of weeks to get the house in order, evenings started to feel a little long. It was time to renew social contacts. A list of former friends was drawn in order of priority. Calls were made and dates were set for coffee, lunch, dinner or walk in the park. Calendar was full and Monica and I felt valued again.

The day we had long awaited soon arrived. We were meeting Dr. and Mrs. Singhal in the only four diamond restaurant in the city. Dr. Singhal is a brain surgeon known far and wide for his deft fingers. Only two weeks earlier he was flown with his equipment and staff to operate on the ruler of an Arab Emirate in the royal jumbo jet. Mrs. Singhal is a social worker whose services to the community have been recognized by the Queen herself. I was very proud that Dr. Singhal had maintained the friendship of our school days in spite of such divergence in our current social status. Naturally, I was aware of the honour bestowed on us by the illustrious couple by their acceptance of dinner invitation and made preparations accordingly. I took the day easy at work to conserve my energies for the evening. On my way home from work I got the car washed inside and out in a vain attempt to make it look young again. After a quick cup of tea, I shaved and inaugurated the aftershave lotion I had received as a birthday present from one of the children. I put on my best suit and carefully tied the knot of the silk tie acquired for this occasion. Monica's day had been hard with critically sick patients. On my insistence, she had a hot bath in the Jacuzzi, got into here bright green low cut dress and sprinkled liberally the perfume she had been saving for a special outing. At seven sharp we got into the car and drove to the restaurant.

The distinguished guests arrived fashionably late, by precisely twenty nine minutes. "Yet another Emirate is after us and wants us to move there permanently" they said in unison as they shook hands. No sooner had the gins been ordered, a cell phone jingle based on 'a little night music' was heard. It was the cell phone of Mrs. Singhal. It turned out that the Premier wanted to consult her on some private matter. Other three sat still when she listened to his story, asked for clarification of some points and shared her wise counsel with him. We could all hear the deeply felt expression of gratitude by the Premier. Mrs. Singhal let out a sigh, tucked the cell back in her cleavage just below the pearl as big as a ping pong ball and sipped from her glass of gin.

No sooner had the dinner been ordered, there was another jingle, this one based on "hail the sun, hail the light". It was the Emir himself making a courtesy call to the famous surgeon. It would be extremely disrespectful to the Emir with billions of barrels of oil under his Emirate for others to talk when he had condescended to disrupt the dinner of a mere surgeon who was anxious to add a few zeroes to his annual income. We sat there not daring to take sips from our soup bowl which was steaming in front of us temptingly, but in vain. When the last calorie of heat had dissipated from the bowl, farewell greetings were exchanged across an ocean and two seas. Dr. Singhal profusely apologized and we proceeded to do justice to our soup the chef had intended to be consumed really hot half an hour ago.

The soup bowls were whisked away as soon as the spoons were put down. The dinner appeared covered by shining brass bells. Four waiters stood ready to unveil the dinner. The maitre'd lowered the baton and the bells went up. My thimble sized steak was carefully placed in the centre of the largest bone china plate I had ever seen. One baby carrot, one Brussels sprout, one small potato and one slice of zucchini were carefully placed along the edge of the plate. We admired the things of beauty in front of us and contemplated the joy for ever for our taste buds even though our tummies would be left growling. However, the reverie was rudely interrupted by some more little night music. Cell shot out of the cleavage, glued to the ear and the famous baritone of a former Prime Minister was heard. Of course, making sounds with the silverware, however elegant, was out of the question when such an illustrious personage was calling to discuss his next step to counter the bad publicity from the book by a journalist with filthy mind. Diners sat there hungrily looking at small dinners in huge plates when the plight of the ex-PM was dissected and wise suggestions on overcoming the adversity were offered. At long last good night, sleep tight was exchanged across thousands of miles of empty space. Every one wolfed down the dinner without really tasting it. No one had any inclination to exchange any words either.

The coffee and desserts were ordered while we sympathized with the plight of the former Prime Minister. Before we could curse the unprincipled journalist we heard twinkle, twinkle, little star. It was Monica's turn to answer the phone. It was the hospital, "come straight away, head is popping out," every one in the dining room heard an excited nurse scream out of the phone. Monica picked up her handbag and my car keys and rushed off after a hurried thank you and good bye. The waiter saw her leave and asked me with a smirk if she was coming back. My explanation failed to wipe the smirk but he did go to the kitchen to cancel her order. Soon he returned with three desserts and three kinds of coffee. We finished them in silence as if stunned by the thought of another person wanting to come into this overcrowded world.

Every one was exhausted after all these long distance conversations and long spells of silence. Dr. Singhal was yawning, very discretely of course. I paid the bill and we walked out. I thanked my guests for their kindness in sharing their precious evening with us and they nodded acceptance. My humble abode was only a couple of blocks out of their way but they were too tired, or bored, to offer me a ride. I did not notice this slight. I was too elated at having spent the evening in such a distinguished company to call the cab and walked home in a cold drizzle. When I got home the phone was ringing. It was a call from waterlogged New Orleans.

~ 9 ~

Chinook winds have their fans but Monica is not one of them. The melting snow splashes on to the cars and makes them filthy. Mud from the car gets on to the clothes and dry-cleaning bill shoots up. She has concluded that a timely trip to carwash saves nine to drycleaners. On a day after a spell of Chinook winds last winter, she finished her morning shift a little early and decided to use the extra few minutes to rush to the friendly neighborhood car wash. At the gas station, she hurriedly filled the car and paid for the gas and wash, relieved to note that she was only the second in the line up.

As it happened, being only the second did not mean a quick wash. The driver of the car in front was an elderly lady who was having difficulty in driving her car into the track between two steel rails. She went forward and back several times without success. In the meantime, cars were piling up behind Monica and her time was running short. Some rude comments were being aired by crude men waiting impatiently for their turn. Rather than exchange sharp words with them, Monica decided to offer help to the lady. She refused point blank all Monica's entreaties to help her, saying she had to learn how to do it. Then Monica shot her pointed arrow, "You can trust me, I am a doctor." As soon as she heard this, she beamed, "I have just been to my doctor, you know" and moved to the passenger seat. Monica jumped in the driver seat, put her car through the wash and hurried into her car before some queue jumper could take her place. She picked up a sandwich on the way back and barely made it to the office before hordes of patients became impatient.

~ *10* ~

It has been a long wait. But the patience has paid off and Calgary's beloved Flames are in the playoff. I am not much of a Hockey fan but all the hoopla got to my preteen daughters. They begged me to take them to the game till my resistance wore off. The game started at 8. We set off at 5 PM to make sure of getting the seats. I stopped by at the bank to cash enough money for three seats and snacks and soft drinks which of course would be sold at the prices as high as the status of the game.

We paid about twice the normal rate for parking at the gate but it was cheap compared to the playoff rates elsewhere. We walked excitedly to the box-office. There was a long line up snaking for almost a kilometer from the ticket windows. However, the line was moving forward quickly, probably because the computers were down and clerks were working the old fashioned way. Quite possibly, most people were paying cash to save the hassles.

In just over an hour, we had reached the window. There was only a frail elderly gentleman in front who was talking to the clerk in great agitation. He had two kids with him, younger than ten and probably his grandchildren who were jumping up and down in great excitement. Kids were barely listening to the conversation between clerk and the old man which I could not fail to eavesdrop. I gathered that the gentleman had just enough money for two children's and one senior's tickets.

However, seniors were not allowed discounts in playoff and that left him ten dollars short. When kids heard this the disappointment on their faces was as great as the anger of the man. I knew I had to intervene before it was too late. Only thing I could think of was to throw the ten dollar bill on the window sill to make up the difference. The man turned to me to thank me and I graciously nodded. The clerk gave him three tickets and lowered the window. The sold out sign flashed over the box office area. I stood there gaping at my daughters. They stood looking at me.

We stood around for a while hoping against hope to get entry somehow. It was not to be. We went home disappointed. For once my daughters did not blame me for my actions. They too felt that their Daddy did what he had to do.

~ *11* ~

We had just moved in our home in a new development. I took a couple of weeks off work to get the yard in shape. I made careful sketches for the flower beds, got help from a horticulturist to place the bushes and then worked to get the flowers and grass in and watered them in a timely fashion. It was late Sunday at the end of my time off when I stood there admiring my handiwork. My brown skin bathed in sweat and a smile of satisfaction on my face. Then I heard someone call "Hey there, you did a great job."

I looked around. It was my neighbor two homes down. He walked over and gave my handiwork a thorough examination. While looking around, he appeared to be doing some calculation in his head. Then he broke the silence, "I need a good gardener badly and soon. You will do just fine. Do you charge by the hour or by the job?"

I was amazed at the question. It was my turn to calculate in my head. After a suitable pause I replied, "I don't charge anything. The lady of the house lets me sleep with her."

The poor man didn't know what to say. He quietly turned and started walking back. I stopped him and introduced myself as his new neighbor. He stared at me and then burst into laughter. He was still laughing when he disappeared through his back door.

~ *12* ~

It was the fortieth birthday of our old friend Bronwyn. I say old not because she looked any older than us but because we had known her for a long time. Her husband Jamie had arranged a surprise party for her in a restaurant an hour away on good roads. We were a little late for some reason I don't remember now. It could have been the baby Monica was delivering, an urge to complete some work in office on my part, an argument about new bathroom scales which increased the weight by several pounds, or snowy weather and bad roads. In any event, we got to the parking lot a few minutes after the surprise hour.

As I opened the door and got out of the car to help Monica, I heard Bronwyn at some distance ask her husband, "That is Rakesh over there, what is he doing here?"

"It must be some other brownie, they all look the same." Jamie replied without missing a heartbeat.

The clever reply saved the element of surprise. We stayed behind in the shadows for a tactful interval, and then slowly walked to join the party by the back door. When I saw Bronwyn a few minutes later, I felt the need to introduce myself. She beat me to it, however. "Rakesh, I presume."

"Yes, one of a kind." I replied.

~ *13* ~

It was a rather cloudy but warm summer day. Lorne and I were collecting magnetic data along the forestry road on our mineral claim near Prince George in British Columbia. Lorne is a big man, over six feet tall and weighs more than two hundred pounds on a kindly scale. Although not much less in weight, I barely reach his rather impressive waistline. I got almost out of breath keeping up with his long strides between observation points. At long last, we saw a stream which would be a nice place for a leisurely lunch. I had just set the equipment for one more observation before we would settle on a log when I heard him mutter, "Hell, bear scare is at the bottom of the pack."

"Hell, camera is at the bottom of my pack" I said rather insolently looking at the gurgling stream with the mountain backdrop. Then I looked up front and lost my remaining breath. There was a black bear standing on her hind legs by the side of the road no more than thirty feet in front of Lorne. My survival instinct came to the fore and I quickly moved behind Lorne. "Don't run," I murmured, certain that I would be the one left behind for bear hug if we started running.

"Don't be scared, raise your hands," said Lorne in the authoritative voice of a man in command of the situation. Both pairs of hand shot up. My hands barely reached his shoulders and were almost certainly invisible to the bear. His hands nearly reached the overhanging branch of a pine tree. A scary thought raced through my mind - Lorne could raise himself to safety by pulling up on the branch and I will become rather juicy lunch for the bear family. However, lady luck smiled on me for once. Bear compared her size to the stature of this grizzly of a man facing her and found herself coming short. She did what a wise bear in any children's story book would do – gently growled what sounded like, "Thank you for the visit. Sorry, must rush back to kiddies," turned around and disappeared in the forest.

I breathed for the first time in what seemed like eons. "Tell me the reading again" said Lorne putting pencil to paper.

~ *14* ~

Urgent meeting with a client in Gainsville. Flight due to depart at 9:00 AM. Leave home at 7:30 to allow five minutes for leaving the car at the airport parking lot and be at the terminal at 8:00. That should be plenty.

Packed the night before. Checked passport, travelers' checks, and ticket. Put the case and the carry on bag in the car. Then slept like a log till rude alarm rang at 6:30. Enough time to get ready and have a leisurely breakfast. It is 7:30. Time to leave.

Can't leave without checking all doors and windows. Must brush my teeth and wash my mouth – the passenger in the next seat may be sensitive. The plants are drying. Must water them, poor things. Must lower the blinds on the windows and check locks on all outside doors. Turn on some lights to fool prospective burglar. Oh yes. Can't leave dirty dishes in the sink. Gosh, it is 7:45. Must run.

Ah, there is the office. Must pick up the messages. Receptionist needs money in petty cash. There are some urgent papers to be signed. Urgent request to phone partner as soon as possible. Oh, it is eight already. Partner can wait till after check in.

Hell, why does every body have to be on the same road at the same time? Why does the car in front have to be a stickler for speed limit? Oh no! Flat tire. Not now! Lucky break – tire changed in record time. Traffic seems to be less. Flight may be late. Must give it a try any how.

Hurray, there is Park and Jet. Still 25 minutes to flight time. Why such line up to get in the lot? Where is the bus to the terminal? Only 10 minutes to flight time. I have had it. It is just not my day.

At last the bus creeps in. Picks up passengers every few meters. Five minutes to flight time. Jump down at the right point. Fly in with suitcase and carry on bag trailing behind in each hand. No one at the airline counter! What is going on? Take out the ticket. Collapse in a heap on the ground. No one around to support. Just as well. Their laughter not good for the ego. Flight time 9:00 PM.

Check in the airport hotel to catch the breath. Phone partner. Faint. Meeting has been cancelled.

~ *15* ~

It is a cold night. Well, cold nights in Calgary are nothing to write home about, most of them are cold. Not only cold, absolutely freezing. I don't know how locals live through them year after year. Being an immigrant from the tropics, I have barely survived two decades of them. I ask myself every morning when I get up, "what am I doing here?" "Making a living that is what." answers Monica from under two thick blankets. Yes, she is right. Living I make is not as good as most people here but it is much better than I could do at home as an engineer.

This night is colder than any other night and nothing can stop me shivering. "To hell with the gas prices, I will work an extra shift if I have to," saying this to no one in particular I get out from under the not so cozy blankets to raise the thermostat. When I open the bedroom door to go into the hall a cold blast from the supposedly hot air vent freezes me on the spot. It takes a while to defrost myself and get to the thermostat. "What is going on here," I say, again to no one in particular. The thermostat shows the temperature of below zero. "The furnace is kaput" I think. "Should have known from the cold blast."

Back to the bedroom. I put on several layers of sweaters and the heaviest coat. Then trudge down to the basement to check the furnace. It is pumping air but there is no flame. A light goes on in my head. "If the problem were pilot being off, the fan would be off too." Then the nasty conclusion, "Way beyond my expertise, must call a plumber."

Out come yellow pages. My shivering finger lands on Happy Plumbing, 24 hour service. I dial their number. Some one picks it up and I hear a pleasant voice, "Happy Plumbing, how can I help you?"

Relief. No, not from cold. Not yet anyway. From the fear that no one will answer the call. "My furnace is blowing cold air and not lighting up," I mumble into the phone. "Karl will be there in twenty eight minutes. Make the cheque out to him" I thank my lucky stars and hug the phone. The owner of the voice is not within reach.

In less than half an hour I open the door to the plumber and thirty below weather. He introduces himself, as if it is necessary "Karl, from Happy Plumbing." Then asks gruffly without ceremony, "Where is the furnace?" He is a big man, over two meters tall and more than 150 kg of muscle; his two eyes the size and color of large California plums. He carries a big bag of tools and, for some unknown reason, a large hammer with a long handle. His face, build and thick East European accent remind me of the bouncer in a strip joint who had made the news recently for brutally beating a disorderly patron and then tossing out his mangled body on the road where it was crushed by a passing truck. What with his voice, manner and appearance, I am scared stiff; I have this normal urge to live a long, though useless, life. My options are: put up with the fear for a while or close the door on him and freeze for the rest of the night. Cold wins the day, sorry the night. I lead him to the furnace. He follows me closely within the reach of his hammer. I leave him in the basement to do his thing and hurry back upstairs.

He works for an hour. All sorts of metallic noises and some loud grunts keep me from dozing off. Then the silence returns. He comes up having finished the job. I know he is done because the room is losing some of the chill. Not a man to waste his energy on words, he silently hands me his invoice. I expect a large bill. Yet the amount gives me another reason to shiver. I raise my head before opening my big mouth. I look at his bloodshot eyes, at the number in the bottom right hand corner of the sheet of paper trembling in my hand, at the hammer and the closed front door. I realize that bargaining is futile and get the cheque book and a pen from the desk. I take the cap off the pen and fill his name. Now he opens his mouth for the first time since coming up from the basement, "Leave the amount blank," he growls.

"Yes sir" I reply in a trembling voice and hand him the blank cheque. He says without looking at it "Sign it". "Sorry" I respond and sign the cheque. He shoves it in the inside pocket of his oily jacket, lifts the huge hammer with ease and puts it on his shoulder, picks up the tool bag and says as he walks out of the door, "Don't cause me any trouble and I will be reasonable."

I pick up the phone but my fingers are trembling too much to dial. Good sense prevails and I put the phone down. I go up to the bedroom. "Thanks dear" says Monica under the impression that it was I who had fixed the furnace. Well, in a way I had, with some professional help. I pull the blanket up to my ears, "you are welcome sweetie."

I see that plumber quite often. Thankfully only when, for all outward appearances, I am peacefully asleep.

~ 16 ~

Having partied till long past midnight we should have
set the alarm clock to get up in good time. In fact,
we did do it but managed to sleep through the gentle
tinkling sounds. When we opened our eyes we saw the intricate patterns on the wall made by bright sunlight coming
through the blind. The small hand of the still ringing clock was
at nine, big hand at twelve. The time gave us a shock. Bolders
were due for brunch at 10! We jumped out of bed, forgetting
our weekend ritual of a cup of tea in bed, showered and rushed
down to the kitchen to prepare the sumptuous breakfast we
are famous for, at least we think we are. Let me be fair and not
take the credit I do not deserve. The good wife does most of
the work. I help with what I can, mostly by setting the table
and doing the dishes. My only contribution to the delicacies on
the table is the scrambled egg. I have my own recipe for this oft
maligned dish which I carry in my head for fear of being stolen
if ever put down on paper. I have refined it over forty years and
now I am told by all who are lucky enough to taste it, that it is
unsurpassed. That said, being a humble person that I am, I will
never take pride in it, not in print anyway.

To make scrambled eggs I need, apart from the secret
combination of herbs and spices, butter, tomatoes, mushrooms,
cheese, red and green peppers and of course eggs. The recipe
demands large free range chicken eggs; twelve of them for

four people. When I opened the fridge, the box contained only four. Scared to death, I rushed down to the basement three steps at a time to check the spare fridge. It was not my lucky day. The fridge had every thing a cook could wish for but no eggs. The only course I could follow was to hop in the car and get them from the Hardway, the grocery supermarket five minutes drive on a Saturday morning.

This is what I did. I parked the car and dashed past all the fruits, vegetables, milk and meat displayed most invitingly to the corner of the store where eggs are shelved. I could see chicken eggs and duck eggs, brown eggs and white eggs, small eggs and large eggs, farm eggs but no free range eggs. I was dumbstruck. I looked all around for a Hardway person to help. When one has plenty of time and no need for the help, white coated attendants are hovering over you. Now that I needed one all of them were playing hide and seek. I found a young man in the nut section who wasn't even sure that they ever sold free range eggs. "They are so expensive no one buys them," he tried to tell me. "I always buy them and they are on the bottom shelf of Aisle 97," I informed him curtly. He came to the aisle with me; I showed him the usual spot. "Wait a minute, I will find out," he mumbled before disappearing into the maze of shelves. Five minutes of twiddling my thumbs later he appeared with four boxes of six. I snatched them and rushed to the counter. The person ahead of me in the Express Lane was an elderly gentleman, hard of hearing and with a touch of cerebral palsy. It took him what felt like an hour to find his wallet, the right bills, change purse, the right change, Air miles and Hardway cards and then place his purchases in the cart. When I presented the eggs to the cashier, she looked at them and noticed a couple of cracked ones. She disregarded my protest and spent precious minutes working out the discount. At long last she handed me the bag with eggs. I left a ten dollar bill on the counter and rushed off without collecting the change.

My troubles were far from over. I was now stuck behind a lady pushing her husband in the wheelchair. They were arguing over something of critical importance to them, like the price of broccoli, and were in no hurry. I had no choice but to follow them at less than a snail's pace. When the lady got to the exit door she had trouble negotiating the wheelchair. I helped her through the door and ran to the car.

It was already ten past ten and I still had to drive home and scramble the eggs. Punctuality is one of the many attributes of the Bolders and just like all other clock watchers they are not very patient. To think of it, no hungry person is. I hopped in the car backed out and heard a bang. No, it was not me. It was a car ahead which had run into two other cars or two other cars had run into his, depending on which side one takes. No injuries, just some dents. But no one appreciated their good fortune. They jumped out and began self righteously screaming at each other for being so stupid as to cause a fender bender. From all the agitation, an onlooker would have thought that it was the first accident they had ever been involved in. I had no time for schadenfreude or the analysis of the human psyche. I turned the car around and found another way out of the parking lot. It was now 10:20.

It was 10:30 when I got home. Bolders don't live very far and they usually walk to our home. So the absence of their car was not a surprise. I rushed to the kitchen with the bag of eggs. Oddly the good wife was gaily humming an old Beatle tune while making pancakes. She asked gently, "What took so long?"

"So many things that I will have to write a story. Where are the Bolders?" I asked.

"They are held up, won't be here till eleven."

I felt a big load off my narrow chest. I wiped my brow with a kitchen towel and started chopping mushrooms.

~ 17 ~

When the going gets tough, the tough get going. I do not know why I thought of this old saw. I was a hundred points ahead, there were only a couple of tiles left and the probability of Jimmie catching up was farther than remote. May be my mind was wandering after concentrating for the last hour. I had challenged Jimmie to a game of Scrabble. Jimmie is a Greek immigrant who learnt English only a few years ago and still has difficulty putting sentences together. Yet, he is passionate about the word game. It improves his vocabulary, he claims. He plays with any one who is ready to match the knowledge of words with him. He is never without a pocket sized set of board and tiles and at the slightest hesitation on the part of an acquaintance, even a stranger at times, the board comes out and the game is set up. This time, though, it was at my request that we were playing. I needed diversion from my many other problems and I thought concentrating on inane words to be made from seven tiles will bring my sanity back. It was a hot summer afternoon. I picked up some cans of cold beer after work and went to Glenmore Park looking for him. There he was, sitting on his usual bench memorizing words from a dictionary. He shut the fat book when he heard me at some distance suggesting a game. We found a picnic table, tossed for scorer, each picked a tile to decide the starter and picked our letters. Words Jimmie and I began with were indeed inane and caused some laughter in the crowd starting to gather around us. He started with MISERY, I responded with PITY. TROUBLE, SORROW, GRIEF followed. It was only towards the end that I put down JOY and he responded with RELAX. The game swung from one way to the other. Towards the end I had a small lead. Then I set up ZENITH for triple word score and my lead jumped to 102 points. There was clapping from the crowd. With such a big lead, I had no reason to worry even when I picked the letters T, O, Q and H and noted that only two tiles were left in the bag. That is when the tough saying crossed my mind.

Jimmie was deep in thought looking at his letters. He was in a tough spot, more than a hundred points behind with only one or two turns left. He kept shuffling letters on the shelf, completely oblivious to the world. Then he looked at the arrangement of letters, smiled faintly, took a sip from the can of beer and put all seven letters along the right edge, taking off from my H and adding from the bottom up Y, L, T, S, E, N and O. Bingo, he had scored 95 points and was now only seven behind. There was a burst of applause. With only two tiles versus my seven, he had a good chance to overtake me. It was I who was truly sweating now.

I took a big gulp from my can and concentrated on my letters scratching the back of my bald head as I do rather unconsciously when facing an intractable problem. Nothing fancy can be done with T, O, G, H, Q, R and A. I could see no space around the U's on the board to use my Q whose weighting of ten points had become a handicap. If left unused, that alone will give the game to Jimmie when he empties his shelf on the next turn. Thanks to my lucky stars, staring blankly on the board produced the desired result; I spotted my salvation. Q on a double letter spot, A followed by T to tie in with S on the board. QATS, a word in official Scrabble dictionary though not in any other, gave me 24 points, giving me a lead of 31 and left only eight points unused on my board. I had Jimmie on the ropes.

Jimmie knew it too. As did the crowd watching the game in suspense. He looked at his two letters, then the board. Actually he looked at the board more than the letters. Along the top, along the bottom, then the left edge and his eyes moved steadily towards the right. Something arrested his attention. A broad smile settled on his face as he saw the freestanding J. He set down W on a double letter spot along with an A to make JAW and WE, 26 points, only 5 behind. I was crestfallen. I showed him my remaining tiles. He duly entered the points due to him, congratulated me on a close game in spite of poor letters and wished me better luck next time so long as I was playing some one else. There was some cheering as the crowd dispersed. Jimmie picked the tiles from the board, counted them carefully and put them in the bag. With the wretched board and the bag in his coat pocket, he left whistling the Colonel Bogey March.

When I got home I found Monica upset because her best staff member resigned, kids were angry because the teachers had loaded them with home work, and their elderly grandmother was complaining of pain in her joints. I consoled them as much as I could and kept my disappointment to myself. Comforting the family takes priority over licking my own wounds any day.

~ *18* ~

Our settled and peaceful conventional life was shattered the other day when the Supreme Court of Canada ruled that the school boards must permit the students of Sikh faith to carry a kirpan (dagger) in accordance with their beliefs. The Judges being the supreme arbiters of law, who am I to disagree with them. Actually I am quite pleased. I can now practice a command of my religion which I have never practiced, not even in India, my native country. However, the third world countries do not indulge the minorities and religious freedom takes second place to social taboos of the vast majority. Therefore, it was not practical to give up all adornments like clothing, as instructed by Bhagwan Mahavir, the founder of Jainism and an incarnation of God. It is better to let the soul return to life one more time than to live in a prison with untouchables and eat food prepared by cooks of the wrong caste on utensils washed by non-Hindus.

Now I can, with Supreme Court's blessing, practice the dictates of my sect, Digambar (Skyclad) Jain, and go naked into the crowds with impunity. If I continued to wear clothes I will have no excuse when I meet the Highest Judge on my way into the next life. All items of clothing must be sent to the Salvation Army for those not lucky enough to be born in my sect. The gift will have to be anonymous because any pretence of generosity is forbidden in the pronouncements made twenty five hundred years ago. The clients of the Army can show off my Armany suits, Gucci shoes and diamond studded rings without acknowledging the source. Indeed, it will give me great pleasure when I think of them proudly walking to the job interviews in clothes they secured largely due to the largesse unforeseen by the supreme judges. The joy of reducing the number of life cycles by following strictly the laws of my birth religion should far exceed the discomfort of shivering even on the warmest day of the summer.

Rather than fearing, I look forward to the reaction of my colleagues when I walk buff naked out of the car on to the parking lot and into the office on Monday. Of course there will be complaints from men and screams from women who have lived all their lives being afraid of the human body. I must take a copy of the court decision to prevent violent reactions. Strange looks, sarcastic comments, resistance to raising thermostat I can understand and live with but avoidance of my company and refusal to meet and work with me will bring forth the fury of a Jain scorned which may result in another appeal to the fair-minded judges and several years of salary and bonuses without having to work.

If worse becomes worst and the police is called, I plan to stand firm. I am prepared to be incarcerated in Canada for my beliefs. The jails for white collar non-violent crimes, from what I see on television, are comfortable rooms with their own thermostats. If they force me to wear uniforms so much the better. My lawyers will include the government in my complaint to Human Rights Commission and the compensation will be considerable larger. The money is of no use to an all-sacrificing sky-clad Jain except that larger the amount I hand over to charities, more brownie points I receive when my deeds in this life are being weighed by the bookkeeping gods above. For maximum impact, I will make sure that the charities are based in the country with the weakest currency. How they use the money is not my worry, in this life or the next.

My biggest problem, I fear, is my family. Not considering the prospects of the enactment of laws supporting the tenets of my religion, I married an English woman and we had agnostic/atheistic children of no faith. How they respond to their short, fat, bald, ugly, spouse or father in his late sixties going around in full glory is a concern. Even if they understand the constraints imposed by my religion in light of new legal freedom, will they be able to stand up to the ridicule heaped upon them by their friends? They can disregard the reaction of strangers but not friends. My family members are extroverts and the life loses all meaning if an extrovert is eschewed by her friends. Then there are two adorable grandchildren of the most sensitive age. I do not expect their school buddies to understand their dilemma and imagine fights in school - unsympathetic teachers supporting the bullies. I can see the poor babies coming home with tearful eyes and bruised bodies to their mother. The mother who already sides with strangers against this senile Born Again Skyclad who was normal till the judges wrote a judgment without considering the consequences – to her. She will not be able to explain to them the normal human urge to follow the dictates of one's religion; they are too young to understand it anyway. She may have to find some facile explanation which will not be flattering to their grandpa. Worse still, the thought of moving to a far-off place might spring into her mind.

I can face the world out there to follow the basic principles of my religion irrespective of hardships to my person. But I can not bear the thought of my grandchildren being distressed and moving away for good. It is a problem far beyond the capacity of a mere human. This evening, after my simple dinner of chapattis, rice and alloo gobhi, I will ask Bhagwan Mahavir for guidance. I know He will listen to my entreaties and issue a verdict that will lead to the reconciliation of life with nirvana.

~ *19* ~

A little more than a year ago I reached a new stage in my life. I became a senior. It reminded me of other important milestones — becoming an adult and starting to financially support parents and a younger brother; getting married and after a decent interval becoming a father; achieving financial independence; each stage building on the one before and providing a deep feeling of gratification. The latest stage, however, is more a millstone than a milestone even though a four figure sum is deposited in my account every month merely for breathing. In addition to the pension, I also get an annual transit pass for almost nothing, free prescription drugs, discounts on groceries, liquor, concert and airline tickets and other considerations too numerous to list. Most seniors have graciously given up their jobs to younger generations and retired to days of thorough review of the morning paper with breakfast, detailed discussion of news with other seniors over coffee, long lunch with more seniors, sessions of afternoon bridge or golf with yet another group of seniors, dinner with the wife who is most likely also a senior. Evening is spent snoozing in front of the TV. This is followed by a drink of hot milk and bed. What can be more idyllic than this routine?

Having an idyllic routine is one thing, being able to live it is another. As a starter, I have medical appointments irrespective of how healthy I think I am. Some of my scheduled visits: the dentist for chipped tooth, the ENT specialist for bad hearing, family doctor for back ache, physiotherapist for sore knees, heart specialist for bad breath – sorry, shortness of breath, the psychologist for poor memory. The visits are due almost every other day. It takes longer to drive there than it would have in younger days because I am loathe to change lanes even when I am following a school bus, I slow down and stop on orange light, stay well within speed limit, do not turn left when a car is approaching – you don't want me to list all my driving habits that annoy harried younger people in a hurry and sometimes cause them to almost crash into this poor senior from behind. Then there is waiting even when I am on time. I understand why family doctors run late. Patients have longer list of problems than they advise when appointment is booked. Not because new ailments crop up, just that they don't want their secrets spilled to a receptionist. Don't blame them, I don't either. Sometimes serious illness is discovered on close examination when the patient had come in for a sore throat. But what unnerves me is the wait in the examining room in my underwear on a visit to the specialist. After I have sat there freezing for half an hour, the specialist rushes in, does her thing for five minutes, tells me to come back for more detailed examination and rushes out. It does get my goat. I appreciate that the specialists have worked hard for umpteen years to get their training and have to be ultra efficient to pay off their student loans, mortgages on their mansions and leases on their stable of BMWs. But patients, even seniors, have urgent commitments as well but no one takes that into account. Enough of this griping, it is not good for my heart. Back to medical visits. Often, one must drop by the pharmacist on the way home with all the attendant delays. All told, a medical appointment takes me most of the day whatever I do. I wouldn't mind it once in a while, but it seems that every doctor, and I see many, loves to examine me at least once a month.

Then there is shopping. Yes, the home is paid for. Furniture is old but serviceable and in any case I have grown fond of it because it has adjusted its contours to mine. Still, things break down once in a while and need to be replaced. When I go to the store; I find they have relocated the department I need, then I can't find any body to help me. If there is one, she is helping a young couple or busy with rearranging items in the store. Eventually I get her attention, order the item and ask for it to be delivered to my home. No, she can't give me date and time of delivery. I need to call an 800 number but must pay delivery charge of fifty dollars in advance. I call the 800 number and talk to someone in a remote village in India or China. She can give me a date but not time. After some cajoling I get a commitment that the delivery agent will call to confirm on the previous day. The delivery agent can confirm but not give me the time. It will be when it will be but certainly on the date assigned in the remote Indian village. The item comes in a big box and is dumped in my garage. I open the lid of cardboard box with some difficulty. The wretched thing has to be assembled!

I call the store. After several tries, a grouchy person answers. I tell him my problem: I had the impression that the item was delivered as shown in the store. Sir, nothing is delivered as in the store, it takes too much space and costs too much to ship assembled. I am too old to assemble, I say. Well, they can give a number to call; the person will come and assemble for a fee. How much? I ask. He can't tell, the number does not work for the store. I call the number. He will come and assemble in two weeks and charge $60 an hour plus half hour for travel. In the middle of coldest spell of winter, I have lost the use of garage for two weeks. Entreaties don't work, two weeks it is. Too many seniors on a buying spree, it seems.

Two weeks go by. He calls to confirm but can't give the time. Depends on how long other jobs take, he says with some justification. I cancel my coffee group, my lunch date, my bridge session and wait patiently for the busy assembler. He arrives in the late afternoon, looks at the partially opened box, grumbles, opens it more, takes everything out, spreads it out all over the rather dirty garage floor and starts putting Humpty together. Halfway through, I hear the scream. He is standing there screaming four letter words. He hasn't brought some tool he must have. I take him to my tool room. He scrambles through the mess, finds a wrench and says it might do.

Two hours later, the thing is assembled. He goes to his truck and prepares the invoice. He comes back with the invoice. I write him a check. He wants credit card. I tell him the card is maxed out paying for the thing and delivery charge. He takes the check with a warning that if it bounces he will charge fifty dollars to cover his expenses. Now I ask him to help move the thing to its proper place. No, he can't do it. He is an assembler, not a mover. He knows one though. He goes to his truck and comes back with the card of a small time mover.

I call the mover. He is very busy because most small movers have gone to Hawaii for the winter; there is so little work here. He gives me a day three weeks later — no he can't give me the time. On the appointed day, he comes at noon with an assistant. The two of them move the thing to the place I want. They present me an invoice for sixty dollars for the hard work. I suppose it is not much for two people considering travel time. However, the delivery, assembly and moving added up to as much as the thing itself. Call it the cost of seniority.

In my young days I enjoyed cutting the grass on hot summer days and shoveling the snow on cold winter days. My back can no longer stand up to such vicissitudes. I hired a one man company to do the snow job. He truly does. He comes after the driveway has been driven over a few times. When I complain of the uneven job, he blames my excessive driving. I advertised in local grocery store to find a neighborhood teenager to do it. Alas! The only respondent was the snow man himself. I pay him a four figure sum for the winter to remove the snow and leave the ice behind. If I don't, the city will be after me to clear the sidewalk. The experience with grass is a little better. The young man cuts the grass and carts away the clippings. But he likes to do it at the crack of dawn. When I transmitted to him neighbor's complains, he showed me the city regulations. I made copies of the relevant regulation and dropped one each in the mail boxes of the complainants when they were out.

Even the taxman is after the seniors. I claim old age deduction on one page, take it out on the next. I enter income supplement on one line, give it back on the other. I saved income tax in retirement plan, now I pay it back with interest when I take money out to live on. Politicians make promises before the election to rectify the situation, forget them soon afterwards. They have good reason to think we have poor memory. Most of us do.

Yes, life could be idyllic as a senior. But I can assure you that it is not. On the other hand, it is better than the alternative.

~ 20 ~

Claiming a minority status has always been in fashion. A generation ago it was being a Catholic. Then it was being black, visible minority if you include Asians, Africans and other undesirables. For a while being on social welfare was something to proclaim with pride. Seniors had their day in the sun for a while. Now it is the turn of the gays. Ever since an ape walked as the first human, gays have been secretive. But the new fashion has outed them. Not only do they claim from the rooftop to be gay, they demand the rights others enjoy. If Catholics could have the monopoly on Prime Minister's job, seniors could get away without paying health-care premiums and visibles could live in the prosperous erst-while exclusive invisible majority communities, why shouldn't gays get married, have children, get divorced, get remarried and inherit the wealth of their past and present partners after their demise. No reason whatsoever, Bible thumpers to the contrary. However, let me warn them; getting legal rights is a far cry from public recognition of their rights.

As a member of the visible minority, I have first hand experience of having all necessary legal rights yet getting little public respect. Thanks to my invisible majority spouse, I do live in an invisible majority community. In fact, I am the only visible human in the "village." But instances of meter readers, plumbers, garbage collectors, window cleaners taking me for a butler are quite frequent. I do play the role of a butler on occasions, but invisible butlers get respect from the mailman, not condescension. When I go out, I am always the last one to be served in the bar or on the counter, there is always a certain distance between me and the others howsoever packed a crowd, my queries are often answered with exasperation, if at all and my Cadillac always attracts whistles when I drive but never Monica's Porsche. I have long suspected that invisibles assume this superior attitude unconsciously because it is in their genes although many sophisticated invisibles are uncomfortable with it and try hard to hide it.

I am a male. That too makes me a minority, although by a very small margin. However, I have been a very small minority in a family of wife, three daughters and a female cat. Buckets of tears have been shed and screams of joy echoed from the walls in our home without any one feeling the slightest need to bring the lonely male into picture. My hope that in-laws and grandchildren will restore some balance was cruelly dashed by fate. Two of my daughters brought home female partners and had female progeny. The third daughter is self contained for now. Our dinner table has one visible male surrounded by four to eight females often discussing male reluctance to recognize them as equals while giving him no chance to express an opinion even if he dared to have one. When gay daughters are home, conversation always comes around to gay rights, homophobia of clergy and duplicity of politicians. I prefer this to other topics dear to liberated females because on this issue I have no contrary opinion to express and be given a cruel cold shoulder.

A year ago, I acquired another claim to minority; I became a senior. I still have my office and work normal hours but I do show my age, have done it for years. Now people look at me and assume that I have a whole day to kill. Consequently, I wait for service even when the clerk has no one else to attend to. All the backlog of computer work becomes a priority as soon as the person ahead to me has been served. That is not all. The receipts have to be arranged and rearranged, the cash has to be counted and recounted, returned items have to be neatly folded, wrapped and put back on the shelves and, once in a while, floor around me has to be cleaned before my cash is taken and my purchase put in the bag. All this time, I stand there wondering which minority role is the culprit; visible, male, senior or any combination thereof. I did ask once. The invisible young lady whisked back the bag and called security. It took a lot of apologizing before I could get away.

Being a minority is not always a disadvantage. Minorities with swing vote are coddled by politicians before elections. Even groups notorious for corruption and utter contempt for local traditions are sought after and their leaders are given prominent seats in the cabinet. Some visible communities and seniors have finally learnt to play this game. No doubt, minority of the day, gays and lesbians, will organize and learn to pull the right strings before long. As for senior men, they do have one great advantage: they become more and more of a minority as they grow older and therefore are more in demand. The invisible old ladies in old people's home cherish even the visible old men even though their manly qualities have become mostly a fond memory by now. If they are able to add another minority feature, money in the bank, things really look up for visible senior males. Women the age of their granddaughters who appreciate easy life with few disturbed nights and no long term risk are happy to move in with them. Well-off seniors in old people's homes, male or female, are showered weekly visits by sons and daughters looking to supplement their unemployment cheques and by grandchildren looking for help with college fees. Local charities wine and dine them hoping to be remembered in the will. Financial and legal advisors are at their beck and call trying to earn exorbitant but well-deserved fees.

Having been a visible minority for almost fifty years, and having added other minority features along the way, it seems to me that the system has taken care of major handicaps like employment inequities but minor daily irritations remain. To resolve these, a large number of invisibles will have to undergo gene therapy. Since this is rather unlikely, my only hope is that the irritants will be offset by new advantages, particularly if I add the elusive money-in-the-bank status. Then I will be able to look forward to my days in old people's home as a visible senior male who is in demand for one last time.

~ 21 ~

As I enter the later half of my middle age it has become apparent to me that my reactions are even slower than they used to be. Unfortunately, either those who are near and dear to me have not noticed my new deficiency or they do not make allowances for it. It adds to the problems in daily life in many ways. Here is an example. If my answer to her query is not as prompt as anticipated by my beloved wife, a fiery "Why don't you ever answer me?" comes at me across my newspaper so loud that I feel the urge to adjust my hearing aid. I answer the second question first, "Thinking the best option, dear" and use this interval to come up with the proper answer for the tricky first question. Then I hope that the storm created by my tardiness has passed over as I take a soothing sip of tea.

The problem with my slow reactions is most acute when I get behind the wheel of my Cadillac, my faithful servant for twenty five years. Along with many other adjustments in my driving habits, I have learnt to stay far enough behind the car in front so that I can make an emergency stop without bumping into anybody. However, impatient drivers snaking in and out to get to the traffic light ahead of the competition butt in and fill the space forcing me to slow down more and more. Every so often this causes the person following me to bump into me. Although the dents caused by these mishaps are fixed by impatient driver's insurance company, sorting things out after the smallest of accidents takes time and I am late for the meeting, even miss it sometimes. Thank heavens I have not suffered any serious injury so far. However, as a safety measure, I have now stopped driving in the rush hour. For early morning meetings I get there before most people wake up. This allows me to take advantage of cheap early bird rates at parking garage. For late afternoon meetings I stay in town till the impatient younger always-in-a-hurry drivers have left. Not only does this help in recovering from the stresses of meetings, every once in a while I get away without paying because the parking attendant has left.

In addition to the peace of mind there is another advantage in being on the road in quiet periods. I can move in the lane I need for the turn and stay there even if the turn is several kilometers away. If I don't change lanes, I don't have to risk my neck muscles by having to look over the shoulder for pesky cars who love being in my blind spot. A friend who was nowhere near as old as me was giving a shoulder check. His neck muscles froze and he couldn't straighten his neck. Fortunately, he was one of those slow pokes who hog the fast lane while driving at the posted speed limit with utter contempt for the traffic moving twice as fast. His car ran into the divider and came to a stop before he caused any injury to himself or the others. When he told me of the incident I knew it was the pretty driver who held his eyes, stiff muscle was a story invented for his wife. It never ceases to amaze me what lies husbands will tell to stay in the good books of the loved and feared ones.

Another problem of being a slow-witted driver raises its ugly head when I am following a car that wants to turn left. In my younger days, as soon as I saw the left turn signal, I would look in the mirror, give a quick shoulder check and smartly move to the right lane. Now, by the time the signal stirs the few remaining neurons in my brain, all I can do is to stop the car inches behind the flashing culprit. There I sit and wait when the oncoming traffic makes the left turn impossible. Then the light turns orange, traffic stops and the culprit rushes to make his getaway leaving me staring at the red light. I allow time for one or two such holdups and do not mind them. I can use them for invigorating sips from my coffee mug. A lady friend uses these breaks to freshen her make up. But there have been times when I had several such mishaps, sometimes on one traffic light, and got so late for the meeting that all the chocolate donuts were gone.

When the light turns green I like to take my time before starting to move. I bring my phone call to a quick but courteous end, check the cross road to make sure the traffic has really stopped, make sure of the oncoming traffic for some one making the left turn and ascertain that the pedestrians are safely on the side walk. It should not really be a problem but all these impatient young punks make it one. There is always someone behind who would rather kill than be late. The honking starts, sometimes in unison by several cars. I start wondering what is going on and react in what some people would call a panic. I either accelerate as fast as my old Caddie would go or not move at all. There have been occasions when rude signs have been flashed and "stay off the road" screamed. As I grow older, I learn to be patient with impatience of others. It makes my life tolerable and probably longer. What it does to others is really not my business.

I like to look where I am going, not where I am coming from; while driving as much as in living. Therefore, I never ever look in the rear view mirror. It does not cause me any problem generally, only when I am driving with Monica. My dear wife's antenna goes up in alarm whenever there is some rushing maniac tailgating us. Without her by the side, I carry on without a care in the world unaware of any problem. But her lively imagination has already given both of us whiplash before a car is within twenty meters of our back lights. In old days when I was young I myself would be speeding and this situation would never arise. No more. Now I refuse to push pedal to the floor or risk my neck to change lane. So I do the only other thing I can do. I slow down more and more till the car behind is touching the bumper. As soon as the distance between my back bumper and his front bumper approaches zero, as my calculus teacher was fond of saying, the goon behind maneuvers to rush past us with a deafening roar of his engine much to the relief of both of us.

My granddaughter gave me a unique gift on my last birthday. It is a bumper sticker made with fluorescent ink. She is certain it will resolve many of my problems and reduce the number of trips to auto body shop. She has even offered to put it on when I get the car back from there. The sticker says in big capital letters - "Old Man Driving."

~ 22 ~

The winters in Calgary are a mixed bag. Some years the snow doesn't appear till January. Other years it snows in September and then not till March. Once in a while it snows every week from October to June and the temperature stays well below freezing. This year, it snowed in early October when the trees were still loaded with leaves. Cold spell froze the leaves and the crab apples in our yard and for all I know they are destined to stay on the trees till spring when they will rejuvenate for an unexpected second life cycle.

In the first week of December the second cold spell arrived exactly as the weather channel had predicted. It really was cold, thirty below zero without counting the wind chill. At these temperatures it doesn't matter whether it is centigrade or Fahrenheit, your exposed skin freezes in seconds either way. Forty winters of freezing and thawing in this blessed city have taught me a lesson; I now cancel all my meetings for the duration and give away tickets to the concerts and other entertainment without fretting about how much they cost. I raise the thermostat to its highest and stay in bed with two hot water bottles and a book of stories about Hawaii by Jack London.

It was nine on Saturday morning when I opened my eyes with great reluctance. I whispered in my wife's ear a compliment before reminding her gently that it was her turn to make the tea. On her way to the kitchen she raised the blind when I was pulling my eyelids apart. I looked out and an incredible view brought me to my senses before taking them away. I will describe it as well as I can. But if I do not succeed, please make some allowance for English being my second language and the poor quality of ESL lessons in the early days of immigration from the Third World.

It was a bright day but I could tell from the thick frost near the bottom of the picture window that it was awfully cold outside. The almost opaque frost had a smooth concave edge which uniformly graded into transparency. At some distance on the left, Green, blue, orange and red Christmas lights on the Mayday tree were shining through the frost, giving the view a dreamy appearance with their diffused glow. On the right almost touching the window, a blue jay flitted in the crab apple tree with dark brown leaves and over ripe crab apples size of a ping pong ball frozen on the branches. Bright icicles of various length and diameter hung from the eaves trough sparkling in the beams of sunlight. Little dots of ice on the pane scattered the light in exploding rainbow colours. The row of evergreens along the fence, their branches stooping to breaking point with the weight of snow but their tops competing with each other to touch the sky, had a new majesty. Twittering squirrels, jumping from one branch to other, were scattering the snow dust which added to the otherworld sense engendered by the scene. The velvety blue of the sky, untouchable in grandeur as much as in reach, gave a unity to the picture which distinguishes the work of a genius from that of an accomplished artist.

My wife had come in silently and joined me under the blankets. We sat there quietly, leaning back against the pillows holding hands, at peace with each other and the world, enjoying the nature at its best. I do not know for how long, only that the tea was cold when I poured it.

It Really Happened!

~ *1* ~

"Dear, I am starving. Do you mind getting me a nice juicy fruit from the garden" Adam was pleased to hear the request. It gave him something to do. He was bored stiff with nothing to do all day. Not allowed to go outside the Garden of Eden, no books to read, no radio or television, no one except Eve to talk to. And all they could talk about was how wonderful the life was. Whiling away the time was a tough job. So when he heard Eve's request, his heart jumped with joy. He sprang up, walked around the garden examining mangos, peaches, plums, bananas, pineapples and grapes hanging from the branches and vines. Somehow, none seemed ripe enough to be offered to his sole companion. Then he came to a tree loaded with red fruits shining brightly through dense green leaves. He climbed up, picked a fruit and tasted it. He was transported to another world; I don't know what world except that it was not heaven because he was already in it. The fruit was so juicy, so sweet; each crunchy bite was a delight. He picked six of them, absolutely the best of the crop, gently dropped them to the ground, came down the tree and carried them to his sweetheart as fast as he could. He presented the best one to her with a deep bow, "The humble gift from a proud slave."

"Oh dear, isn't this the fruit Father forbade us to eat? How can you go against his wishes, he has given us everything we could ever need?

"Oh my darling Eve. Surely He forbade us to eat it but

only before it is ripe. Unripe fruit may cause stomach ache or something worse for all I know. He would not want such a lovely fruit to rot on the ground, would He?"

"Adam, you are always trying to find ways around the few instructions that we have been asked to follow. The other day I saw you trying to climb the garden wall. Fortunately, it was slippery and you couldn't do it. Your disobedience will be our undoing."

"Darling, be kind to your soul mate. I feel this urge deep inside me to know what is around me and this thirst for knowledge must have come from somewhere. I sometimes think that I got it from our dear Father. I tasted one before picking so many. This is the most gorgeous fruit in the garden. Try it, you will love it."

"OK, I will try it. But what do we say if the Father finds out?"

"How can He find out? He doesn't watch us every moment of the day, does He? If He does find out and asks, we will blame the slithery snake for telling us how good it was."

Eve swallowed the argument and bit on the apple for the first telling taste. She loved it and greedily ate the whole one spitting out the stones with gusto. Then she ate another and then another. Soon they were all gone. She wanted some more, as did Adam. He led her to the tree and was throwing down the apples to her when they heard the gate open. They turned around. Father was looking at them with fire in his eyes.

At this point I woke up, my pajamas soaked with perspiration.

~ 2 ~

Of all the languages I know English is the odd one. The other language is my mother tongue, Hindi and I had no trouble learning to speak it. English, however, has always been a foreign language to me and after fifty years of trying to speak it correctly, there are days when I am ready to give up.

Hindi is written exactly as it is spoken. There are no spellings to worry about, no articles to fuss on. If you can read it you can speak it although many speak it without being able to read it, being ignorant of the script. But English is strange that way. Foreign kids learn to read the alphabet, practice writing capital and small, both in large size for clarity. Then the idiosyncrasies of pronunciation and spelling hit them - urn is pronounced the same as earn, ic in rich sounds different than ic in rice as does thes in these and thesis. Well, it is not for them to reason why. Just learn if you want to urn, sorry earn, a living when you grow up.

My teachers worked hard with the best intentions but they had never heard English from an English mouth. If they ever came across BBC on radio, they could not make head or tail of what they heard and quickly tuned it out. They learnt the grammar by reading a book on grammar and the usage of words by reading classic books. Consequently, English language took a new form – the grammar and spellings were the same but pronunciation often reflected the spelling, and intonation followed the mother tongue of the speaker. Thus, develop became 'dave lup', typical 'type ical', bicycle 'by cycle'. Articles like 'the' and 'a' became rare if they appeared at all. The language I was taught was "Indian English" and speaking it had little to do with English proper as I learnt to my chagrin when I landed in England. It was several months after our first meeting when my professor and I could be sure of what the other was saying rather than gas, sorry guess, it.

When I met Monica she decided that she had to train my diction before she could train me as a prospective spouse. She urged me to slow down like a commuter train that stops at each station rather than go fast like an Express train that had to hurry along to the next full stop. The demotion of this magnitude was hard to take but I was young and lovelorn and the happiness of a prospective mate was worth it. Then followed the instruction to listen carefully to how people were pronouncing the words, not just hear them for what they meant. To promote my ability to concentrate on listening, I was made to sit through classical music concerts, operas and plays. My most offensive mispronunciations were spelled out and I repeated after her till I got them right. Often it took quite long because it seemed like a good excuse to prolong our time together. After a year or so, she stopped correcting me. Not because my diction had improved, but because she had got used to it and errors did not jar her ears, or is it years, any more.

We got married, kids arrived and before long we had

teenage girls finding faults with everything around them. Even a thirteen year old knows an easy victim when she sees one and they pounced on the strange language I spoke. And you know what – I was often annoyed although I attempted to humour them. It struck me only recently that they helped my career by making my speech more comprehensible to my clients. When I think of all the big contracts I missed I often wish that the teenagers had arrived a decade earlier. Their good natured criticism also helped me when I started writing short stories for my amusement, although I claimed that it was for their amusement. They did read them, if only to make me feel better.

Last year I took a course in Creative Writing to ease my rite of passage to becoming a writer. Our works were work-shopped – every one commented on the work of a willing victim. My comments were accepted by nods which I have come to understand very well, nods of someone totally ignorant of what I am saying. Their comments on my work implied that the flow of language was strange, which it may have been because I was writing in 'Indian English', a language quite foreign to them.

What can I do at this late stage of my life to write a readable piece of some length? I have had some success in getting very short pieces like "Letters to the Editor" published in newspapers and magazines. However, fiction and essays are another story. Fortunately, I do have more time now to work on improving the language skills, particularly if I give up golf in the afternoons and bridge in the evenings. Who knows, some years of dedicated work may teach me the intricacies of Queen's English, a language which could not be better designed to torture poor foreigners, and enable me to write a story or an essay acceptable to a reputable editor.

~ 3 ~

O f all the women in our company, and there are many, Dora is everyone's favorite. She has an answer for every query, whether related to work or the family. No, she is not an older employee counting her days to retirement. She is a young lady, does not look a day older than twenty although looks are probably deceptive. She could not have her MBA from a well-known school, have run our department for five years with enviable competence and not be at least twenty nine. However, the age is immaterial. It is the appearance that counts. Her well tailored suits or dresses bring out the gorgeous figure without displaying too much cleavage, her platinum blonde head is always well coiffed and minimal make up and jewelry add to her attraction. There is not a man in the office, young or old, short or tall, single or married, who wouldn't die for a date with her.

I am an opera buff. I listen to every opera broadcast and watch every opera program on the boob tube whatever the time or the duration. I have had two season tickets for the opera since I started earning a living even though I have to pinch pennies elsewhere and Monica finds listening to hours of singing in a foreign language a torture. She puts up with it because she likes dressing up and where else can you go these days in a long black dress which shows at its best what it covers up.

I woke up with a spring in my body and brought Monica her morning tea. I reminded her that we had opera in the evening. She responded by a huge sneeze and demanded a box of tissues for her runny nose. Insensitive though I am, her appearance worried me. I touched her forehead, it was hot. She muttered that she must have caught the flu which was going round among her patients. It was obvious that she needed rest; not only from work during the day but also from The Flying Dutchman in the evening. She told me to find someone else to go with. As soon I got to work I put out the word of the spare opera ticket although I was aware of the distinct lack of interest in cultural events among my colleagues. A hockey ticket is fought over; a movie ticket finds a taker with some difficulty; a classical concert or opera ticket – even if you throw in the dinner at an elegant restaurant they look at you as if you are an E.T.

It was nearly quitting time and I had become resigned to sit next to an empty seat. Then the phone rang. It was Dora.

"What do I hear about an opera ticket tonight?"

"Monica has called in sick. I have her ticket. These are not the best seats but you can see most of the stage and hear almost every sound."

"I have never been to an opera. It is about time I learnt what the fuss is all about. What time can you pick me up?"

I couldn't believe my good fortune. It felt like I was on my way to heaven. Suppressing my joy as much as any human could I said, "Seven will allow us time for a drink and I can tell you the libretto. That will help you enjoy it more."

"What is a libretto?"

My heart sank. Visions of the boss still upset by the endless hours of guttural German reviewing my annual performance bonus floated in front of my eyes. Alas! It was too late to back out.

"Libretto is the plot of the opera. It helps you to follow the action on stage if you know it. It is almost impossible to follow the words even if you know German."

"Okay, see you at seven."

I got to her place a little before seven and hummed Leporello's aria from Don Giovanni till it was time to ring the door bell. She came out after a few minutes looking as impressive as she always did. "Sorry, I was on the phone, couldn't get away" she said carefully balancing a steaming cup of coffee in one hand and in the other a gold laced handbag which matched her bright red pant suit perfectly. She winced at the creak as I opened the door of my 1990 Honda Civic and squeezed in with some difficulty while I held the cup.

As soon as the car moved forward she put the cup on her lap and took the cell out and asked peremptorily, "Do you mind if I check the messages?" She touched the keys with the expertise of a teenager and stuck the gadget to her ear horizontally to avoid the dangling sapphire earring. "Sorry, I must answer this call from my sister," she told me after messages had been duly noted in the appropriate corner of her brain. Then followed an animated discussion about their father who, it seemed from the snippets I caught while trying not to be snoopy, was refusing to sell the home he had lived in for

SUDHIR JAIN

fifty years and move into an old people's home. It did amaze
me that, in spite of considerable agitation, she managed to do
justice to her coffee without spilling a drop. The call ended
just when I entered the parking lot. "I must call my brother
before she gets to him" Dora told me and another discussion
ensued. Leaving Dora in a quiet corner in the lobby, I got two
glasses of vintage port from the bar. Dora was completely
focused on explaining the merits of her point of view which
her obstinate brother failed to appreciate. Her occupation did
not bother me; I love watching handsome couples strutting
in their fineries while enjoying the drink of the gods. When
the crowd started moving into the hall I gently nudged her.
She gave me an annoyed look that I deserved for interrupting
a crucial dialogue and finished the call by telling her brother
not to talk to anyone on the matter till they had finished the
discussion later that evening. She drained the port down her
throat, gave me her arm and we walked to our seats in style.
No sooner had we sat down we heard the announcer advising
the public to turn the cell phones off. I confirmed that mine
was off and Dora grudgingly followed suit.

There was no time for me to explain the plot but I pointed
out the relevant pages in the program for Dora to read while
the prelude was being played. No sooner had she handed me
the program back the curtains went up to a beautiful set. Dora
enthusiastically joined in the applause. However, it wasn't long
before she was having trouble keeping her eyes open. She gave
in to the impulse and her head lolled on to my shoulder. I
must admit that contributing to the comfort of my companion
added enormously to my enjoyment of the show.

The first act was soon over. Hearing the applause Dora woke up with a start. When the cheering stopped she looked at her watch and asked me how long the intermission was. We made our way to the bar. I lined up to get her a glass of bubbly and myself a scotch. When I joined her she was already on the phone. To be fair, so were most of the people in the lobby. I watched the scene while sipping my drink and wondered how the people managed before the mobile phones made their way into the handbags and the pockets. My dirty mind wondered how many people are on the cell when making love.

Dora enjoyed the rest of the opera as she did the first act, with her eyes closed. Thankfully, her snoring was barely audible. She opened her eyes when the curtain came down and joined heartily in the applause. On our way out she thanked me for the novel experience and offered to join me again when Monica was busy elsewhere.

She spent the drive home reconnecting with the brother who dared to have an opinion of his own. The goodbye was a very brief interruption in the discussion. At home the dear wife was feeling better but not well enough to sympathize when I told her of my evening with the cell. Fortunately, no one in the office knew about our date and I was saved the embarrassment of telling my mates how the evening went. I soon put the unpleasant episode out of mind and the hefty bonus check did not surprise me in the least.

~ 4 ~

Monica and I are getting on in life and the urge to wrap up the worldly affairs gets stronger by the day. Of all such affairs the will is probably the most important. By will I mean the legal document that is pulled out of the safe and opened with great ceremony after your body has been appropriately disposed off. The family lawyer and trustee read the document with due solemnity to all family members who are entitled to share what is left of your estate after paying hospital, nursing home, funeral home, trustee and the lawyer. It took some convincing for Monica and me to believe that the residual estate would be worth the trouble. The clinching argument was that the likelihood of such a happy happenstance was greater if things were clearly spelt out and the work of the trustee and the lawyer was reduced to a minimum.

We wrote a clear set of instructions on what was to be done with any estate left after paying for the care in our old age. The instructions were emailed to the lawyer of my company. After the exchange of several phone calls and emails, the gentleman drew up a legal document and advised one of us to meet him at his office at 5 PM on Friday. Monica drove to his downtown office at the height of rush hour and found a parking place which was not in a tow-away zone. She had to run to his office and cursed the elevator in three languages for keeping her waiting to get to his office at 4:59. The front door to the office was open. It seemed that the secretary had already left. Monica surreptitiously looked in the hardworking man's office but there was no sign of his august presence. She sat down in the waiting area and opened a two year old Time Magazine to remind her of the world shattering events in one of the final weeks of the last millennium. She was engrossed in the story of President Clinton's cigar when an elderly man hobbled in. "Oh Dr. Lodha, so sorry to keep you waiting. I was hit by a car when hurrying from a meeting to get back. Will you mind looking at my knees and my back where the pain is most excruciating?" He started stripping his clothes off and Monica had no choice but to examine him and recommend that he take some pain killer and see his doctor as soon as possible. "You won't happen to have some with you by any chance, the pain is killing me," he whimpered. Monica searched her handbag and found a few tablets to tide him over. He told her where the washroom was so she could get him some water to wash down the tablets. After the tablets were duly swallowed, he put his clothes back on and asked Monica to step in his office to sign the papers.

He produced two copies of a standard mimeographed form with a poorly typed document for her to glance over and sign. Then he signed it as a witness and gave her a copy. After that he produced an envelope with great ceremony and remarked, "This is my invoice for the fee for services. I hope you will find every thing satisfactory." Monica stuffed the envelope in the handbag, thanked him and walked to the car. After all the events of last hour, a parking ticket would have been the last straw. Thankfully, some one up above was looking after the camel.

When Monica got home she looked at the bill. Looking at the sloppy typing and the number staring her in the face, she felt the decimal had moved a couple of spaces to the right. When I got home, she showed it to me. I was only mildly surprised with the amount, having been fleeced by lawyers at regular interval in my business dealings. However, when Monica told me the story of lawyer's accident, I was quite disturbed. I went straight to the phone and left him a message to call Dr. Lodha's office and leave his health insurance details so she could bill for her services. Unfortunately, her service rates are fixed by the government and the fee did not amount to a tiniest fraction of what we had to pay him. To rub salt in the wounds (ours, not his), her fee was pre-tax and he had to be paid out of post-tax income.

Monica wonders to this day why she didn't take her doctor's advice and go to the Law School for a couple of years instead of ten years of hard slog called medical training.

~ 5 ~

My friends carry computers they call laptops in their right hand and cell phones in their pockets to convince themselves, as much as the others, of their importance. Being a quirky little fellow that I am, I carry a little pocket diary with all my appointments, important postal and email addresses, mobile and stationary phone numbers, name and passwords for important web accounts and various reminders of what to do or not to do. The book leaves my hands free to wave to passers by I know remotely and to shake fist at the cars endangering my life. If the need arises, I pull it out of the pocket and scribble the relevant notes or check the memory lapses. It doesn't need a power outlet and has no battery which runs down at the crucial moment. I don't need expensive and inconvenient appliances to boost my ego. Whatever works is fine with me.

Colleagues often tell me the woeful tales of how they lost their laptop at the customs, in the restaurants, in hospitals, even on a sidewalk. Every time I hear a harrowing story of lost critical information, not to mention big bucks, I feel my pocket for my little friend and the sense of relief mixed with elation at my cleverness brings a smile to my face. This smile causes annoyance to the poor friend relating his misfortune and no amount of apology and explanation improves the unpleasant situation.

Not so long ago the tables were turned. On this fateful day I was up at five. After a thorough review of the business section of the newspaper and one hour of workout prescribed by my physiotherapist for various ailments a person of my age is supposed to have, I noticed that I had only five minutes to drive to my future office four miles away where I was due to meet a painter. I quickly stuffed the pockets of my jacket with wallet, diary, keys of the office and car, and woolen gloves and rushed to my appointment leaving the breakfast untouched. After discussing the color scheme and the scheduling of paint job, I drove the car to the dealership for routine service. Darlene, my associate, picked me up from the bus shelter across the street. After an unusually hassled day which culminated in my walking to and fro for fifteen minutes in front of the building while waiting for the pickup to the dealership, I got home at about five. Then I walked to the neighborhood gas station to pick up Monica's car which had a leaky tire.

I was physically and emotionally drained when I finally got home. We are empty nesters and Monica was away. There was no one at home to take out my frustration on. On the other hand, I could sit down in front of the TV, put my favorite CD on the headphone and read the sport page undisturbed. When my nerves had calmed sufficiently, I found enough leftovers in the fridge to satisfy the pangs of hunger. A glass of port with unsalted raw cashew nuts got me in a mood to start planning the next day. Dear diary, where are you when I need you the most?

After emptying both jacket pockets of gloves, keys and

wallet, I pushed my hand deep inside them for the little book. Not there. I opened my briefcase which I use to carry a cheese and tomato sandwich for lunch. Not there either. Pant pockets: Empty but for the handkerchief. Shirt pockets: Pen and a crumpled note with a strange phone number. No sign of the diary. I looked in both cars, on, beside and under the seats with a search light. Nothing except a toonie, three loonies, one nickel, three pennies and a lot of dirt. Well, no need to worry yet. I must have left it in the office next to the phone. Still I dreamt all night of stolen Aeroplan miles and strangers with horns snooping in our private accounts. I woke up more tired than I was when I went to sleep.

I got to the office half an hour earlier than my normal time giving Darlene a shock. She asked, "Are you all right, your face looks pale." "How can she call my coal black face pale?" I wondered. But I let it pass and rushed to my desk. I turned every thing upside down, then downside up. I looked beside the computer, behind it, under the desk, in the credenza, you name it. Every inch of every surface was inspected. In vain: there was no trace of the little black book.

In desperation I called both service stations, went by the new office, and checked wherever I had walked. Finally, I had to conclude that the book had disappeared. I spent all evening changing passwords of all the accounts I could think of. Still, I dreamt of my hard earned miles, 150,278 in Aeroplan and 41,126 in Air Miles disappearing into thin air and my normally gentle wife being not a little upset with me. When I got up it occurred to me that no one could use the miles because even if they were issued the tickets to nowhere, they would be in our names and the thieves will need our IDs to use them. The sense of relief was immense.

A couple of days went by. Monica returned and duly sympathized when I told her of my loss. The morning of the next Saturday was very cold, nothing unusual for Calgary. We dressed and had our usual weekend breakfast of porridge oats with bran. While sipping tea it struck me that I should check the driveway again in case the diary fell out of pocket when I was getting out of the car. Once in the driveway I decided to check the path to the gas station. When I asked the gas attendant about the missing item he looked at me as if I was a customer paying cash for the gas. Disappointed, I walked back towards home my eyes still glued to the path. By the time I got to the front door my nose was running. "Completely wasted effort, just as the good wife had predicted," I muttered. I took out the handkerchief from my pant pocket to blow my nose. Phut, something dropped to the floor. You guessed it.

It made my weekend. If I knew there is so much joy in finding lost items, I would have been a lot less careful in my younger days.

~ 6 ~

My old friend Sammy is a man of many talents and great many interests. He has been called a renaissance man, though admittedly by friends asking for a loan. Still, he can talk about classical music, European, Arabic, Persian and Indian literature, history, geography, philosophy, even subjects as complicated as paleontology, medicine and psychoanalysis. Of course, he is usually wrong but he picks the audience carefully and collects accolades when someone less astute would be eating humble pies.

His professional talents are many. For decades he was in oil and gas industry advising oil companies on where to explore. He impressed fellow professionals with technical jargon above their heads and prospered even when none of his clients ever found any oil or gas based on his advice alone. Then, to utter surprise of all his friends, he retired claiming burnout. Only a few of his fellow professionals knew the truth. There was a slowdown in the industry and employers were forced to evaluate their technical staff more carefully. As a result, almost all his contacts in the industry were found wanting and given retirement packages. Sammy knew more than any other that there is not much you can do in consulting business without contacts. So he decided to quit before it became obvious that he was being made to quit.

One can't just retire and twiddle his thumb all day, not Sammy any way. So he fired his financial consultant and took over the management of the family's, mostly his wife's, savings. Again, fortune smiled on him. The darts hit the right spots and his portfolios reversed the downward course they had followed with the financial advisor. He bragged about his successes to his ex-clients and one of them entrusted a portion of his retirement package to him.

Sammy soon discovered, much to his surprise, that managing three portfolios totaling a few thousand dollars doesn't take the whole day. In his spare time he started writing short stories based on the memorable events from his life and essays based on his knowledge, vast in his view and shallow in every one else's. One, particularly the one with the ego size of Sammy's, does not write for personal satisfaction alone. He writes for the admiration of his fellow men and, even more so, women. At first Sammy satisfied himself by emailing his creations to all his friends. But it wasn't long before he felt the need to expand the circle of fans.

He started sending his stories and essays to big circulation magazines. When he didn't receive any acknowledgements he sent reminders. When even the repeat reminders did not generate any response he concluded that the editors did not have the ability to appreciate his art. He lowered his sight and sent his work to second tier magazines and newspapers. The sight had to be lowered again and again till he was pestering the community papers, still with little success.

It was Friday the thirteenth, an unlucky combination for many, but it turned out to be a great day for his stocks. One jumped 10%, the other 30% and yet another he was loaded with doubled. What a day. He made $5,129 on the market, enough to cover the losses for the whole month. That is not all; a stock his client had bought on his recommendation jumped and generated a commission of $211. "It doesn't rain, it pours. I could do with a few more days like this Friday the thirteenth" he said to no one in particular.

Then the phone rang. It was the Editor of Backwater News, the community monthly magazine. The Editor had read his essay "Why volunteering is a waste of time" and had liked it. Not only was he going to publish it, he was happy to pay $10 honorarium for it. Sammy couldn't believe his ears. He asked the Editor to repeat what he had said. Yes he had heard it right. He felt the joy greater than any he had ever felt. And for an excellent reason; he was now a writer. Not just a writer, but a published writer. Not merely a published writer but a paid writer. What could be more thrilling than being a writer the droppings from whose pen, sorry keyboard, are sought by the Editors in the whole of Backwater County.

Sammy told me that he was more excited by the honorarium of ten dollars than he was with hundreds in commission and thousands in investment income. I don't know about you, but I would be too if I were ever lucky enough to receive such a call from an Editor.

~ 7 ~

"Uncle, you know Daddy is obstinate," My niece said into the phone from across the world.

"How would I know? He wasn't when we were kids together," I defended my brother the instant I heard the unpleasant observation.

"That is because you wouldn't notice, your whole family is obstinate," she responded.

"You must be obstinate too, coming from the same family," I fired back.

"It has been greatly diluted, thanks to Mummy," she cleverly deflected my arrow.

I admitted defeat and quickly changed the subject. Monica always called me obstinate, even when she was not angry. My daughters called me that among many other things when they did not need the allowance. My colleagues called me 'determined' which is a courteous form of that nasty word. I always denied this and challenged any other association with these unpleasant characteristics. I believed that I stuck to what was right, as every one who is always right must. I realized a little too late to do me any good that I did this to keep my fragile morale up.

Now that I have reached the dignified status of a senior, I have no need for morale, high or low. I can face the truth with open heart, mind and wallet. I can accept that I am obstinate. Why else would every one near and dear say it? May be, just may be, that if I accept the observation to be true, allowances will be made for this obstinacy. The good wife and daughters will do what I suggest without lengthy arguments and give me what I want without a need for hour long persuasion every time. I could just say, "You know your obstinate husband. Once it gets into his pea-brain that he wants Chicken Kiev with pecan pie a la mode for dinner, that is what he must have," And that is what she will serve me. Or I could tell my daughter who has no intention of finding a job, "Dear, you know how obstinate your Dad is. May be it is time you lived on your own and earned your own keep." And she will move out and find a job before the words were out of my mouth. I could tell my colleagues, "You guys know how determined I am. Why don't you just do what I have outlined, rather than make me repeat it over and over." And they will rush to their cubicles to implement my plan.

I could do the same thing with the professionals whose services I seek. "Doc, you know I am obstinate. If I think I have heart murmurs, why do you have to waste our time on tests? Why not just prescribe some pills and get it over with." If the doctor is as obstinate as I am, she will insist on tests and a battle of two obstinates will ensue. I am sure to win this one too. Out of thousands of doctors in this city, there must be one who is reasonable and I will find him/her.

There is a reason senior and senile have first syllable in common. With age comes wisdom to some but delusion to most. Am I deluded to think that other people will take my obstinacy into consideration? May be, I won't know till I try it out. If it works, fine. If not I do really believe that I am always right and I will continue to insist that others acknowledge this simple fact. Sooner, rather than later, they will. Just to get me off their back. And I will be no worse than I am now.

~ 8 ~

I am a volunteer driver for Cancer Society. I am the only member of this elite group of seniors who has a job. Therefore, I am assigned short hauls – radiation therapy patients. I drive the patients from their home to the Clinic, wait for the duration of treatment - fifteen to twenty minutes, and take them back home. The whole thing takes less than two hours. Once in a while the patient has to see the oncologist after the treatment. It can take two or three hours to see the busy doctor. In these cases I give the patient my phone number to call when finished. Then I drive to my office and catch up with work till the phone rings.

It was a cold rainy day last Friday. I had agreed to take a patient to the clinic for her appointment at 11:00. For some strange reason I had a disturbed night and got up on the wrong side of bed. However, I had recovered my composure by the time I arrived at the patient's home in a prosperous area half an hour before her appointment time. A tall slim well-preserved and better-groomed lady in her seventies was waiting for me. I opened the door of the car and helped her with the seat belt. Surprisingly, there were no traffic hold ups on the way and we arrived at the clinic a few minutes early. On our way to the radiation station, she told me that it was the day for her to see the oncologist. I gave her my card with the phone number and returned to work. I reviewed an application for a job in Monica's medical office and called the applicant to set up the interview. Next item was the email to a locum doctor with suitable dates. I was starving by now and it was time to eat the sandwich I had brought to work for lunch. Just as I had taken the first bite, the phone rang – the patient was ready to go home. I returned the sandwich to its container and picked up some coffee on my way to the car. While pushing the elevator button I lost my balance and spilt most of the coffee on my white shirt and grey pants. Thankfully it had cooled enough to spare the skin and stains were limited to the clothes.

On the way to the Clinic I noticed the traffic building up on the opposite side of the highway. With the empty stomach protesting loudly, a crawl for half an hour did not appeal to me. Therefore, after picking the patient I took a long detour on the way back. Thanks to numerous stops on red lights, several school and playground zones with low speed limits and a short diversion due to a bridge repair, the detour probably took a little longer but we did not have to breathe in the exhaust fumes of hundreds of stalled cars and trucks.

After dropping the patient at her home, I took the roads through a residential area hoping to beat the traffic. For the first time that day things went my way and in less than fifteen minutes I was three blocks from my office. Then my luck took its normal turn for the worse and I sat in a stationary car twiddling my thumb for what seemed like eternity. Gods in the form of the longest train any one has ever seen had decided to teach me how to relax by arriving at the crossing a second before I got there. The flashing red went on and the gate came down to block my way. I was too agitated to count the number of rail cars, must have been thousands.

Like all good things, the train also passed. Everything on my desk was exactly the way I had left it. There were no messages on phone or on the internet. Nothing of any note had happened and no one had noticed my absence. I had worked myself into a knot for nothing. Relieved, I poured a cup of fresh coffee and ate my sandwich. No sooner had I opened the file with job applications the phone rang. "Debbie from the Volunteer Driver Program; will you be able to pick up ...."

~ 9 ~

Ravi has many wonderful qualities and he would be voted the most popular man in the club except for one fault. He likes to tell every one in the earshot of his brilliant successes on the stock market. One can tolerate a person bragging about an intellectual achievement like publishing occasional letters in the community paper, or his great contributions to the common good, even his sexual exploits. But to brag about the successes on the stock market, particularly when every one is feeling depressed about their retirement funds having been cut in half, it is just not acceptable. Not in a civil society at any rate.

One Friday last week the North American markets had taken an unusually big dive and there was a feeling of gloom and doom in the club. There was only one cheerful face among fifty in the room. Ravi's happy visage is not particularly noticeable when others are feeling upbeat as well. However, on this evening it stood out like a sore thumb. Rather than improving the sour mood around the table the stories of his triumphs made the players feel worse and induced silly mistakes in bidding and play. No surprise that Ravi happily cleaned up on every table he played.

The club has made a practice of taking a break after every hour of play to help players recover from the stresses of trying to make six no trumps when four hearts would be impossible and trying to defeat three clubs when six no trumps is a lay down. Of course the drinks sold in the breaks help in keeping the membership dues at an affordable level. The bar was particularly crowded that evening because every one was bent on drowning their sorrows if not themselves. It was in the last break when I was jostled into Ravi. He greeted me cheerfully, then looked at my downbeat appearance and asked what was making me so unhappy. He heard my tale of woe, duly sympathized and said, "Take my advice, old boy. Be a day-trader. Buy and sell all you want during the day but don't leave any money in the broker's safe for the night. That way you can control your losses and gains in such a way that at the end of the day the sum total is in black."

"What if the market goes up in the morning and I am sitting with all that cash?" I queried.

"No problem. You look at the stocks and buy those moving up. Don't buy the ones that go down. Sell your purchases by the end of the day and you will have a bigger bundle than you started with."

"What if the stock I buy on the way up nose dives? My bundle will shrink."

"Of course it will. But if you sell before it has dived too far it won't shrink as much as when you buy and hold. Most likely, the small loss will be offset by gains on another trade."

I was not convinced. I had heard the sad tales of day traders who lost all their capital in the collapse of tech bubble. Still, I thought there was no harm in trying with a small sum. I sold 1000 shares of Sellus first thing on Monday and decided to use

the proceeds to test Ravi's formula. I didn't have to wait long
to shoot my first arrow. Imperious Bank announced increased
profit in the morning. But the stock, instead of rising on the
good news, dropped 5% to $19. Here was my chance. "The
stock is sure to make up the losses and more when the market
had digested the news," I thought. It took a few seconds and
half of the Sellus proceeds were Imperious shares.

The events have a way of turning out differently than my
anticipation, should I say fond hope. Imperious was in a foul
mood and had no intent to recover. For good reason, investors
had read the release more carefully than this budding day
trader and had cottoned on to the bad news. The bank had
investments which were shaky and likelihood of major losses in
the next quarter was considerable. The humiliation of Imperious
continued and in another hour the shares had lost another 5%
and were trading at $18. Then, as if by the divine command,
the tide turned. In next ten minutes Imperious regained 1% to
18.20. This was the signal I was waiting for. Remaining cash was
used to acquire more stock. Now all I had to do was to wait till
a few minutes before close and calculate my profit.

Imperious oscillated within a wide range while the rest of
the market climbed steadily. I watched with my heart in my
mouth. I noticed with consternation that Sellus was in demand
and had gained 5% while my investment was fluctuating around
measly $17, thousands below my cost. To my utter dismay the
price ranged from 16.75 to 17.50 till thirty minutes before the
close of trading. Then the fun began. It moved up 15c in one
trade to $17, then 17.20 then 17.50. My heart began beating

faster. Ten minutes before close it was 18.00, within range of my cost of the later purchase and rapidly moving up. In great suspense I was watching the Imperious price like a tiger watches its prey for the kill. It was at this critical moment that the secretary announced an important visitor, the prospective publisher of my first book.

Spouses know their place and do not expect to be ushered in the office straight away. One can keep a client waiting. But publishers are from a different planet. Their time is invaluable. They have to look after editing, printing, distribution, marketing and of course financing of all the books on their list, not just yours, and cannot be expected to waste their precious time in an unknown writer's reception room. So the moment I heard his name, I hurriedly placed the order to get rid of Imperious at a higher than current price but still at a loss. Publisher was with me till the market closed to explain in painful detail his estimate of my share of the publicity budget and then left hurriedly to see the printer with the cheque safely tucked in his wallet. As soon as his back was turned I typed in the ticker symbol for Imperious. It was as if I was hit by a thunderbolt. After my sell order went through for a thousand below cost, the price continued to improve and ended the day a dollar above that of my initial purchase.

Thanks to the publisher's unfortunately timed visit I had lost more than I would ever receive in royalties for the book. Worse still, Ravi gleefully told me at the club that he had betted all he had on Imperious and made enough to go round the world in style with his new girl friend.

~ *10* ~

Vancouver is lovely in the spring time with flowers in full bloom and gardens competing to delight the aesthetic senses of the visitors. This is why Monica and I jumped at the opportunity to visit our daughters Yamuna and Sheila there last week. Geeta, our other offspring, was also visiting from California with the youngest member of the family, three year old Hope. It was a reunion with a twist. To get the ball rolling, Sheila, a dentist, pulled out another tooth from my mouth; she had removed a molar a month earlier. She is apparently trying to change this old wimp into a tiger, albeit a toothless one. The proud, rightly so in my humble opinion, dentist celebrated her thirtieth birthday the following day with a big party which tested the staying power of many in the older generation. The family welcomed her next decade with a dinner in a classy restaurant the next evening. It was Father's Day on Sunday and the younger generation arranged a brunch to put further strain on the few remaining teeth of their father. In summary, the extended weekend was a succession of grand affairs with many great meals and lively conversations.

At last it was Sunday evening and the time to return home. Geeta's flight was due to leave about the same time as ours and we drove together to the airport in our rented car. To the grandparents, one hour ride was a breeze thanks to the joyful singing of Hope. On the other hand, Geeta was trying to finish a story before returning the book to us. Commonsense prevailed and she put up with it; it was easier to cope with the child's singing than crying. Thus, all passengers got what they wanted.

After dropping Geeta and Hope at the U.S. departure area we drove to the lot of Fudgit Car Rental. The returning cars formed two lanes but there was only one attendant. I parked in the left lane while a luxury sedan rushed past on my right. The attendant finished with the car ahead of me, pointed out that there was some one else before me in the other lane and looked after him. After that car he proceeded to attend to the luxury sedan. Unaware of the fury it was to cause, I interrupted to suggest that I was there earlier. The attendant agreed, quickly did whatever was needed with my car and waved me on. Monica and I carted our luggage towards the elevator for the departure floor.

As happens frequently to me, the elevator had more important customers and took its time to come down to my level. Monica and I were blankly staring at the elevator entrance when we heard a barrage of profanity in a high pitched soprano directed at us. We turned around sharply risking cricks in our necks. The driver of the luxury sedan was rushing by after venting her anger at me for claiming priority even though I had only rented a humble subcompact. I wondered whether I would have received the blast if my car had been an expensive model beyond my means or I were not a short, fat and bald brownie. The elevator arrived to break my reverie. We checked in our cases and had a simple dinner skipping much needed aperitif and dessert only to learn at the gate that our plane was an hour late. It was nearly midnight when we arrived in Calgary and found ourselves at the last waiting station of the trip, the luggage carousel.

It was now that I had one of my brilliant ideas for which I am justly famous. I suggested that it would save some time if Monica got the car from the parking lot while I waited for the luggage. She asked for the keys and I put my hands in the pockets. I looked in all six pockets of my jacket, all four of my pants and both of my shirt. "Oh, I must have put them in the shoulder bag" I said apologetically. The bag had four large and four small pockets. After the cursory search failed, each pocket was emptied in turn. The keys were nowhere to be found. "Could you have put the bunch in the suitcase?" Monica asked after checking the bag again. By now other passengers had gone home with their bags and our cases were enjoying the business class ride on the carousel. I will spare you our agony and make the story short. We turned both bags inside out but in vain.

All was not lost. Monica had the key of the front door in her handbag. We loaded our stuff in a cab and headed home wondering where the dumb keys could be. Monica thought she had seen a bunch on the hotel bed and I felt sure I had zipped the pocket and the keys were secure wherever they were. In our younger days this could have led to an unpleasant argument right there on the back seat much to the amusement of the driver. But not this time; I was feeling depressed, sure that it was one of the episodes of senility which were becoming more frequent of late. Monica was, as she always is, very understanding and consoled me as much as she could.

We got home after a very long day and dragged the luggage into the house. Familiar surroundings and the anticipation of tea just as we like it gave us both new bursts of energy. We started emptying the bags to find the pesky keys. Monica looked into the cases while I checked the carry on bags. Placing the shoulder bag on the table, coincidentally under the chandelier, I unzipped the outer pocket, pulled out the newspaper, shook it vigorously and threw it on the recycling heap. Then I put my hand in the pocket in the left corner and slowly moved it along the bottom to the right. I found several American and Canadian nickels and pennies which I separated into four towers. As the hand got to the right corner something pricked my index finger and the hand shot out. I pulled the pocket wider to look for the culprit. There was a pin and wedged in the corner the bunch of keys hiding as if it was ashamed of the mischief it had caused.

Monica gave me a ride to work the next morning. My colleague drove me to the parking lot and the car and I are united – for now.

~ *11* ~

It had been a long day. Actually it had been a normal working day broken into two short spells by a long buffet lunch with a not so secret admirer of my book of short stories which had been recently published. However it doesn't take much to make two short spells feel like a long day of uninterrupted calamities. The partner in a mining project was mad because the ministry had rejected our report on last summer's work as inadequate. Publisher of my book was unhappy because the local paper had refused to review it. The office manager was upset because her office was too hot one minute and too cold the other. To top it all, the stocks in my shrinking retirement plan were threatening to disappear.

At last the clock of the church across from my office chimed four. I turned off the computer, locked all my work troubles in the desk drawer, picked the briefcase containing what would have been my lunch and walked out humming "What a beautiful morning". My car was waiting where I had left it in the morning and the book to be mailed to an editor in Edmonton was gleaming in the sun on the passenger seat. I stopped by the post office and parted with the equivalent of the price of the book to send it two hundred kilometers by cheap mail. As I turned in the driveway I remembered that the good wife was hiking in the mountains and I was on my own for the evening.

I changed into comfortable shorts and T-shirt appropriate for early spring weather, poured a tall glass of scotch diluted with a few drops from the tap and set down with the newspaper. What with two wars, major shootings in an American college, scandals in Washington and a British lord of Canadian vintage being tried in Chicago of ignoble conduct, there was plenty to read. Suddenly it was six thirty. I was not hungry but it was important to go through the formality of dinner. I found some interesting leftovers, heated them in the microwave and sat down to eat with a fresh drink.

No sooner had the first mouthful passed the taste buds the door bell rang. Before I could get up it rang again. It turned out to be a canvasser for a charity, not the rowdy teenager who gets his kick by disturbing neighbors at meal times. Her spiel was interrupted by the ringing of the phone. Just as I picked up the phone I heard the canvasser "We take check, cash and credit cards" and Monica "I am on my way to a meeting now and will see you in a couple of hours." Thanks to all the music lessons in my younger days, I could decipher overlapping sounds.

I was a little unnerved by all this activity and even more so when I could not find my wallet to get money for the impatient lady on the door who continued to repeat her mantra, "We take ....." Feeling exasperated, I wrote a check to get rid of her and gulped down my dinner. Then I turned the house upside down but the pesky wallet was nowhere to be found. Exhausted I sat down and had the last sip from the glass.

SUDHIR JAIN

Suddenly the light flashed - I must have left the wallet at the post office. I wished I had taken that sip before going on the fruitless search. With no license - it was in the wallet and so much scotch inside me, I couldn't drive. So I walked a kilometer to the drugstore which housed the post office. Just as I approached the counter, the young man on the other side bent down and produced the wallet with a beaming face.

I love long days which end in such a pleasant note. Don't you?

~ 12 ~

It must have been ten years ago. It was a beautiful winter afternoon, bright warm sun, sky the shade of blue I have never seen anywhere outside Calgary; dripping water from the snow-laden trees which would form brilliant icicles the next morning. I tried to move my cat to the deck to laze in the sun but it resisted. Several fat squirrels were rushing around the yard having fun and the cat did not feel safe with those boisterous critters around. It upset me that my own pet, a legitimate resident of our home, was too scared to enjoy the glorious sunshine and I decided to do something about it. I fired a letter to the local newspaper demanding that the city controlled the furry pests who had taken over our community. The editor obligingly published it a couple of days later.

To tell you the truth, I did not expect a response from the pest control department and was not disappointed when I did not receive any. The newspaper did get at least one irate letter which they published a few days later to show their broadmindedness. The letter took me to task for hating the squirrels, may be plump and scary in my prosperous neighbourhood but they were slim, dainty and no threat to a cat in her community; and even more for wanting to disturb their equanimity by putting a cat among them. She, in turn, demanded that before the city even hurt a single squirrel in the prosperous part of the city, the noisy magpies that woke her and her cat up at an ungodly hour every morning in her poor and deprived corner of the city should be laid to rest.

I was annoyed by the response of the lady but it did not cause a wave in the pest control department any more than my letter had done. The squirrels kept multiplying as I expect did the magpies. A neighbour whose garden was suffering from the assault of the greedy creatures took the bull by the horns, trapped a couple and released them in the park a few kilometers away. By a strange coincidence, a park ranger happened to be passing by. He saw the grave violation of the city code and charged him with the offence. Fortunately, the kindly judge took the accused's long record of community service into consideration and did not hand out an exemplary jail sentence demanded by the prosecutor. He did impose a hefty fine though.

Earlier this summer I observed a reduction in squirrel activity in our yard and more birds on the feeders than in recent years. I pointed it out to my gardener wife who had noticed that fewer of her plants had been damaged this spring. She also observed that a small golden squirrel she had become fond of had not been seen for some days. "Hope the poor thing is OK and some cat or the neighbourhood trapper did not get it," I said without really sharing my dear wife's sense of loss.

At last the situation became clear as sometimes happens. Our daughter was visiting from Vancouver last week to help us celebrate our wedding anniversary. She is a keen birdwatcher and after breakfast on Sunday she took out the binoculars to look for birds in the tall poplars bordering the yard. It was not long before she called us in the hushed voice of an experienced birder, "Come and look, a hawk."

We had seen a variety of birds on our feeders as well as a hummingbird hovering near the window. The only hawks we ever saw were on the fence posts on our way to the mountains. But there it was, nonchalantly examining the surroundings from its perch on the top branch of the tree like a monarch of all it surveyed. As I admired the majestic bearing of the hawk, it dawned on me that there on the other side of the lens was the perpetrator of the disappearance of the golden squirrel before it had laid any eggs and, along with its associates, the cause of the decline in squirrel population and activity. Lo and behold, Nature had stepped in where the parks department feared to tread and no law-abiding person would dare after the harsh punishment of a long suffering citizen for taking the issue in his own hands. We had the confirmation a couple of days later when four young hawks were sitting on the back of the lawn chairs surrounding a squirrel busily feasting on the birdseeds from the ground. Strangely, the hawks did not look as if they needed the breakfast within easy reach of their claws and the squirrel did not seem at all anxious, her only acknowledgement of the youthful predators being a puffed up tail. After a few minutes of hopping about the yard, the hawks took off; perhaps to return after they had worked up an appetite. Or they felt like magpies for lunch and knew where to find them.

~ *13* ~

Atlanta is renowned as a beautiful city, pride of the South and the fastest growing city on the whole continent. There is a lot to see and admire in this antebellum city. However, the most important place to visit on a Sunday morning, whatever your religious belief, is the historic Ebenezer Baptist church founded 120 years ago. Martin Luther King preached here in his younger days and prepared himself for the leadership of the Black movement for racial equality. We were in the city because Monica had been invited to make a presentation in a medical conference. She was very busy but had reluctantly accepted the invitation. I did not have much to do and tagged along to carry her suitcase and provide company when she was not attending the events related to the conference.

I spent Friday and Saturday roaming around the downtown, gaping at the skyscrapers, visiting the sundry museums, and tasting wonderful southern delicacies in cafes and restaurants while Monica basked in the admiration of her fans. On Sunday, after a leisurely breakfast of coffee and gorgeous pancakes with heaps of butter and Aunt Jemima syrup, we dressed formally as we would to go to a church at home and headed for the ten o'clock service at the famous church. We arrived there half an hour early expecting a big crowd at the door. We were not disappointed; the queue went around the whole block.

People in the orderly crowd were visitors to Atlanta, largely black women and men worshippers with a sprinkling of white spectators. Members of the regular congregation, cheerful black men and women of all ages, men dressed in their best suits and heavily made up women dressed in beautiful dresses and decked in colorful hats, were allowed to enter the church as they arrived. Fifteen minutes before ten, the doors were opened to the visitors. Fortunately, every one could be accommodated in the cavernous hall although every seat was taken by the time pastor and his assistants entered the podium with appropriate ceremony from a side door.

After spirited singing of traditional spirituals by the church choir made up of at least a hundred excellent singers, the pastor welcomed the congregation, particularly the visitors and asked those present to hold the hands of persons on their either side and introduce themselves. This done he asked every one to join in singing Amazing Grace. Fortunately the building was exceptionally well built and the chorus of more than a thousand singers did not bring the roof down in spite of their best efforts. Then the announcements of church activities for the next week followed. I noticed that many of them related to what would generally be considered the domain of the schools.

Now was the time for the sermon. The pastor was a short frail looking man with thick curly hair on a large head with a big nose, full mouth and jutting out ears. He walked on the podium from one end to the other, sometimes slowly, sometimes quickly, to suit the subject matter of the sermon. He held a microphone with a very long cord in his right hand

and punched the air with the left. His booming baritone voice was pleasant to the ear. I don't remember him standing still for a moment except for the time he stared at his captivated audience and chastised the men among them for neglecting their families; abusing their wives and the children and abdicating the responsibilities they took upon themselves when they befriended the women and got them pregnant. He went on to talk about the unfortunate consequences of rampant alcohol and drug abuse and chastised the youths wasting their time in frivolity rather than using it to build the foundation of a fruitful life. It was at this juncture that he told the story that made his sermon so memorable.

"My friends, you all have enjoyed the fabulous amenities hotels provide these days. You arrive at your destination. You head for a hotel, by yourself or with your friends. You check in, collect the room keys, go to the room, and inspect the bar. You take what you want from it, order the room service to bring food and more drinks, charge the restaurant bill to the room and enjoy every moment of your stay. Just before check out time on your last day you pack and head for the checkout desk. The clerk greets you with a smile and presents you the bill highlighting the amount you owe for all the fun you have had. You look at it, the shock waves go through your body and you stammer that there must be some mistake. The clerk goes inside the office and comes out with several pages of a computer printout. Every item that you have consumed is listed on it. You go through it with a fine tooth comb. Of course you don't find any errors and grudgingly pay what they asked for."

Now he stood facing the audience, stretched himself up to his full height, raised his voice to match that of the thousand member choir we had heard earlier, "Friends, when you go to meet your Creator in the next world and challenge Him when faced with the consequences of sins you have committed, there will be a computer printout of everything you have done in this life, from the day you were born to the day you die. There will be no escape, none." Now he bent forward almost horizontal from waist up, his voice softened to a whisper and added as if conspiratorially in each ear, "It is you, my friend, and you alone who decides what goes in that printout." He paused for a few moments to let it sink in and straightened up. "And now, ladies and gentleman, boys and girls, let us pray."

I was unusually down hearted on the way out. The thought of a printout listing every act in my life scares me to this day although it does not stop me from actions which I repent soon after they are done.

~ 14 ~

Ravi was shocked. If you were in his place you would be too. After spending most of the morning working to save a major contract, he was now looking at the picture of Natasha, his wife, dressed to kill in a low cut gown, in the tight embrace of his best friend Vijay with their lips in firm contact. The picture had not arrived surreptitiously in the mail as such pictures do. It was presented to him, in person, by David on the cover of a folder with HAPPY ANNIVERSARY in bold letters across the picture. Ravi's mind was in a whirl. Anniversary of what? Natasha's illicit affair with her husband's best friend? How can it be? What is there to be happy about it? Why is David presenting it to him with such ceremony?

Perplexity writ large on Ravi's face confused David. He could not understand it. Ravi had engaged him to take pictures at his tenth wedding anniversary party. He had worked hard taking hundreds of pictures while others were enjoying delectable dishes and vintage wines in the company of interesting members of opposite sex. His long time assistant had worked overtime to select the best thirty shots and to prepare this folder. There was a long pause before he blurted, "What is the problem?"

"The problem you ask. My wife is kissing my best friend on the cover of the album and you ask what is the problem? Where did you get this picture and why would you show this to me any way?"

"Oh God. How could I be so blind? I am so sorry for the blunder." With that apology, if one can call it that, David whisked away the folder and rushed out of the door.

Vijay cuts a dashing figure although he is short, balding on the top; a little paunchy and of a patchy brown complexion. He is always immaculately dressed in a freshly ironed pale blue or white shirt, dark suit and a red tie with every strand of jet black hair plastered in its proper place, a confident smile on his lips, the faint perfume of after shave in the air and black shoes he had polished till they shone to match his hair. He is single but never without a ravishing blonde by his side in any social event. Unlike most men in his fortunate position, he is reticent about his love life even after he has had a few drinks too many. However, he did share with Ravi and Natasha an unfortunate incident at his company's Christmas party. He was waiting near the entrance of the dining room for Roma, his girl this evening, to return after 'freshening up' when a friend of one of his former girl friends, "a heavily made up woman long past her prime" as he described her, walked towards him. He extended his right hand to greet her but she held both her arms out for a hug. As his cheek accidentally brushed hers she whispered, "Mouth, not cheek." When their lips separated Roma was staring strangely at them. To Vijay's utter dismay, normally voluble Roma was quiet for the whole evening, declined his invitation to visit his apartment after the party to see his collection of rare miniature art from Maldives Islands and curtly refused to see him again.

To clear the air between them Ravi mentioned the incident with David to his wife over dry sherry before dinner. Natasha burst out laughing, "When I greeted Vijay at the anniversary party he said - mouth, not cheek - quoting from the incident with his former girl friend and I played my part in the jest. David must have snapped us and his assistant put the picture on the cover thinking Vijay was you." The mystery solved, Ravi now wondered what Natasha found so funny in the incident. But he was too tactful to ask.

Natasha relates this tale of mistaken identity with great gusto in every gathering and the listeners enjoy its every telling. As for Ravi, the initial shock has worn off but the attentive guests in the party can't fail to notice a touch of unnatural in his laughter.

~ 15 ~

The summer was especially beautiful that year; hot but not too much, sky deep blue, sometimes dotted with sparkling white clouds. It was an ideal time to spend a week in the mountains. The hike to the SuperFine Hikers camp ground was long and tiring. But the limbs were raring to go again after a hearty meal of beef stew and freshly baked buns with loads of butter followed by a huge piece of apple pie with whipped cream. How the cook managed to prepare such delicious dinners for six days of our stay in the remote camp remains a mystery to this day.

Every morning, sixty campers were offered four hikes of varying difficulty to choose from. Being short and fat and prone to run out of breath on even a hint of ascent, I chose the easiest of these. Most members of the group were keen long timers and there were no more than four or five modest enough to go on easy hikes. Experts set out to break records for quickest ascent to the toughest peaks, glance momentarily at the view of the valleys and rush down. We took our time as we strolled along the streams, stopping every few minutes to take a sip of clear liquid from the bottle while admiring the glorious views of the mountains above. The only record we established was done unwittingly on the first day; for taking longer on a both way five kilometer excursion than any previous group had done in fifty years of the SuperFine Hikers. We beat the previous record of six hours twelve minutes comfortably by forty two minutes.

Not much happened during the camp that was remarkable. If it snowed or rained buckets flooding the tents, every detail would have stuck to the grey cells. There is nothing interesting in the cloudless, warm, sunny, mildly breezy, mosquito free days. I would have forgotten that I even went to Sun Rise Camp if it were not for what I remember as an amusing incident now but may not have been if the gods were in a foul mood that day. It was our fourth day. Robbie, the leader warned us in advance that although the easiest hike was long and had beautiful views, it had one rather steep descent on a scree slope. When I expressed alarm he assured me that I would be able to manage now that my fitness level had improved after thirty kilometers of walking. I was not happy at the prospect but I was won over when Robbie promised to help me if it became necessary.

We set off, my backpack loaded with peanut butter whole wheat sandwich, four cookies, one apple, one flask of weak tea and a big bottle of impure water, the impurity shall remain my little secret. With our sun hats, tough boots, brown shirts, blue jeans and walking sticks we would have made quite an impression on viewers if there were any. But their absence did not bother us because we had not gone into the wilderness to impress the strangers.

Five hours of the hike were uneventful except for the short nap during a long lunch break. The break was interesting because I dreamed that I was sleeping in my comfy bed at home, not lying on the bare rock with my head on the backpack. Perhaps due to the wishful dream I felt more refreshed than I ever feel in the morning at home.

We must have walked an hour in a single file on a narrow trail in the thick forest, long enough to forget the dream and comforts of home. On Robbie's orders we sang the marching song of SuperFine Hikers - Yippie I O, here come the foolish but brave o - to keep the bears at more than an arm's length. Then, without warning, we were out of the trees. We turned to our left, walked a few more minutes and stopped, I presumed, to look at the view. My admiration for the bright snowy peaks in the distance, their majesty enhanced by the glorious blue of the sky, turned into dread as my eyes slowly moved down and focused on the cliff a few feet from my feet. "Is this the scree slope we are supposed to go down?" I asked no one in particular.

Robbie turned around, looked at me with great sympathy and said in a consoling tone, "Yes that is it. It is not as hard as you think. You walk down leaning forward a little and the scree does all the hard work for you."

"No way am I going down this cliff. I promised my wife I won't do anything dangerous. And there is nothing dangerous if this is not." I said with some firmness.

"Only option is to go back; not much of an option if you ask me. Look, Jennie is already halfway down," Robbie said pointing to a dainty young lady sliding down as if she were a swan gliding on water.

"Jennie is fit, not fat like me. I have never been on a scree slope; leave alone a cliff like this one. You go ahead. I will retrace my steps and get back to the camp, late but in one piece."

"I can't let you go alone. Rest of the group is already most of the way down. Come on, hold my hand. We will do it together." Robbie shook his body to balance his backpack, heavy with all the medical and other stuff a leader has to carry, and extended his hand towards me.

I did not really fancy walking back for another five hours, longer if I got lost. So I grabbed his hand and gingerly walked towards the dreaded cliff.

"Hold my hand tight, take small steps, lean forward, do not pull," Robbie offered final bit of advice.

We took our first tiny steps on the slope. I must have leaned too far forward, then leaned back to correct it. It is getting late; I should skip the details, they are really of no interest, and relate what happened next without baroque ornamentation. I slipped and fell on my back taking Robbie with me. As we fell our hands became free and my eyes were shut tight. When they opened, I was not on a hospital bed, as you would rightly assume, but on the soft ground at the bottom of the cliff. The feared descent could not have lasted more than a few seconds. Robbie was lying there too, a few feet away. Jennie offered me her hand and pulled me up on my feet. Robbie did not need help and got up on his own. We dusted our clothes and checked our limbs. Everything was in order.

On our way back, Robbie and I fell behind musing on our good fortune. At the camp entrance, a large crowd had gathered to greet us with cheers as if we had scaled a major peak.

Joys of Being a Grampy

~ 1 ~

Hope, my younger granddaughter, was ten months old. She was a fast crawler and as any active toddler, she loved to open shelves, pull drawers, open doors, and most of all pick up objects from the floor and try to swallow them whatever their size. The other day she swallowed a cotton ball and almost choked on it. I avoided being the sole babysitter for such an active child with no instinct for self-preservation. However, parents had to go to her older sister's school Christmas pageant and grandma needed to fill the space under the tree. So, I was left in charge of the safety and welfare of Hope. I must admit that my good wife had generously offered me the option of shopping but the thought of being jostled hither and thither by stressed shoppers equipped with heavy weapons called handbags deterred me from accepting. No sooner had I taken the charge, Hope pulled a loaded drawer with one hand, and then let it go. It shut on the fingers of her other hand. Thunderous screams followed. I picked her up. A little cuddling, some gibberish and tickling tummy put her back in good mood. Her world was back in order and all was well with her fingers. She now lay on my outstretched legs and leaned back. Too far back, as it turned out. She tumbled over to the floor. Another crying session ensued. Some more patting the back, rubbing the tummy, monotonic gibberish followed. Life returned to normal.

It was time for a feed. I took the cooked peas and fruit

mush out of the refrigerator, mixed them thoroughly, warmed the gooey mixture in the microwave for precisely six seconds, put the by now crying sweetheart in her chair, strapped her in disregarding the louder cries. I then put some food in the baby spoon, opened my mouth and pushed the spoonful in hers as she opened it in imitation. The process was repeated a hundred times over. When she refused to open her mouth and started pushing the spoon away causing food to fall all over my clothes and the floor, I took the hint. I wiped her face, hands, table, floor and my clothes, in that order. She was now ready for a workout and started crawling around the floor. I made sure the door to the basement was firmly shut and kept watch that she didn't wedge herself in some inaccessible nook.

A few minutes went by. Suddenly, the room was full of a foul odour. Its source turned out to be the little one. I located the plastic sheet for her to lie on, wet wipes and a diaper; and a clothes peg for my nose. In spite of her powerful protests, I managed to take her clothes off, undo the diaper, quickly wipe her bum, fold old diaper and used wipes and put them away just in time to take the peg off my nose and breathe again. I gave her a toy to hold when putting the diaper on her wiggly body which would rather be in the birthday suit. I breathed a sigh of relief when all this was done and put wipes and plastic sheet away. In a short while, the little darling whined. She was hungry. Out came the bottle, in went the milk. Temperature had to be just right, warm to the touch. Bottle went in the jug of hot water. Patience is not a virtue in a toddler. More crying followed. At last the bottle was ready. I sat down in the rocking chair holding her in a comfortable position, put bottle in her mouth. She held the bottle, I sang a lullaby and rocked the chair. The whole atmosphere was soporific. I dreamt of the full night's sleep without interruption. Suddenly I heard a thud. No, I was not in bed; I was on the rocking chair. Baby was on the floor – crying. Bottle was lying by her side; milk dripping on the carpet. This crying was louder and more persistent than previous ones. Her feelings were really hurt by a rather negligent and from her point of view grumpy grandpa. A long session of patting back, rubbing tummy, rocking her in the arms (far from the rocking chair) and singing lullabies followed. At last, she was happy again and ready to go back to the bottle - bottle of milk, pure and unadulterated.

Sheer bliss; sound of heavy breathing from the little nose permeated the air. I carried her upstairs and put her to bed very gently so as not to disturb the sleep. Oh yes! Her breathing apparatus (to supply her extra Oxygen) had to be put on. With one hand, I brought the tube around to her cot, put the nozzles to her nose, wedged her face firmly between pillows and taped the lead tubes for the nozzle to her cheeks while patting her rhythmically with the other hand and singing baa, baa, black sheep soothingly. It was my lucky day; she stayed asleep through all this. I covered her up with a light blanket and quietly slipped out of the room. Low whining from the room started. Had my luck run out already! I held my breath, stood still and waited. Whining stopped and a sigh escaped my mouth.

I walked down to the living room and found the newspaper. It was the end of a great evening for a budding grandpa. Family returned a short time later to find me snoring in the chair with newspaper over my face.

~ 2 ~

It was Sunday when I opened my eyes. I knew it was Sunday, not Monday or any other work day because alarm had not gone off and radio clock said it was 6:30. Monica rolled over as I contemplated my next move. I whispered so as not to wake her if she was asleep, "Are you ready for a cup." She said she was. So I rolled off the bed and staggered downstairs to the kitchen. Yvette, our daughter-in-law, was already up and playing with her two children, four year old Frieda and one year old Hope. She was doing her best to keep them from screaming, either with joy or in frustration. I exchanged greetings with the three of them. While the kettle was boiling and tea brewing, I unloaded the dishwasher, put away pots and pans drying on the drainer and set the table for breakfast. I took the tray upstairs. We had our lazy cups while discussing what the day would bring. Then we got out of bed to implement the plan others had made for us without our input.

Monica had a short walk in the park even though the temperature was -30 degrees. At that temperature, it doesn't matter whether it is Centigrade or Fahrenheit; the wind is more important. Frieda cutely advised her to wear a lot of warm clothes and not catch the cold. I took the easier path. I went to the basement and did my set exercises prescribed by physiotherapists at various times for my knees, arms and back and stationary cycling routine prescribed by the family doctor to keep the little heart ticking.

After a shorter walk than she normally takes, Monica made a special breakfast of whole wheat pancakes. She wanted a change from poached eggs I serve over the weekend. The family gracefully waited for me to have a quick shower rather than endure the smell of a sweaty unwashed old man. The breakfast was well made, well served and most enjoyed. The discussion centered on Canadian winter and how to cope with it. Diversion was provided by an essay on Death by Music Monica is working on and on the story of a cab driver I have just completed. After breakfast we got together to clear the dishes while Sam put baby Hope to sleep.

Catherine, a friend of Geeta and Yvette, who had been visiting us for last three days, packed her bags and Yvette took her to the airport. She dropped Geeta and Frieda at a kids' birthday party and picked them up in on her way back. The group returned home around two. During this time, Monica worked in the kitchen; the work in the kitchen is endless. When the group was getting ready to leave, Hope woke up and attracted attention by crying lustily. I picked her up I played with her upstairs till her mom left. Then, I changed her rather dirty diaper and gave her the bottle. She was in a great mood and played her new game – crawling up and down the stairs at great speed. She has mastered the art but it would be dangerous to let her do it unattended. Accidents do not happen when babies are learning but when they become overconfident and lose their focus and the grip. A lunch of leftover soup and quiche followed. Hope enjoyed her grammy's concoction of banana pulp, mashed vegetables and milk. A milk bottle and afternoon nap was next. After putting her to bed, I challenged Monica to a game of Scrabble. She accepted and we had our first game in several months. I narrowly won as I normally do when I am keeping the score, thanks largely to ESL bonus which I surreptitiously grant myself. Rest of the family arrived when we were at the finishing stage. Now it was Yvette's turn to pack. She was leaving for four days of work in San Francisco. It didn't take her long. A short brisk walk in the park by Yvette and Geeta with Frieda in the stroller followed. Preparation for the walk took longer than the walk itself. But by all accounts it was worth it. Monica and I got a short rest in bed during their walk. Their return corresponded with Hope's awakening which acted as the call bell for us. The standard process of changing diaper and feeding the bottle followed. Now the major occupation was to keep kids diverted when Geeta and Yvette prepared to leave for the airport. This was achieved by watching Sound of Music for the umpteenth time with Frieda and letting Hope explore the plant pots and inaccessible corners of the sun room.

After Geeta and Yvette left for the airport, Monica took out of the fridge the curry and trimmings left over from a really splendid Indian feast she had prepared on Saturday. As is always the case, chicken and Chick pea curries tasted even better after a day of absorbing the spices. Frieda did not want to interrupt her film and we let her watch it. Hope enjoyed her peas and cheese combo. I made Monica her cup of tea and cleaned up the kitchen. Monica then went to the computer room to catch up with her yoga, correspondence and office work. Geeta arrived when I was wiping the table as the final act of food clearing process. She got the food I had just returned to fridge out again, heated some of it and Frieda joined her for dinner. After they finished, Frieda had the usual battle before being prepared for bed; change into pajamas, brush teeth, read a number of stories, tuck her up, start her CD. I cleaned up kid's mess from the floor and the table. Now it was the turn of Hope's night routine – feed the bottle, change the diaper, put her in warm night suit, rock her into bed, pat her back till she falls asleep. It was 7:45 when this was done. Geeta had also finished with Frieda. Monica was still busy in her well deserved and much needed "quiet time" when she shouldn't be disturbed. Geeta got her work out. I asked her if she wanted any group activity. She whispered a decline. Time for my last task had arrived. I prepared Hope's bottle for midnight feed to which she is accustomed.

The hour of decision had arrived. I could watch Bayreuth production of Wagner's Ring on video, listen to recent CD acquisitions I had not even opened yet, read a book in the cozy sun room or go to bed. For some strange reason, I chose the last option. I was asleep as soon as my behind hit the mattress. Next thing I heard was the muffled baby cry, which became louder and louder as adults wrapped their heads more and more tightly in their sheets. At last I gave up and slid out of bed, picked up crying Hope, juggled the bottle and flask of hot water with one hand to prepare the milk while holding 22 lb Hope in other arm, sat down on the bed and fed her. She started greedily, slowed down to a steady pace half way through the bottle and closed her eyes just when I was worrying about the logistics of preparing the second bottle. Her breathing tube had come undone. I put her gently to bed and tried to attach it. She let out a big scream of protest. I gave up and patted her to sleep. It was 3:04 on radio clock when I got back under the blanket. My dear wife turned over and mumbled, "That was a good job. " I felt the stars were all in their proper place as I fell asleep on second sheep. Alarm woke me up at 6:00, half an hour earlier than the day before. It was indeed Monday.

~ 3 ~

The chirping of birds on the apple blossom next to our open window woke us up just before our two grand-daughters announced their survival through the night by appropriately shrill cries. It was a beautiful summer morning with the bright blue sky decorated with a few luminous white clouds. I asked Monica whether a picnic at our rustic cabin in Waiparous would be a good idea to give four year old Frieda and one year old Hope the taste of a typical Alberta summer day. She heartily agreed and we jumped out of bed. Yvette was already up and about trying to keep the kids occupied. After a leisurely breakfast of tortilla with a wonderful mixed vegetable sauce, the ladies got busy with preparing the picnic and I sat down with the morning paper and a large jug of Irish coffee. What with kids under foot and demanding constant attention, it took a couple of hours to get things organized. No doubt, it would have been quicker if I helped. But I felt that having to watch tarmac on our drive when others enjoyed breathtaking mountain views was enough contribution. The news of bombings in Baghdad and horrors perpetrated by politicians in Ottawa caused a minor depression but it was quickly alleviated by the joyful anticipation of little ones enjoying themselves on the river bank.

We packed the car and made the kids comfortable in their car seats. Yvette squeezed in between them. I went back into the house to check doors, windows, stove and the iron while Monica made sure that all the necessities had been loaded and that I hadn't lied about car having enough gas. Then we shouted in unison: "Waiparous, here we come", engine kicked in and we set off. As we turned into the beautiful country road, Frieda demanded music. I turned the player on. CD happened to be a selection from operas of Wagner. Yvette expressed the hope that her kids don't get addicted to Wagner as some people seem to do. She was quick to add that she was not being sarcastic to anybody in the car. Being tone deaf, I had no difficulty in believing her at all.

A police car with roaring sirens passed by us as we turned on to a narrow road for the last seventeen kilometer stretch. I was relieved that it did not stop to give me a ticket for holding the traffic by driving well below the speed limit. Soon an ambulance came rushing by, then another police car and then another ambulance. We suspected some trouble in the camp ground which is notorious for rowdyism over the long weekends. I hoped that if there were an accident it was beyond our cabin. No such luck. As we approached the hamlet of Benchland two kilometers before our destination, the traffic slowed down and then came to a stop. We could see an SUV in the ditch and several people looking under it. My doctor wife and Yvette jumped out to ask if they could help. I jumped out with a camera to take the pictures of the grisly scene. The ladies were suitably disgusted by my action, as was the policeman guiding the traffic. He accused me of leaving the car unattended with two children in it. I suspect that I escaped a ticket or even a harsher punishment from the guardian of the law because of the torrent of rebukes I was deservedly receiving from two normally mild ladies.

We got moving again once I regained my composure and were soon at the cabin. Frieda had a series of questions about the accident which Yvette handled admirably. The cabin was just the way we had left it a week ago, even the leaves on evergreens had not sprouted yet. We would have to wait to see the damage caused by the vicious hail storm of last summer. After unloading the car I found the flask of tea. With Yvette busy organizing the kids and wife finding things to organize in and around the cabin, I sat down with a nice cup of tea to recover from the hard work of driving for an hour and the shock of the accident. My need to relax was understood, if not much appreciated, by the busy ladies. On my part, I enjoyed watching hummingbirds visit the feeder and a deer stroll through the woods. I may even have snoozed for a while.

Soon it was time for lunch. Frieda was excited to sit in a "grown-up" chair and have her sandwich and juice. It didn't make any difference to Hope. She tottered around tumbling over every now and then. We had our lunch without worrying about the mess kids were making while looking for wild life on the ground and in the air. The evergreens which looked dead as the doornails at first glance had, in fact, begun to sprout shoots and revived the prospects of a green summer on our property. The warm sun was pleasant and gentle breeze was soothing to the senses. There was no lawn mower or pop music screaming next door, no trucks groaning uphill on the road and no planes roaring above. This was as close to heavenly peace as I can ever hope for. I suspect peace in the heaven above, if all those angels with their harps will let one have any, is not likely to be my fate in view of the lazy sinful life I lead.

After a stroll around the property, we walked over to the Waiparous creek. This creek starts from Lake Minnewanka in Banff National Park. It flows through a deep gully. There are a few places around the bends where gravel is exposed. These are wishfully termed beach and named after illustrious residents of the small community. The residents with tough backs use them to sunbathe. The creek is ice from October to early May and ice water for remaining months of the year. I manage to put my toe in it for a fraction of second twice a year although some masochists claim to having braved the water for long swims most afternoons. We made our way to the nearest beach. It wasn't long before Frieda had stripped to her skin and Hope to her diaper. They played with the rocks, building and demolishing castles and finding flat rocks to throw in the water. We were soon joined by a young lady with three young sons and an energetic but well-behaved collie. She was typical of people who live isolated lives; very keen to talk about her holidays, her family and whatever else came to mind. She brought us up on all the separations and new unions that happened in the community during the winter and told us that the accident we witnessed earlier was caused by a tire blow up as the Jeep took the sharp turn at a great speed. The young male driver, too macho to wear the seatbelt, was thrown out of and trapped under the vehicle as it rolled over in the ditch. Two female passengers with seatbelts on were shaken but not hurt. This provided another reason for me to be glad that all my progeny is of the intelligent sex.

We walked back to the property in the late afternoon, loaded the car and locked the cabin. We drove back at a leisurely pace looking for blue birds. Little ones soon fell asleep and, with the storm clouds gathering in the sky, the drive home was, thanks to our lucky stars, most uninteresting.

~ 4 ~

Soon after the picnic, our daughter's family moved back to California. A year later our grandchildren, Frieda now 5 and Hope 2, were visiting us. Calgary is a very different place than Santa Cruz. It is cooler and we don't have a beach. Monica and I were determined to make these differences disappear and to ensure that their visit was so enjoyable that they would be asking to return every week. I acquired two sand boxes and filled them with clean sand. Monica brought out from storage the blow up plastic pool and filled it up a day before their arrival to give water time to warm up in the sun. We decorated the bedrooms with their favorite pictures and arranged their toys neatly in the living room. Monica shopped for the food they love: frozen blueberries, cucumbers and tomatoes.

Monica had a long standing arrangement to spend a day hiking with her group. Whoopee! I had children to myself for the whole day. I could take them to the zoo in the morning and to Drumheller in the afternoon. The zoo has a play park with a wide variety of slides for the little kids to enjoy. Drumheller has the dinosaur museum with a small play area attached to it. Frieda was thrilled at the idea and Hope, as usual, reflected Frieda's sentiments.

Monica prepared the picnic lunch, drinks, snacks for the

drive, light blankets to help them sleep in the car and of course the music. No Mozart and Beethoven on the long drive to Dinosaurs, it had to be educational music for the little ones. It was fine with me. I find it hard to keep eyes on the road when they are whining for their music behind my back.

I packed the car a little before nine. Frieda set the example by hopping in her seat and clicking in the seat belt. Hope told me in no uncertain terms, "Don't need help, don't need help" as she tried to get into her seat. After a few tries she managed to get in and looked triumphantly at me. As I proceeded to help her with the belts she repeated, "Don't need help, don't need help." I stood and watched her trying to work the system out. Then she gave up, "I need help, I need help." I buckled her in and we set off for the zoo.

Just to make sure that none of us fell asleep on our way we sang Mary had a little lamb, Twinkle twinkle little star, Humpty sat on a wall loudly and in unison. At least we think we sang in unison. The parking lot was already busy and only spot I could find was at the farthest end. After shepherding the two through impatient cars looking for a resting place, we joined the snaking queue to purchase the tickets. The idea of a long wait did not appeal to me much but Frieda and Hope did not mind at all. They ran around life size models of an elephant and a giraffe. It was ten by the time I reached the ticket window.

As soon as we got in, both of them started shouting, "Play Park, Play Park." While crossing the bridge Hope saw a ledge. She forgot the park, rushed to the ledge and started her careful walk on it. Frieda tried to push her aside but I told her firmly to leave her sister alone. The crisis was averted by Frieda moving to the ledge on the other side of the bridge. Play Park was further delayed by a stop for juice and cookies from the bag. By now I too needed refreshment. I had my cup of tea from the flask when they ran around with the juice boxes in their hands, taking sips when they stopped for breath.

On our way we passed a gorilla enclosure. Hope looked at it with amazement and asked why the man was in the cage. Before I could think of a reply, Frieda remarked in all seriousness that the cage dweller looked very much like Grumpy. Hope nodded in agreement. I walked ahead silently afraid that the zookeeper may have the same opinion. Eventually, we got to the play area and they ran to the biggest slide. It was heartwarming to see Frieda helping her young sister go up the steep steps and encouraging her to slide down.

An hour passed by before I had batted the eyelid. They came over to the bench from where I was watching them and sat down on my either side. I cuddled their small soft bodies permeating with joy. Cuddle soon came to an end when Frieda said she was hungry and Hope duly repeated it. We found a table in an open space where peacocks were showing off their fans. The girls wolfed down their peanut butter and jam sandwiches, drank some juice and yawned. The sun was very hot now. They needed a nap and driving to Drumheller in the air-conditioned car was the best use of time.

The walk to the car at the far end of the parking lot was

slow and their whines tested the limits of my patience. There were no protests when I loaded them in their seats. I covered them with blankets and they were out of this world before the car was on the highway. I put on the disc of a ninety minute long symphony which was just right for the time it would take us to get to the dinosaur museum. The drive was uneventful except for road works every ten kilometers and a hefty speeding ticket in a construction zone. The girls slept till I was driving into the parking lot of the museum. After some more juice and cookies they ran to the play area. I had time to enjoy a refreshing cup of tea before they came back in need of a washroom. It transpired that the only washrooms were in the museum. I bought a senior's ticket; kids were admitted free, and took them to the men's washroom. They insisted on going to the same stall and I had to wait till Frieda was finished before I could help Hope do her thing. I sat them down on the front seats in a theatre to watch a dinosaur slide show and ran back to the washroom for my own needs. When I returned my heart stopped. They were not where I had left them. It took a while for the eyes to adjust to the faint light and then I spotted them in the back row where they had moved to be safe from the frightening images. I collected them and we went round the museum admiring the amazingly realistic exhibits of dinosaurs, monarchs of all they saw eons ago.

It didn't take long for the little girls to get bored with the exhibits intended for older children. Before going out we had a repeat performance of our earlier visit to the washroom. But the visit to the play area was a different thing altogether. Frieda ran ahead and disappeared, I thought in one of the playhouses. Hope can't read and insisted on going on a slide which said "For the ages 5 and over." Clutching the side rope she managed to climb the rope ladder to a platform ten feet above the ground. She triumphantly marched to the top of a long covered slide and stared into what must have appeared to her a long dark tunnel to nowhere. She looked around. Where was the older sister when she was needed the most? Well, she was nowhere to be found. I looked all over the play area and started wondering where she could have gone? But the little Hope, now screaming on the high platform, was the priority of the moment. The small crowd of five and six year olds had joined her but nobody was able to do anything. I was trying to console the inconsolable when someone tapped my shoulder, "Are you the grumpy of Frieda? A uniformed gentleman asked. "Yes I am, do you know where she is?" it was my turn to ask. "She is crying for you near the main entrance." I asked the gentleman to be patient till I somehow got the younger sibling down. His patience was not tested for too long. A seven or eight year old girl knew what to do. She climbed up, held vigorously protesting Hope in her arms and slid down. Hope was smiling with relief when the pair dropped out of the tunnel. The girl rushed back to the top before I could express my appreciation. I picked up my brave two and a half year old and turned towards the main entrance. There was Frieda, her cheeks wet, walking towards us holding the hand of a young lady. I thanked the guide and the earlier messenger and carried both my lost but found girls to the car which fortunately was only a few yards away.

They were asleep before the car was out of the parking lot

and opened their eyes only when I opened the garage door. They missed the fine views of the renowned countryside but got what children need the most, sound sleep and the assurance of love.

~ 5 ~

A few months later Monica and I visited Geeta and Yvette in Santa Cruz for an extended weekend. It happened to be a week before Monica's birthday. Unbeknown to us Yvette prepared a surprise birthday dinner of chicken and sweet potato salad and ordered a special cake. Six year old Frieda and three year old Hope got into the spirit of things. Hope even managed to keep it a secret, much to the surprise of this grampy who is well acquainted with the ways of little ones.

Yvette, a strict vegetarian, marinated the chicken for twelve hours and baked it in the oven for precisely fifty seven minutes. Geeta helped with the vegetables and the dishes. Frieda made the place cards and insisted on determining the seating order. After a major argument between the sisters, Frieda won out and placed herself in between Geeta and Yvette while Hope had to be content with the seat in between the window and crusty old grampy.

Geeta and Yvette brought the dishes loaded with food to the table and we took our places surrounded by the aroma of lovingly prepared and elegantly served dinner. Hope reminded us of the custom of holding hands and every one taking turn to say what he/she is thankful for. Every one said in their own way how she was thankful for us all being together and I said how I was so thankful for others being so forgiving of my stupid words and actions. Then we loaded our dishes and dug in.

After justice had been done to the delicious dishes, Hope, much to the delight of all, started singing:

I love my Grammy
I love my Grammy
It's Grammy I love
I love my Grammy,

over and over again. Then she sang this ode to Grampy, Mommy, Geeta and Frieda. When she stopped for a breather, as if on a cue, all of us started singing the same ode to Hope. She was taken aback for a moment. But only for a brief moment and then joined in. It was a moving scene, every one expressing their genuine love for every one else in the family.

The cake with twelve candles was brought in. Both little girls joined their Grammy in blowing them out. Monica cut a suitable size piece for every one. I say suitable size because my piece was at least twice as large as the others. It was a fitting finale to an excellent birthday celebration.

It was a truly memorable occasion. What makes this family dinner memorable? I think it was the love oozing out of every heart and pervading the whole being of all who were present. Love may or may not make the world go around; it certainly makes traveling thousands of miles to be with the loved ones for a few hours well worthwhile.

~ 6 ~

It was a hot day and the grandchildren were bursting with energy. Six year old Frieda demanded to be taken to the water park and three year old Hope supported her with great energy. It is amazing how the younger sibling always demands the same while the older want just the opposite. It was my good luck that the older one spoke first.

Water Park is a children's paradise in the summer. There are several kinds of sprinklers suitable for all ages and swings, monkey bars and slides to provide some variety. I got them to wear their swim suits, picked a towel and we were entering an empty parking lot in less than fifteen minutes. It surprised me till I realized that it was a working day and the kids were at home watching TV while the parents relaxed over dry martinis after a hard day in the air-conditioned offices.

Frieda and Hope ran through the sprinklers and soon the heat was off and they were complaining of being cold. I guided them to swings in the sun and before long "I am cold" was replaced by the cries of "higher." When Hope was at her highest point a little blonde girl attracted my notice by coming dangerously close to the swing. I helped her get out of the way and she sat down at the edge to play in the gravel. There were two young men and a young woman chatting blissfully at some distance. The parents had done their job by bringing the child to the playground in a pretty dress and stylish shoes. Now she was on her own. I watched the girl play in the gravel while absent-mindedly pushing Hope higher and higher. My mind was buzzing with the idea of the story of a neglected little girl whose parents put social contacts before her enjoyment even on a playground.

In another half hour the kids complained of being tired. I suspected that they were hungry rather than tired and brought them granola bars from the car. This revived them for another half hour of sun and sprinklers. We got in the car ready for chicken dinner waiting in the refrigerator at home. There were a few grapes on the passenger seat. I asked if the girls would like them. "Silly Grampy! Of course we like grapes." I picked a bunch and passed it to Frieda. Then I offered another to Hope. "I can't reach, I can't reach," she whined. I turned around to help her reach. Suddenly there was a jolt. Car had come to a stop against a tree. I cursed aloud and jumped out. The damage was minor - nothing broken. Frieda was crying because her chest had bumped against the retainer of the car seat. Hope was crying because her head had bumped against the back of the seat. I was angry because I saw the gleam in the eyes of the collision guy and a four figure bill for repairs. But crying children came first. I kissed them both better and they were soon laughing at their grampy for crashing into a tree.

We got home and they rushed in crying in unison, "Grammy, Grammy, Grampy crashed into a tree." I sheepishly told her the story and assured her that the damage was not too bad. The children had to call their mommy in California that evening to tell her of the accident. It took all of the powers of persuasion my wife is known for to convince dear mommy that the accident was minor, there were no injuries and she did not need to take the next flight to Calgary.

~ 7 ~

"I can't cope any longer. I am being driven mad." The call from Yvette in California alarmed us. She is separated from her partner, our daughter, and was looking after their two daughters, Frieda and Hope, seven and four years old respectively. Frieda had the attention span of a flea, temper tantrums fit for a mad monarch and lagged behind in skill development. One and a half hour commute, difficulty in obtaining medical services, departure of the part-time care giver all combined to create an impossible situation. The next call informed us that she was taking a year's leave of absence and moving with us in Calgary.

Monica, a physician, had been anxious about this family ever since Frieda was born, a little premature and with very low hemoglobin count. Her anxiety was much worse because all her efforts to improve the situation had been in vain. As soon as she heard of their imminent arrival, she felt that at long last her opportunity had arrived and started preparations in top gear. Rooms were readied for the children and their mother, a list was made of all medical care specialists to be approached and some appointments arranged, the authorities contacted about schooling and process of registration and strategies discussed on how to handle a difficult child.

Frieda allowed us a few days' grace after their arrival and

then reverted to her usual tricks. She screamed whenever she was asked to do something, whether for fun or to help with chores. Her drawing was a few random lines on paper; her writing was that of a five year old. She was good at reading but I wondered how much of it she comprehended. She was extremely shy with adults and could only relate to other kids, whatever their age, on her terms. Putting her to bed was a major exercise in frustration and she woke up at five and made sure every one else was up too.

The pediatrician prescribed pills to increase her attention span. There was a significant improvement in her ability to focus and her skill level improved. Probably due to these factors, there was a gradual reduction in the frequency and intensity of her blow ups. Other medical care and family therapy, an excellent teacher at school, attention of three adults and discipline enforced by them, regular hours of eating and sleeping, all helped. A measure of improvement was that she was now trying to maintain some control on herself during the angry episodes and often apologized when she had calmed down. She stopped screaming when mother left her in our care and going to bed routine became a piece of cake. Although all was not well in the estate in Calgary, it was becoming almost manageable. Our concern now was no longer how we will survive the day; it was how will the mother cope when they return home next summer?

Then the miracle happened. I was looking after the girls by myself that evening. Frieda busied herself in painting while I helped her sister to bed. This included reading two stories, cuddling her for a few minutes and setting the music to lull her to sleep. Entire process took a little more than half an hour. Frieda occupied herself for the whole time, something we could not even imagine only four months ago. When I came down she showed me the picture she had been working on. She had shaded in a complex outline drawing of the fairyland with felt pens. The drawing showed a good sense of colours and a reasonable level of competence. Progress from a few scratched lines to this drawing in such a short period was incredible. I complimented her on the good work and she neatly placed it on the dining table for her mommy to admire on her return.

Frieda went to the wash room and I sat down in an easy chair in the corner of the living room. She came out a few minutes later and stood next to the wall facing me. I looked at her and was astounded. The person facing me was not the little girl who has had us on tenterhooks ever since her birth but might have been an angel. Her eyes were sparkling and face glowing, her body radiating a joy she could not have experienced before. She told me in minute detail her event of the day. A kid in her class punched her face without any provocation. Instead of 'getting frustrated' she kept her cool and did not retaliate. She was proud of the way she handled it. More than pride, it dawned on me, she realized that she had turned a crucial corner in her life's journey; whatever had been tormenting the child was no more in her and from now on she was going to endure the misery daily grind of life brings and emphasize in her little brain the happiness that is also all around her.

SUDHIR JAIN

I did not expect that she will become a 'normal' child instantly and she hasn't. We have not cancelled appointments with therapists and other professionals. But I feel a fundamental change within me. I am confident that the family is on its way to stability and my little granddaughter will grow up into a fine young woman.

It Is All Greek To Me

~ *1* ~

Monica and I returned to Greece after thirty years, this time with our daughters Geeta and Sheila. Our third daughter, Yamuna, was representing Canada in Canoe events in the Olympics and was traveling with her team. Dmitri was our travel agent. We arrived in Athens on a beautiful evening after twenty four hours in planes and airports with ten hours of jet lag. It was the first week of summer Olympics and there was no available room at an affordable price anywhere within Herculean stone's throw of Athens. Since our main interest was the canoe races to be held in the following week on a lake couple of hours away by boat and ferry, we had decided, on Dmitri's advice, to spend the first week traveling away from the maddening crowd and visiting shrines of ancient Greece. We picked up the car Dmitri had booked for us and drove on deserted roads to the beautiful sea side town of Napflio. By the time we found the hotel, a beautiful Venetian building on a narrow street in old part of town, it was quite late and time to hit the sack but not before the dinner of lemon chicken with boiled salad, a mixture of boiled vegetables, on the terrace overlooking the sea and the fort built by Venetians on a small island to keep Turkish Bey at bay.

After a hearty breakfast of eggs and various cold cuts next morning, we headed for Epidavros, a World Heritage archeological site, sanctuary of Asclepius, son of Apollo and the founder of medicine. The 30 km drive along the winding road through lovely vineyards and pretty villages with stores selling locally made Venetian glass and cafes serving local delicacies was memorable in itself. Then the vista changed and we were driving along a small river with mountains clad in green on both sides. The dream ride ended on a huge parking lot which was completely empty. Every person in Greece was glued to the TV watching Olympics and the stray visitor had all the glorious places to himself. We strolled through the large area where excavation is under way to the track that was used for races 2500 years ago but could have been the landing site for flying saucers bringing various gods to the theatre or to be treated by descendants of Asclepius. The theatre itself is an amazingly well preserved limestone structure that can seat 14,000 and is renowned even today for its acoustics. The museum was small but very interesting. It housed statues and artifacts from the digs including a perfectly preserved statue of Asclepius.

An hour's drive took us to the Citadel of Mycenae. The structures in the citadel were destroyed during the wars in ancient times but enough is left to give a visitor with better imagination than me the idea of the magnificence of the city in its heyday. The splendid museum with particularly delightful display of pottery added to our understanding of the ancient civilization.

Next morning was dedicated to Palamidi, a massive fortress built on the hill. It had marvelous views of the old and new Nafplio, two smaller fortresses and the charming port. The fort itself was built by Venetians in early 18th century and is noted for well constructed and strategically placed bastions. We skipped the smaller fort that goes back to Bronze Age.

~ 2 ~

It was a pretty drive to Sparta. Surprisingly, it turned out to be a modern town with elegant hotels on both sides of a tree-lined avenue and the town square full of noisy cafes overflowing with young people. The highlight of Sparta was the olive museum. We learnt the history and importance of olive oil since the oldest known culture and saw some oil presses of historical importance. Mystras was a short drive away. It is an ancient fort built on the steep hillside with an active monastery. Two surviving palaces are impressive and the museum houses pottery and other artifacts recovered in archeological excavations.

We got to Delphi, called the navel of the Earth by ancient Greeks, just before the sunset. The quaint village is located on the western side of steep Mount Parnassus overlooking the Gulf of Corinth. The view of the setting sun across the vast valley with clouds of changing hues was awe-inspiring. There were very few tourists and we enjoyed the opportunity to window shop at a relaxed pace. Sales ladies were very civil and showed their merchandise without any pressure to buy. We did not allow any feeling of guilt to come over us and returned to the hotel empty handed.

Next morning, we drove to the archeological site which was founded in the Mycenaean times (1600 BC) as the Sanctuary of earth goddess Gaea and after many transformations ended

as the Sanctuary of Apollo. It is the most impressive of all
historical sites in Greece and has an air of divinity about it
which touched even this atheist. Doric temple of Apollo,
theatre built in 4th century BC, the Sanctuary of Athena and the
stadium provide an understanding of life in ancient Greece.
Museum attached to the site was worth visiting in its own
right. Surprisingly well preserved exhibits related to ancient
myths and daily life were very well explained.

After a leisurely lunch in a restaurant with a beautiful view
of the valley, we drove for several hours to Olympia where the
Olympics began. The village also has a museum of the modern
games with a nice collection of stamps and literature of games
since 1896. The main site of ancient Olympia is extensive and,
for once, is located on flat ground. It goes back to Mycenaean
times and started life as the temple to worship Rea and her
son Zeus. The first games were held in 776 BC. The games
were restricted to Greek males only and included arts and
business as well as sports and lasted for five days. Women and
slaves were not allowed even as spectators. The games were
banned in 396 AD and in 426 AD the temples were destroyed.
Therefore, it takes some imagination to reconstruct the glories
of the temples of Zeus and Hera, stadium, hippodrome and
magistrate's residence where feasts were held for athletes.
The recently reopened museum is a grand affair with splendid
statues, pottery, columns and arches.

It was another long but pleasant drive to Meteora. The
place is known for vertical columns of black volcanic rocks
jutting out several hundred meters into the air. The surface

area of columns is quite variable, a few square meters to a tenth of a square kilometer. In 14th century, solitary monks built monasteries on these columns to escape the Turkish invaders. The monasteries have beautiful churches full of art and architecture of this period and museums with articles of religious and historical significance, particularly beautifully preserved books which are gems of calligraphy. The combination of monasteries and the unusual topography of black towers in the foreground and a majestic river in a vast valley clothed in diaphanous haze made for otherworldly experiences at sunrise and sunset.

~ 3 ~

We arrived at the hotel located on the outskirts of
Athens late in the evening after a six hours drive
from Meteora. The races were to start the next
morning at 8:30. The stadium was a 32 minute ferry ride away.
To allow enough time for the much dreaded security at the
games, we planned to catch the ferry at seven. In order to be
sure of a place on it, we got to the terminal an hour before.
Getting up at five was easy, thanks to the excitement of being
the Olympic family. The problem was in making the protesting limbs do what was needed, particularly when reversing the
tiny car in a tinier lane on the rocking boat. However, it was
duly accomplished after prayer to Zeus supplemented by the
sacrifice of a cup of decent coffee on the dashboard.

We were in the stands at eight sharp. The Hungarian
contingent had taken over the whole area across from the finish
line. They were chanting at the top of their voices – "Ra Ra
Ra, Hun Ga Ria" accompanied by drum beats from the father
of a competitor. The father's body was painted the red, white
and green of Hungarian flag and he wore a matching tall hat
on his bald head. Young women in skimpy red tops and green
bikini bottoms were swaying to the tune and many young men
were shaking their rattles at full blast. The scene was exciting
to the eye but hard on the ear. A small Canadian group was
sitting quietly nearby. We joined them and put the Maple Leaf

up. A few more rolled in just before the start and someone distributed small flags to other Canadians. We formed an elite group of about twenty, many dressed in appropriate red and some faces painted with maple leafs. A Polish group now joined the Hungarian fans on our other side. The Polish men were almost as noisy as Hungarians but the women covered some of their skin and were not as wiggly as the Hungarian beauties. Sandwiched in between, Canadians lived up to their sedate image.

The opposite bank of the lake had two big boards; one showed results and the other television pictures of the races. This screen also offered sensible advice to the spectators roasting in forty degree centigrade:

Drink a lot of water and recycle (It didn't say how).

Don't touch the walls of ruins you visit, it ruins them.

Don't leave packages unattended, they will be confiscated if not stolen.

In between the races TV cameras focused on the spectators. Needless to say, the colorful and musical Hungarian contingent dominated the television coverage. Only time the Canadians made it on the screen was when the camera got stuck in its move to the victorious Poles from lamenting Hungarians whose chanting had become a little muted.

The races finished soon after eleven. All Canadian boats, including Yamuna's, moved ahead to the next round. We joined our compatriots who were gathered outside the stadium to wait for our Olympians to show up. We talked of our relatives with pride without listening to the boasting of others. The families of likely medal winners were the loudest, those of remote medal prospects were slightly less vocal and I and some others claimed softly that we were happy to be there, as we indeed were. If truth were to be told, our group was the happiest because our kins had worked the hardest and had overcome not only the poor coaching at training sites far from home but also the team selection process biased by meddling sponsors.

The athletes came over in ones and twos. They were congratulated and hugged by the family members. Occasional tears of joy were shed. Good and not so good things were said about the team mates. Then the athletes boarded the team bus, Monica and the two daughters hopped on another bus for the tour of Athens and I set out to enjoy the sun and the sea to cap an altogether satisfactory morning.

My stomach started protesting rather loudly my inattention to it. A lunch of Greek salad and moussaka at the beachside café, helped down with local red wine, filled the void. Espresso with a few pieces of baklava was icing on the cake. I changed into my swimming suit and walked to the chair near a beach umbrella to let my lunch settle before I tested the water. No sooner had I put my towel and book on the side table, a young lad appeared. "Five Euros, sir?" he asked pointing to a sign in Greek. "Yes, indeed", I answered handing him over the money I had brought for a drink. "This covers the whole day", the lad said, "so long as you don't move the chair too far."

Wondering whether it was too far, I moved the chair from the shade of the umbrella and opened my six hundred page tome. I did not use sun cream thinking that my native brown skin could do without foul smelling lotions. I hadn't made much progress with the book before I dived deep into the slumber land. I lay there oblivious to the world dreaming of winning gold medals in sports I had never watched, leave alone played. But the pleasant dreams turned into a nightmare. I failed the drug test and the mailman was knocking to deliver the notice of forfeiture of gold medals. Shocked, I opened my eyes. The lad was tapping on the chair, "It will soon be dark, sir. I have to take the chair to the shed". I scrambled out of the chair. I was the only visitor still on the beach. But it did not deter me from attempting a swim in the lovely Aegean Sea. I made a dash for water. Ouch, the gravel on the beach was hard on my feet. Ouch again, salty water was rough on my skin. The comfortable warmth of the water was being offset by salt in the wounds. Wounds caused by sun burns, I discovered as I bent down to scratch the back of my legs. I got out of the water, gingerly dried myself, picked up the book and walked towards the car. Halfway there, the lightening struck, "God, what did I do with the keys?" I rushed back to the beach. All the chairs and umbrellas were gone and there was no way to know where I had been. The world was as dark as it had been bright a few hours ago. I guessed the best I could, dropped on my knees and started feeling for the keys in the sand with both my hands. Desperation was getting hold of me. I was cursing myself for my stupidity with increasing vehemence. Then I heard light footsteps and eventually the lad, "Sir, I found these when I was putting away the chair." I jumped with joy, grabbed the keys, thanked the lad and stumbled towards the car scratching furiously my back and neck. The lad followed me closely to the car. I got the impression that an appropriate tip was expected. As always, I did the right thing. However, my problems were far from over. My thighs did not want to touch the seat and my back hated the backrest. I learnt my lesson the hard way - never again will I sunbathe lying on my tummy, if I indulge in this foolishness at all. And a layer of sun lotion one inch thick will cover my body. I gingerly drove to the hotel. There was no way I could dress for dinner. So I ordered room service to bring me lemon chicken and cold beer. An hour later, I was served cold food and hot beer. Too tired to complain, I ate what I could and went to sleep, on my tummy of course.

Things improved a little the next morning. I managed to cover my wounds with a light T-shirt and had a proper breakfast. The semifinal races were thrilling and Yamuna and three other Canadians made it to the finals. My family decided to visit the beach. But I was not going to be caught in the mid day sun again and decided to spend the early afternoon in the museum of Acropolis and visit the ruins afterwards when the sun had lost its sting. To avoid the notorious Athens traffic I drove to the nearest Metro terminal and found a spot in a tow away zone where many local cars were parked with impunity. The train was rather crowded and more people pushed their way in at every stop making it difficult to scratch my sunburns. The whole train emptied at Acropolis and the procession of thousands marched towards the entrance of the cradle of Western civilization. The magnificent pillars of

Parthenon towered above as the crowd jostled along the wide avenue. Soon, a huge queue formed to buy entry tickets. The collection of Olympic pins on my hat provided a good topic of conversation and the hour passed pleasantly before I parted with ten Euros at the ticket window.

Inside the gate I admired the bird's eye view of Athens from a vantage point and proceeded towards the museum. I was not alone. Most of the crowd was also heading for the air conditioned comfort. The discipline of the thousands of men and women from every corner of the world was astounding. It didn't take long before we were admiring Zeus and other deities in full glory, the bulls at rest, lions killing horses, men carrying goats on their shoulders, Corinthian pillars and colorful wall and ceiling decorations. Digital cameras flashed, movie cameras whirred, disposable cameras clicked and people behind waited patiently except when some egomaniac decided to pose with a statue and the cameraman took his time. People were admiring the exhibits in languages of six continents and the resulting din was music to my ears.

The sun was bearable when I was pushed out of the museum by the crowd behind me. I learnt that the Parthenon had been reconstructed in the seventies based on wrong principles and was in the process of being re-reconstructed in accordance with the theories of the new millennium. I enjoyed the shade of the tree which had supplied olives for oil which Hercules rubbed on his body before his battles and saw the outdoor theatre which seats ten thousand and where sold out performances are a normal occurrence even now – a time when anything classical is looked down upon by all and sundry.

The crowd had thinned a little on my way out and I stopped to take the picture of the Parthenon from below. I was immediately surrounded by hawkers selling cards, guide books and models of the Parthenon with great enthusiasm but not enough to melt my cold heart. I refreshed myself at a roadside cafe before boarding the train to my car. This is when I started becoming nervous about having parked in the tow-away zone. However, the car was there adorned with a ticket on the windshield informing me of my infringement and the penalty of 125 Euros to be paid in cash within a week at one of the specified locations. I surreptitiously placed the ticket on the windshield of the next car hoping that the owner would pay without checking the identification. He probably did since I have not heard from the rental company yet.

By the next morning, my sunburn had improved to occasional itches. I could watch the canoe finals without worrying about the sun. However, a strange dizziness came over me during the last race with Yamuna's boat head to head for the gold medal. My voice went hoarse, my legs could not support my weight and I slumped to the seat. A sweet young lady standing behind noticed me and stuck a bottle of water to my mouth. Miracle water, or perhaps it was her lipstick around the rim, revived me. She was gracious as I thanked her effusively. On our way out, Monica bought a large bottle of imported mineral water which I emptied in one gulp. Soon, I was impatiently waiting in the line up for the entry into "Q.C.", a quaintly named little room, presumably a washroom for highly qualified lawyers. When I came out, Yamuna had joined us. We congratulated her heartily and finalized arrangements for her to meet us at our hotel the next morning.

After experiencing massive sunburn and debilitating dehydration in quick succession, I was ready for a siesta while the family headed for the beach again. After a light lunch of Greek salad saturated with nourishing olive oil, I put the "don't disturb" sign outside the door, double locked it from inside, turned on the TV to watch the games and slipped into bed. No man can really rest when Greek beauties are fighting French queens in a close game of Beach Volley Ball. This was followed by swimming events where equally erotically unclad women were competing for gold as well as the attention of show business talent scouts. Sprints over various distances followed with athletes trying to outdo swimmers. From what I watched that evening one would be forgiven the impression that Greece had won all Women's Olympic events and the athletes were well suited for the role of TV stars.

~ 4 ~

The car had to be returned at the agency at the airport a day before we were to leave on our tour of Greek islands. Dmitri offered to help us return the car; store our extra luggage during the two weeks we were in the islands and take us to our overnight hotel in downtown Athens. Every element of the arrangement had been gone through with a fine-tooth comb and approved. But the gods hadn't had their say yet.

Dmitri arrived at our suburban hotel in his van at the appointed hour. He proudly showed its gleaming exterior and the spotless interior. Then he announced with certain pride that he had owned it for thirty years to the day and looked after it better than his family. The van had survived notorious Athens traffic without a scratch. He serviced it himself from head to tail every month and changed oil before it had a speck of dirt in it. The van was washed more often than some members of his family: it had cost money to acquire and it helped grease the wheels of his business unlike the members of the family who only talked to him when they needed help.

The van was loaded with our cases which were to be left in his care. The bags we were to carry to the islands were in the trunk of our car. While arranging the bags I noticed a fire extinguisher. I could not imagine why one would carry one in the car but the law required it; a large notice on the inside of the trunk said so. The reason for the law was not hard to find.

Greeks were avid smokers but they hated the sight of cigarette stubs. The only thing to be done when the lighted end had reached the finger tips was to flick it out of the car with great panache. Once in a while it landed in the passing car and the consequences were not pretty. Hence the law requiring fire extinguisher in every car. I did not believe we could become the butt of such joke by the fate and arranged bags all over the extinguisher and the plastic bag containing the control valve.

We drove to the airport, Dmitri in his van and our family of four in our car behind him. Driving in Greece needs sharp reactions and the nerves of steel. The machismo of Greeks is expressed behind the wheels and takes full wings when they see a young woman driving the car ahead. Not to be outdone Geeta was giving full reins to her fiery temper by the time the bustle of Athens traffic was left behind and we were on a six lane rather deserted airport road. This super highway was built to accommodate speedy traffic of Olympic Committee members between airport and their luxury hotels. Dmitri picked up speed and we reluctantly followed suit. Soon the speedometer was hitting 150 km. The exhilaration of speed took hold of us but Dmitri was no doubt used to it. It was at the height of our excitement when Geeta noticed flames coming out of the back of the van. Dmitri was, however, totally unaware of them. Geeta hooted the horn and tried to get along the van to warn him. But there was no way a Greek male was going to let a Canadian young woman overtake him. He speeded as well and hooted back. After a long minute or so of this drama, a Mercedes 500SL saw the writing on the wall, sped past Dmitri and waved him to stop. It was at this moment that Dmitri saw the flames of fury from his well-serviced van.

He stopped on the wide shoulder and Geeta parked carefully at a safe distance behind him. He ran to the back of the van and started to throw our cases out. Monica screamed telling him to run to safety and not worry about the cases while I screamed about the safety of the contents. But he continued throwing out the cases and fighting the flames with bare hands.

The incredible scene came to a sudden end. Sheila had the presence of mind to think of the extinguisher in our car. She found it in the jumble of bags, located and fitted the control valve and rushed with the red cylinder blazing to attack the flames with the zeal of a novice fire fighter. It didn't matter that Dmitri was getting as much of the extinguishing foam as the flames; he deserved it for being in the way. The flames did get enough foam to subside and quickly died without a murmur. We all breathed a sigh of relief. Dmitri looked at the damage and the worried frown was replaced with a heavenly smile, "The damage is superficial, small leak from the pipe connecting gas tank to the engine, will be fixed in no time and the van will be good for another thirty years." However, he was not ready to drive the van till the leak was fixed. He arranged for the tow truck and we drove to the airport car rental. The ride to the hotel on the new train may not have been as comfortable as the van but it felt safer even though I had my pocket picked.

Our family got a Christmas card from Dmitri thanking us for our business and thanking Sheila for saving his van. He said that a new pipe has done wonders and he is looking forward to picking us up in his van on our next trip to Greece - in another thirty years.

~ 5 ~

A 30 minute flight from Athens took us to Santorini. It turned out to be an idyllic island. It is small, approximately 15 km x 5 km. We rented a car before realizing that the tourists are well served by a frequent bus service covering the island. Thira is the main town on the west coast. There are several pockets of tourist areas with good hotels and restaurants. It is a paradise for lovers of sun, sand and shops. Broad beaches are not crowded. We visited three sites of historical interest: the pretty village of Pirgos, ancient fort of Elefsina and archeological digs at Akrotiri and visited the museum in Thira for excellent wall paintings, statues and pottery from Santorini and surrounding islands. It was an enjoyable walk on the narrow vehicle free street from Thira to Tholos on the northern tip. The long street has attractive jewellery shops, cafes, restaurants and art and antique stores on both sides. We happily joined thousands of others enjoying delectable Greek food in elegant hillside restaurants in Thira and Tholos while snapping for posterity unforgettable views of the sunset.

A two hour hovercraft ride took us to Iraklio, the capital of Crete located roughly in the centre of the northern coast. Crete is a relatively large island, 220 km in the east west direction and 30 km north south. Its interior is mountainous and the coast is dotted with beautiful villages often accessible by ferries only. Tourism is the major industry and hotels and cafes are plentiful. During our stay we found that service often left something to be desired. Iraklio is inhabited by over one hundred thousand people to cater tourist population of the same size.

It was 10:30 PM when we checked in the hotel. As soon as I had put the cases down Monica, who had been studying the tourist guide, screamed with delight, "This is something we have to do - a 16 km hike along a gorge in rugged mountains, starting at 1000 meters ASL and dropping to sea level. Legend has it that this trail was taken by Alexander the Great on his great march to India and one can still see the hoof marks on the rocks, although there is some question about which ones are from Great man's horse. We have to do this hike to get the flavor of Crete. I will call the receptionist and get the details."

There was only one possible date for this trip during our four day stay in Crete — the next day. Bus would pick us at 6 AM, take us to the start point 250 km away and pick up at the other end of the trail. Expected arrival of 7 PM seemed to me a little early considering the distances but not after the good wife reminded me how Greeks drove their buses. In any event, the details depressed me but not the others. Our Olympian daughter said she needed exercise and supported her mother. Looking back, it may only have been out of gender solidarity and the wish to teach old fat scrooge a lesson. The receptionist wanted to know within next 23 seconds if we wanted to be on the bus. We rushed down the stairs three steps at a time, paid 300 Euros cash for our transportation and we were booked. As soon as the die was cast, stomachs growled, not only for dinner, but for next day's breakfast and lunch as well. Dinner at midnight fitted right in with the local custom. I stealthily pocketed some bread for breakfast and we bought some peaches for lunch from a stall which was ready to call it a night.

After a four hour sleep, we were up and raring to go at the hotel door at six o'clock sharp. A minibus showed up half hour late and took us to a gathering point next to a garbage dump we could smell but not see in the dark. We waited for the bus on the side of a busy road. A double-decker bus showed up in another half hour. We climbed up and found five seats separated by several rows. The guide introduced herself via the microphone in Greek, German, French and Italian and informed us that there was no W.C. (wash room, if you insist) on the bus but there will be a stop in three hours for stretch, smoke and coffee. There were many groans but no one dared to complain to the guide. The bus did stop every few minutes but only to pick up would-be hikers. Soon, the bus was bursting at the seams, like many of its passengers, but driver and the guide took no notice and the passengers minded their own business – holding on till the W.C. stop.

Eventually the bus stopped at a convenience store, not a minute too soon considering the dash of passengers to W.C. Relieved hikers had rather late breakfast and bought lunch. Some people noticed that the guide kept a close watch on how much was spent by each hiker and surreptitiously pocketed a bundle from the store owner when we had boarded the bus. We got to the start point where we paid five Euros each to enter the national park and to begin the hike. I claimed my senior's discount but was gruffly brushed aside – discount is only for the European Community citizens. The guide told us, again in four languages – none intelligible – expected arrival times at check points. The most crucial was the arrival at the beach before 6:00 PM when a ferry will take us to the bus a couple of kilometers along the rugged coast. Seven hours for sixteen kilometers downhill is a stroll for fit and rested young in heart and body. For this short and fat Canadian who had missed his sleep for many nights and was still suffering the effects of the blinding sun and scorching heat, it was like a marathon race in hell. "Pace yourself, old man, you can do it" I told myself as I set off. Soon I was the huffing and puffing tail in this group of sixty intrepid hikers from fifty countries.

It was a picturesque setting of lovely mountains - green, not the white I am used to in Canada. I was told that it got prettier as the gorge got deeper and the red cliffs make their appearance. Some hikers with sharp eyes and lively imagination noticed hoof marks and could tell from the shape when they were made by Alexander's great horse. But I was panting too hard to notice. When I stopped, it was to recover my breath, hydrate myself, and wipe the sweat off my bald head, brows and glasses. There was no time to waste on appreciating the scenery. I had to stay with rest of the group so as not to get lost in the woods.

The examples of Greek entrepreneurship were everywhere. A couple of men waited at regular intervals with their donkeys to give ride to hikers who got injured or disheartened for a modest fee of thirty Euros. I was sorely tempted but I am too much of a cheap skate to part with that much money. At every point of rock fall warning, their was a young man with steel helmets with horns, just like those valkyrie helmets in Wagner operas, to rent them to you for a Euro each. At the end of rock fall zone his colleague collected the helmets and rented them to clients coming the other way. You paid the rent at each rock fall zone and by the end of the hike you had parted with ten precious Euros.

Just when I was running out of steam and starting to drag myself on all fours, my lonely brain cell activated. I realized that unless I picked up speed, I would barely make the boat and miss out on dinner set for 5:30. Thought of being rocked and rolled for five hours or more on the boat and the bus on protesting stomach was all I needed to get the second wind. I started walking as if I was in the Rockies in my young days thirty years ago. I did last five kilometers in an hour and was at the stipulated dining room in good time to refresh myself before ordering Greek salad with extra olive oil and moussaka. The food of ancient Greek gods made me feel like Atlas without the world on his back. There was spring in my feet when I walked on to the boat and from boat to the bus.

The spring lost its elasticity by the time bus dropped us at the garbage dump. Minibus picked us up after regulation half hour wait and dropped us at the hotel at midnight. When I asked the receptionist about the discrepancy with what she told us the previous night, she shrugged her shoulders and walked away. We decided that this Cretan and courtesy do not cohabit and went to bed to snore and dream of a sumptuous breakfast buffet which, alas, remained a dream.

~ 6 ~

We had the opportunity to visit the Minoan ruins of Knossos, five kilometers from Iraklio. The ruins are unusual because of extensive reconstruction by the British founder Sir Arthur Evans in early twentieth century. Knossos is the remnant of a large palace built in 1500 BC and much of it is cordoned off. Still, there is a lot to see, wall paintings and the Royal Road attracted me particularly. Museum in Iraklio has many wonderful exhibits from Knossos and we spent very enjoyable three hours there. The old harbor is very picturesque and fifteenth century Venetian fort built to protect the harbor from Turkish invaders was worth the visit.

A 25 minute flight on a miniplane took us to Rodos, a smaller island than Crete but equally popular with tourists. The island is roughly 75 km in the north-south direction and 20 km wide. It is dotted with beautiful beaches on the eastern coast. The interior is hilly and covered with vineyards. We visited the picturesque walled area of the Old Town of Rodos several times. The area has several museums, mosque of Suleiman, Palace of the Grand Masters and shopping alley with attractive tourist merchandise. I found the Son et Lumiere in the beautiful gardens across the fort wall from the Palace of the Grand Masters illuminating after spending a most enjoyable day admiring the harbor, visiting the aquarium, and relaxing on a very crowded beach. A drive on the road circling the island was interesting and sunset from the western coast across uninhabited islands was simply gorgeous. The visit to butterfly gorge was most fascinating in spite of some unruly visitors.

It was now time to return home. We arrived in Athens in the late afternoon and joined the hordes in one of the great plazas of Athens. Syntegma Square was chocker-block with visitors. Confectionary stalls, amateur musicians and pick pockets were doing roaring business. Having had my pockets picked and passport stolen in all great cities of the world, I was careful not to add Athens to the list and we kept our hands in our pockets firmly gripping our wallets and travel documents. After being pushed back and forth for a while we found ourselves in a park. Here we parted from the crowd and found a lane relatively less traveled. We came across a bridge on a narrow stream with a snow white embankment. It was a local artist's idea of the Canadian landscape. Shaking off our homesick feelings, we walked across to the Houses of Parliament, a majestic building overlooking the park. I offered the security guard a set of Canadian pins and she let us have a peak into the plush office of a junior assistant to senior deputy under-secretary to the Minister of Culture. This glimpse of Greek bureaucracy satisfied our curiosity. It was now time for our Olympian to join her friends. We kissed a fond goodbye and the rest of us strolled to the hotel.

I set the alarm for 4 AM to catch the 6 AM flight on our long way home. I slept fitfully on the plane dreaming of a white Christmas with family and friends. The plane landed in Calgary in a snow storm and the temperature of -10 degrees. The family groaned but I did not mind at all. After the torturous heat of past week, I was ready for a roll in snow.

Return of the Native

~ 1 ~

A new immigrant from India has a hard time. First, he must learn to drive on the wrong side of the road. Then he has to get used to the freezing weather and all that goes with it. If he is young and hot-blooded he falls in love and marries a wonderful local girl. Before he knows it, she is training him. He learns to enjoy the fine points of bland Western food and to honor her wishes unlike in India where a wife anticipates her husband's whims and fulfills them before they are expressed. What is worse, he can't join his wife for holidays to exotic places on this continent because he must go 'home' to see his family.

I was not your typical immigrant though. I did marry a Western girl and undergo strict training. But I went on holidays with the family and gave my former home a skip. Last time I was in India was in October 2003 four years ago and Monica was there with me part of the time. Monica is currently recovering from a debilitating illness and needed a long rest. My sister-in-law Nirusha invited us to visit her in India. We were in complete agreement except that I suggested three week recuperation under Nirusha's care while Monica wanted to travel to explore opportunities for volunteer activity. After long discussions carried on in bed instead of more interesting activities, we reached an agreement – ten days in Delhi with Nirusha, a visit to the ancient Jain temples in Northwest India, a few days with my social activist nephew Rajneesh, a safari to a tiger sanctuary and a few days in Singapore with my niece. I sent the provisional itinerary to Rajneesh and he made reservations accordingly. There was a last minute scare. The visas did not arrive and I had to make several cajoling calls to the Indian consulate to receive them on the planned day of departure. Finally, we set off on a twenty hour journey made to appear even longer by the twelve hour jet lag. Thanks to travel during midweek, we had empty seats on our flight to Frankfurt and slept comfortably all the way when we were not being fed. The combination of long sleep, good food and favorable jet lag is hard to beat. We were bursting with energy when we pushed our luggage cart to the reception area at Delhi airport a little after midnight. My niece Sarala and Rajneesh's wife Manju were there to greet us with broad smiles and open arms.

The realization that we were in Delhi struck with a new force when we walked out of the building and breathed the heavy warm air. Taxi that had been arranged to take us to my brother Vijay's home did not show up and after waiting for an hour Manju engaged another one at the exorbitant rate of five hundred rupees (thirteen dollars). The trunk was loaded with the driver's personal belongings but a little rearranging made room for the large and heavy case. Four of us squeezed in with smaller cases on our laps. The roads were busy even at this hour and the fifteen kilometers ride took an hour and a half. The journey from the airport was more tiring than the twenty hours of flying. I was snoozing and Vijay and Nirusha were waiting in the driveway when we turned the last corner. Their welcoming faces made Monica's nervousness and my weariness disappear in Delhi's thick air. We jumped out of the car as soon as it stopped and hugged each other like the long lost kins we were. In view of the late hour detailed exchanges were postponed till the morning and after a drink of hot creamy milk we hit the comfortable bed under the canopy of a mosquito net. Sleep was not in the cards though. Noise of continuous traffic in which blowing the horn every ten seconds is de rigueur, recorded prayers blaring on a microphone in the nearby temple, call of a muezzin, again on the microphone, in a mosque across the main road are not conducive to a restful slumber. Fortunately we got used to it in a couple of days.

A tropical travel specialist in Calgary had prescribed a number of pills to be taken daily and some others as required. The need arose after a few hours of tossing and turning. Monica was attacked by Delhi Belly – diarrhea by its Western name. When pills did not help she started the course of antibiotics. After two days she could keep the delicious food in again and we breathed sighs of relief. A little too soon, as it turned out. At the breakfast table the next morning, I coughed gently with a handkerchief on my mouth. Every one noticed it and a barrage of questions were let loose.

"Do you have phlegm?" asked Vijay.

"Did you cough in the night?" asked Nirusha.

"Were you cold in the night?" asked Sarala.

Manju, not to be left behind shot the final arrow, "Did you sit under the A.C. vent on the airplane?"

Monica, a real doctor and most concerned with the health of her only husband, tried to interject but no one would let her. They did not listen to my replies either. Vijay rushed to a cabinet and returned with a musty old bottle and shoved in my mouth a tea spoon full of green syrup spilling some on my sparkling white new kurta (long shirt). He did not notice the spill and confidently assured every one "His cough will be gone in ten minutes." Nirusha went to the kitchen and brought an Ayurvedic powder wrapped in a brown paper and a bowl of tomato soup with a liberal sprinkling of black pepper. "Take these" she commanded and assured all who would listen, "The cough will be gone in ten minutes." Kamala produced a yellow tablet from her handbag and handed it to me, "I took this last week and my cough was gone in ten minutes." Manju watched me consume all this medication and thankfully did not produce any herself. But she did offer this bit of advice, "Stay in bed and drink a lot of sweet chai with cardamom. The cold will be gone by the evening." Her prescription seemed to me the most attractive because duration of her treatment was a shade less unrealistic than that of the others.

Monica watched in consternation as I consumed all the offerings and prepared to stretch on the sofa with a cup of prescribed chai. The doctor was the only one who thought that the much ballyhooed cough was merely a sneeze and was nothing to worry about.

I later discovered that the duration of every event in Delhi is ten minutes whether it is a two hour drive to visit the relatives at the other end of the city or an hour wait for a visitor who announced his imminent arrival on the 'mobile'. As for my illness, every one turned out to be wrong though no one admitted it. It was indeed the cough but it took much longer than ten minutes to go away. In spite of gaining several inches around my waistline due to the consumption of syrups, pills, powders, gels, soups, teas and miscellaneous brews, the cough persisted during the whole stay in Delhi and left only when the dusty grimy air of India's bustling capital city was a memory.

Apart from Monica's diarrhea and my cough, the stay in Delhi was most pleasant. Nirusha loves to spoil her family, particularly her husband's younger brother. Monica and I were not allowed to do anything that could be construed as work but were expected to consume massive amounts of delicious curries, parathas, gulab jamuns, burphies, pealed apples, guavas and pears and varieties of nuts every hour we were awake. Somehow we found time to see an excellent performance of a ballet based on the Hindu epic Ramayana, the museum of modern art with some paintings by the renowned poet Rabindra Nath Tagore and the local fair to celebrate Deewali, the festival of light. We also managed to arrange a visit to the local government hospital and a private clinic which gave Monica a great deal of pleasure as well as the information about the delivery and range of medical services in India.

~ 2 ~

Our visit was planned around the holy festival of Deepavali, or Deevali. It is timed to be a harvest festival and celebrates the victory of Ram (one of many incarnations of God) over the devil Ravan. It is a good time to visit India. Weather is pleasant, heat of the summer is a thing of the past and the cold of the winter is a few weeks away. Monsoons are over but the ground is not parched and the vegetation is still lush green. However, there are a few problems. Delhi has grown to be a city of five million inhabitants with infrastructure for one tenth that many. Therefore, the roads are clogged, water and electricity supply irregular and air heavily polluted. Not surprisingly, the diseases are so common that every fourth store on the main street was related to medicine. Illnesses of the individual and the family dominate all conversation. This may be an indication of another perversion in society. Corruption in all walks of life, the favorite topic on previous visits, is now accepted as the way of life and there is a general realization that complaining about it is futile, if not dangerous.

Our arrival nine days before the festival was a welcome news to my extended family. My niece Sarala and her businessman husband Amul had come over from Nagpur to see us. Rajneesh and Manju came from far off Pune. A stream of visitors from Delhi culminated in a big party thrown by

Nirusha for seventy guests. Monica in her new pink Salwar Kameez was the toast of the party so much so that few noticed their male relative from Canada. In accordance with the ancient custom, we visited the older relatives to pay our respects. Invariably the hosts were most insistent to feed us the creations of their servants and were offended if we, Monica especially, showed any hesitation. On every visit the hosts legitimately complained of the shortness of our one hour stay although it took us more than four hours including the travel time. All because Vijay estimated that every one of them was a mere ten minutes away although it took longer than that to get the car out of its parking spot.

On the festive day itself, Manju made a beautiful 'Rangoli on the floor near the front entrance. It is an artwork approximately one meter in diameter made with fine white and colored powders. Its sole purpose is to make the entrance of the home attractive and welcoming to the visitors. Lunch that followed was a veritable feast with dozens of dishes loaded with spices, sugar and fat. A snooze in the afternoon was mandatory, even for ever busy Nirusha.

After sunset, the small store room which also serves as prayer nook became the hub of activity. Earlier in the day, clay statuettes of various gods, which the family worshipped in spite of Jain edict forbidding it, had been arranged neatly in an arc on the floor. Tiny earthen lamps were filled with vegetable oil and placed in front of the idols. I was assigned the job of lighting their wicks which required lying prostrate on the floor. Then Nirusha handed Vijay a 'thali' (round metal plate) containing more lighted lamps and offerings of rice and coconut. All believers now accompanied Vijay in chanting a prayer to the glory of all-caring and all-loving God while the patriarch waved the thali around the idols. Every one had a turn with the thali and chanting, self-proclaimed atheists and the lone Christian included. After the prayer Nirusha, as the lady of the house, applied the ceremonial tika, a mark with red paste and grains of rice, on all foreheads and gave cash gifts to Manju and Monica.

After the religious ceremony we sat around the dining table doing justice to the lunch leftovers. Vijay and Nirusha talked of how nice it was to have us all, particularly Monica, with them. I reminded Nirusha of her instruction to me, "Bring Monica with you, don't come without her." She laughed, happy that her threat had worked.

As the midnight approached words became few and yawns many. It was time to wish good night. Another Deewali had come and gone leaving fond memories, especially for Nirusha whose life revolves around her extended family.

~ 3 ~

After ten restful days with the family in Delhi, Rajneesh, Manju, Monica and I said our long goodbyes and left for Udaipur leaving a long stream of tears behind. After a smooth two hour flight we arrived at our destination in the late afternoon. A van and the driver were waiting for us. We drove for five hours to the holy city of Mount Abu which is also a summer resort. The views of mountains and the sunset were refreshing and the towns and villages we passed through showed signs of economic revival. Our hotel was located on a hill top and had a marvelous view of the city and the surrounding area. The sunrise next morning was something to treasure in the memory bank. There are numerous temples of various Hindu sects in the vicinity which attract pilgrims from all over India. Our focus was Jain temples of Dilwara about twenty minutes by car. The temples were built in twelfth and thirteenth centuries and are deservedly renowned for intricate sculpture. Monica wore a sari for the visit out of respect for the pilgrims' sentiments. This also allowed us to claim her as a Jain believer and we were permitted entrance in the hours reserved for Jain worshippers. The vast courtyard houses three main temples, two with statues of the last and the most revered Tirthankar (messenger of God) Bhagwan Mahavir for two Jain sub sects and one of Adinath, an earlier Tirthankar. Small cubicles were built along the perimeter of the courtyard which had beautifully made statues of each of the twenty four Tirthankars, many repeated several times. We left when the crowds of non-Jain visitors started pouring in and it became impossible to appreciate the art works. Next stop was a lake with crocodiles where the unplanned attraction of the afternoon was a small snake tightening itself around a mouse. Then we drove to the foot of a hill and walked a long way to the top. There were small shops on each side of the narrow cobbled path. However, the merchandise was no match for a Gori (white woman) in a Sari. Almost incessant questions to her were courteous and Monica's Hindi improved appreciably by the end of the walk. There was a famous but small and unattractive temple on the top. However, the sunset across the Aravali mountains with the winding Banas River in the valley was magnificent and the clicking of cameras competed with the chirping of a variety of colorful birds.

Next day we drove to another set of Jain temples in Ranakpur on a circuitous way back to Udaipur. The temples are a little older and if anything more magnificent in design and art work than the more famous Dilwara temples. There is one main temple for Bhagwan Mahavir in the centre with smaller temples for all Tirthankars along three sides of the periphery of the courtyard. The marble idol of Mahavir was magnificent as were all the intricate carvings everywhere. There were two other temples in the grounds which were simpler but interesting if only because they were a few centuries older. Another feature was a Dharmshala adjacent to the temple; a large number of small rooms around a vast courtyard where the pilgrims of limited means could stay for whatever they could afford.

On our way out Saree clad Monica was surrounded by a crowd of school children in immaculate uniforms. Children talked to her in Hindi all at once and she reciprocated with good humour. This event prompted a strange dream that night. Monica, surrounded by hordes of children was exhorting them on a loudspeaker to march to Delhi to demand the end of poverty and more important – longer holidays. She then led the children who were shouting slogans in Hindi "Remove poverty, give us longer holidays" out of the temple grounds. I was by her side giving moral support. However, when we got the main road neither of us knew which way to turn for Delhi and the procession fizzled out in utter confusion.

After the temple we made a short stop at a museum commemorating the great battle between Maharana Pratap of Chittor and the forces of the Moghul emperor Akbar. After a night in a hotel in Udaipur we visited the fort of Chittorgarh three hours away on a four lane divided highway. Although the traffic was rather sparse, its variety was even greater than in Delhi. There were camels and elephants walking regally to their masters' destinations along with usual pedestrians on the tarmac, horse and bullock carts, bicycles, dogs, cows, bulls and bare foot ladies in colorful lahangas (long skirts) with a variety of loads skillfully balanced on their heads.

Chittorgarh is the fort of the longest ruling dynasty in the world – from sixth century to the present day. We hired a guide who claimed a reasonable command of English. It turned out that he could string sentences using some English and many Hindi words with verbs of whichever language suited his fancy.

He showed us most of the 130 temples the fort is famous for, the museum, the thirteenth century victory tower with beautiful carvings inside and out and, believe it or not, the wash room of Padmini, chief queen of Maharana Sanga who built the victory tower.

The wash room boasted nothing grand. All it had was a hole in the ground with two thin marble blocks on which the queen squatted to do the dirty work. What caught my eye about the room was its size. It was bigger than any such facility I have had the opportunity to use in any of the countries I have traveled in. The reason, the guide told me with complete equanimity and no explanation: ten maids assisted the queen in performing this vital function.

On the return drive a problem of great historical interest occupied my thoughts. What could the duties of ten maids in the Queen's wash room be? The drive was almost over by the time I worked these out. Two maids were required to take off the silk lahanga, one to untie the knot in the string holding it up and the other to pull the garment over the majestic head. Third maid washed the royal bum with all reverence due to it. Fourth dried it with soft rose petals, fifth disinfected with haldi (turmeric) lotion, sixth applied sandalwood paste deodorant, and seventh perfumed with chameli oil. The eighth maid pulled the lahanga back on over the queen's head and the ninth tied the string. Tenth? She was the supervisor who made sure that the queen was not inconvenienced in any way by any maid's slackness in her duty.

It occurred to me that there was no reason why this queen would be the only one to have this privilege. Other queens of Maharana must have had the maids in their wash rooms too although their number probably declined in proportion to their mistress's importance. As for Maharana, there is no record of the number of attendants, male or female, that accompanied him to his wash room. I suspect that the wash room entourage became customary in all royal palaces in India and the European monarchs followed suit with great élan to outdo their primitive counterparts in the luxury every claimant to royalty deserves.

Just in case you think that the maids had easy lives, they had other duties too. After appropriate rest to recover from this exhausting but necessary task, the queen took her place on a suitably padded marble bench and opened her beautiful mouth which was to launch a thousand horses of another ruler and interrupt, albeit briefly, Maharana's reign. The maids took turn in cleaning the pearly teeth with a brush made out of a neem twig and helped in washing her mouth with water from the holy Ganges. According to some reports, at least one modern prince in Europe has taken this leaf from the medieval queen's diary. To keep the princely mouth in shape to launch enough hot words to keep the kingdom warm, a qualified dentist and his well-trained assistant are in attendance every morning and evening. It will be too low a stoop for the prince whose forefathers ruled the waves to brush his own teeth. As to the royal bum, all lips are sealed and there is no word on how the issue is handled.

~ 4 ~

The plan was to catch the afternoon flight and reach Mumbai in good time to spend a couple of hours with a nephew there before driving to Pune. However, the flight was six hours late. A frequent traveler on the route told us that we were lucky; the flight is often twelve hours late due to a dire shortage of pilots. We missed seeing the nephew and arrived at the apartment at 3 AM instead of expected 11 PM. We went straight to bed and woke up around ten. Rajneesh accompanied Monica to a missionary hospital to investigate the opportunities to volunteer her medical services while I rested to complete my recovery from Udaipur Downer – a less severe form of Delhi belly I had caught on my last day in that city with a glorious past and the potential of a bright future. Two days in Pune went by quickly as we visited the social projects of Rajneesh and Manju – organizing volunteers to teach slum children, showing documentaries to raise awareness of social problems, meetings with volunteers to maximize their impact and recruitment of new 'social activists.' We also had an opportunity to attend a social activist wedding in which most of the formalities were discarded in favor of a simple brunch and performances of classical dances and semi-classical songs of a very high standard.

Our last stop in India was a tiger sanctuary located on Kabini River near the border of Karnataka and Kerala provinces. To get there we flew to Bangalore where another van with a driver was waiting for us. It was a six hour drive, some of it on dark and often treacherous dirt roads. We arrived just in time to 'freshen up' before dinner. The cabins in this forest reserve were luxuriously appointed with, among other unexpected comforts, a western toilet with a somewhat appropriate brand name Hindware. On each of our two day stay we had jeep safaris in the jungle at dawn and boat rides on the river in the afternoon. The promised elephant rides did not materialize because the elephants were 'in heat'. In the mornings we saw hundreds of spotted deer, one leopard hiding in the bush, couple of elephants, some coyotes and many egrets and cormorants in the lakes. As for tigers we had to console ourselves with the video of the reserve with these magnificent creatures in it. In the evenings we saw more egrets and cormorants and a few crocodile snouts and one elephant. The sunset was spectacular on both evenings. The meals and service in the resort were very good, particularly in view of its remote location.

On our way back to Bangalore for our midnight flight to Singapore we had the opportunity to visit the historic city of Mysore with its magnificent nineteenth century palace, Brindavan gardens with lovely fountains and a majestic temple on the top of a hill with superb view of the city and the surrounding countryside. A traffic jam on our way to the airport threatened to derail our travel plans but the driver's skill in negotiating the heavy traffic saved the day. Looking back, this day was the appropriate summary of our Indian experience – beauty in its many forms if you look for it mixed with confusion that is miraculously resolved at the very last moment.

~ 5 ~

We arrived in Singapore with the sun after a four hour flight. The airport facilities were amazing and we had completed the formalities and collected our luggage within twenty minutes of leaving the plane. A half hour cab ride took us to the apartment of my niece, Vijay's daughter Maya and her husband Pritam. We spent four days with them chilling out, as Maya instructed us to do.

Singapore is a small island of about 700 sq kms and less than five million inhabitants. About 70% of the population is of Chinese origin, the rest are Malays and Indians with a few Europeans. The difference in an Indian city of the same size, say Bangalore, and Singapore is like night and day. Overcrowding, dust, garbage, smell from open drains, beggars and potholes are nowhere to be seen in Singapore while they are omnipresent in India and worsening as the economy grows. I got the impression that Singapore was growing without any pains while the cities in India were choking due to wholly inadequate transportation systems, utilities and general services.

Singapore is a city state with a small base of industrial activity focused on electronic assembly and legal drug production. Being an island, winds refresh the air constantly. The prosperity of last few decades has led to the replacement of horse and donkey carts and rickshaws by relatively new low emission cars. There are very few trucks on the roads. Hence, the traffic flows smoothly and noiselessly. The culture of cleanliness inside and out of the home means clean public places and roads with hardly any litter.

The dense living in high rises with 100 – 400 apartments in an area occupied by ten homes in an Indian city leaves room for large open spaces. While the side walks in India are strips of dirt which pedestrians avoid, the roads in Singapore are immaculate with paved sidewalks and potholes as as rare as concrete on some Indian roads.

When Singapore became independent in 1959 it was not much different than any Indian city. In two generations it has been transformed to match any in the first world while the cities in India have noticeably deteriorated. There are several reasons for this anomaly. First, Singapore is a compact city state, much easier to administer than a vast country like India. Total budget of the state is focused on the city. There are no long stretches of road and rail connecting far-flung population centers and no countryside to send its millions to overburden the city. Second, the defense needs are met by a small army whose budget does not siphon off funds from necessary services. Third, a benign dictatorship rules with a firm but fair hand. Punishment is swift for the law breakers whether they are drug traffickers, litterbugs or in between. Fourth, the corruption in public services so common elsewhere in Asia has been rooted out and the rule of law prevails like nowhere else in the world. Last but not the least, the geographic location of the island is ideal for a trading hub for Asia.

Singapore has prospered because firm rule from the top first enforced discipline and respect for the laws and then created conditions suited to the talents of its citizens by providing physical infrastructure and economic and tax incentives to promote trade and entrepreneurship. Companies trading products of foreign countries pay taxes on income in Singapore even when the traded items do not touch its port. Low tax rates attract multinationals to set offices here to advance the trade. New shopping malls attract tourists from Indonesia and Malaysia. The city state of five million residents prospers without any polluting industry and provides unparalleled services to its citizens.

Small is indeed beautiful when the rulers and the ruled concentrate on what they do best.

Return of the Native 2

~ 1 ~

I left India in 1961. Over fifty years of my life as immigrant in four countries I have returned on average every four years for about three weeks each time. I was there for nineteen days in 2011 in November and December and my previous visit was in the same months of the year 2007. I was keen to see how the country has changed during this interval. According to the media reports the economy there has grown annually by 10% for many years. It has been pointed out by some that the middle class has expanded while others have insisted, and I shared this opinion, that just like the West, rich have grown richer while poor have grown poorer and also more numerous because the economic growth has not kept pace with the population growth over the long term. The population has indeed grown at an alarming rate; at over one billion it is three times it was at the time of independence in 1947. Although there is a small decline in the growth rate, population is no where near stabilizing. An unfortunate side of this growth is that it is concentrated among the poor who have no incentive to limit the number of children they have and more of their children now survive, thanks to the availability of better basic services and medical care in the villages and slums.

To get some idea of the real situation, and to spend time with the family as well, I spent four days in Delhi visiting relatives, a week travelling in Kerala at the southern tip of the country with my social activist nephew and his wife and a week in Uttarakhand in Himalayan foothills to attend a wedding in a village near Dehra Dun, my home town, and enjoy the beauties of Nainital, a celebrated mountain resort since the glory days of British Raj. India is known as a country of contradictions and true to form it offered many surprises. It was pleasant to find that there were very few beggars except near the temples where begging is big business operated by the Indian mafia. There was little cow dung on the roads because most of the unclaimed stray cows have been exported to the Middle East. There are fewer mangy stray dogs but plenty of well-fed monkeys. Contrary to my fears, poor in cities and villages I visited or passed on my travels were better fed and clothed than ever before. Majority of women now wear salwar (baggy pants) kameez (knee-length long tunic) rather than cumbersome sari, jeans are worn by some teenage girls and a few young women in major cities. Niqab (face covering) is rare indeed, even in villages. A simple proof of trickling down prosperity is that there were very few bare feet on the streets and children looked healthier and cleaner. Groups of teenage girls in school uniforms going to or coming back from schools were a pleasant sight every where. Even the coolies proudly talked of their children, girls as well as boys, going to private schools at their expense. One of our cab drivers had a post graduate degree but he did not complain about his lot. He is happy that that he and his school teacher wife can afford to send their two children to private schools. The sad aspect of this story is the general distrust in public schools who suffer through siphoning off by corrupt officials of already meager funds.

The other side of the happy economic situation is that even the medium size cities like Kochi and Dehra Dun are choking with ever growing vehicular traffic clogging their narrow streets. Large cities like Mumbai, Calcutta, Delhi and Bangalore with population exceeding ten millions are virtually at a standstill for many hours in a day. Thankfully, majority of buses and trucks have converted to natural gas from diesel and ancient cars have largely disappeared. Therefore, obnoxious fumes these cities were notorious for in the past are now rare. But breathing is not any easier anywhere in India, not even in pristine Himalayas. The air is heavily polluted with dust and invisible but deadly gases emitted by stalled vehicles. Fogs are a constant presence throughout the year making air and rail transport unreliable. A heavy mist almost completely masks the Himalayan peaks which were a sight to behold only a few years ago in Nainital. The sewerage is dumped untreated into the streams which people use to wash themselves and their clothes and to draw water for cooking and drinking. The ground water level in areas surrounding the cities is dropping fast; for example the wells go down to more than four hundred feet in suburbs of Delhi rather than a hundred feet a decade ago. Major population centres have uninterrupted electricity most days but towns and villages are lucky to have power supply for eight hours. Therefore, professionals like doctors and teachers stay away and hospitals and schools can not offer services the citizens need. The solution of the shortages appears to be a long way off since the plans for nuclear power generation are facing insurmountable local opposition after Fukushima disaster.

Indians are generally outgoing people. Yet, although there

is great awareness of cleanliness inside the home they do not see the dirt, dust and human and animal refuse beyond the front door. In spite of economic boom, most streets have more dilapidated appearance than on previous visit. Beautiful temples and mosques which are visited by thousands of visitors daily are spotless inside but their surroundings are repulsive to any one concerned with hygiene. To add to the hardships of dense population, residents live in constant fear of theft which is rarely reported due to a general distrust of law enforcement officials. Rule of Law is embedded in the constitution but it is of little practical value for general public.

Corruption is visible at every level in India from an orderly who must be tipped for a message to be conveyed to the receptionist to cabinet ministers, even senior judges. Ironically, educated and intelligent persons claim to be honest while taking pride in how they avoided taxes or secured other favours by cozying up to the right officers. A new high in two-faced attitude was reached when Rahul Gandhi, son of former Prime Minister Rajiv Gandhi who was murdered (martyred?) by Tamil Tigers and Rajiv's Italian wife Sonya who now runs the government through her puppets. Rahul is next in the dynasty which has ruled 'democratic' India since independence except for a few short terms when Congress party lost the election. Unfortunately, he has shown little aptitude for anything other than claiming his right to rule the country. In an address to the delegates from the youth wing of the ruling party he preached that the only way to eliminate corruption in the country was to modify the democratic system. He did not care to elaborate but one would be forgiven to assume that he wishes to be given a free hand when he ascends to his rightful place at the helm. No one in the audience, either the delegate or the media, dared to ask the questions on the lips of ordinary citizens – How did his family accumulate the fortune estimated in hundreds of millions of dollars without ever having been in a successful venture or what qualifies him for the positions he occupies in the ruling party and the government?

My overall impression is that the drastic reduction in state controls on production in final decade of the last millennium liberated the suppressed native ingenuity and the economy developed rapidly. It helped most of the population to live better in a material sense. While there is optimism among people I met, there is also a growing awareness that rapid exhaustion of basic resources like water and clean air, corruption in administration at every level and governance focused on shortsighted economic goals are driving the country towards a cliff and no one has an inkling of how to stop it.

Late Life Thoughts and
Das Lied von der Erde

~ 1 ~

It was a rainy evening in early October of 1962, like most evenings in Liverpool that year. I had been in that lively city for a year but the fine, almost molecular, grey drops still chilled me to the bones. In retrospect, it was a brave act on my part to accept a free ticket and walk down about a kilometer to the concert hall for my first visit to a performance of Western classical music. I had no idea of what to expect. I suspected it would be very different from the classical music I had grown up with in India. However, I was encouraged by the reputation of Liverpool Philharmonic Orchestra as top notch and that of John Pritchard as a very promising young conductor.

I took my seat in good time to study the program. Mozart's symphony no. 41 was performed in the first half. Although it is one of my favourite symphonies now, it made so little impression on me then that I even forgot about it being performed in that concert. It was the second half that got me hooked. The title "The Song of the Earth" impressed me. 'Song' was actually six verses which I read with great interest during the intermission. Although I did not really understand many of the allusions, the poetry made a deep impression. Fortunately for me, they were, as was the custom in England then, presented in English translation of the German text used by the composer. I later learned that the German poems were a translation from French version of what was originally written in Mandarin. The singers were tenor William McAlpine and

Alto Sandra Warfield. I followed closely the words while listening to the singers, a practice I have followed ever since. Even though ignorant of Western music, I was struck by the way music captured the soul of poetry. The desperation of "The life is gloomy, so is death" was driven home, as was the forlorn mood of the autumn. The clincher, though, was the final words, "The beloved Earth everywhere blossoms in spring and becomes green again! Everywhere and for ever the horizon shines bright blue, for ever, for ever .... ." The expression of sorrow at taking one's permanent leave from the earth that will always return to lushness and beauty would move a heart of stone even with amateur performers leave alone the distinguished artists performing that day.

The 'song-symphony' has six 'movements' sung alternately by the tenor and the Alto. First song, "Drinking Song of Earth's Sorrow" laments the short sorrowful human life on this beautiful Earth with the refrain - Life is gloomy, so is death. In "The Lonesome in Autumn" the grieving singer extols the beauty of the landscape before cold winds destroy it and wishes for either death or love to tenderly dry her tears. "Of Youth" describes an assembly of young men writing poems in a beautiful garden. "Of Beauty" is a lovely song where girls are picking flowers when handsome young men on beautiful horses gallop by creating tumult in the hearts of the ladies. In "The Drunken Man in Spring" the young man lives as if in a dream singing and drinking all day and sleeping all night. "Farewell" is the last song. On a beautiful and pleasantly cool evening the forlorn singer is waiting for her friend who arrives to tell her that he is returning home leaving this beautiful place for ever.

Mahler's version combines two Mandarin poems separated by a haunting interlude. The composer added at the end a line similar to one in the first song and this coda is probably the most moving music in the Western classical canon.

What was it that attracted a 24 year old postgraduate student to this pinnacle of melancholy? It could not be loneliness, being far from the family and friends. I had left home six years earlier and never really missed my family. I never had any bosom friends and moving away was never a heart wrenching experience. I was living in a foreign country but I had lived in Liverpool for a year and was familiar with English literature, British history and politics since the early teens. Therefore I was not in an altogether strange environment, my work was going well, I had received additional funding and there was no reason to fall in love with this song of sorrow. In fact, I did not feel sorry, rather felt the elation of reading and hearing something beautiful; beautifully expressed emotion in poetry and music. The emotion was not strange of course. If it were, the beauty would not have been appreciated. But excitement was with the beauty of words compounded by the musical setting, not sorrow expressed by them. Melancholic music in 'Farewell' made me pensive for a few moments; it did not bring tears to my eyes leave alone induce me to jump in the Mersey. I do believe that my interest was more intellectual than emotional.

~ 2 ~

I owe an immense gratitude to the local Rotary Club who do-
nated a pair of season tickets to the International Students
Residence where I lived. I went to as many concerts as the
graduate student workload allowed. I was also introduced to
the world of opera with The Magic Flute. It left a more lasting
impression than Symphony no. 41 had done. A young English
girl, mature beyond her years, was a source of inspiration and
information in my acculturation. A couple of years later she
agreed to marry me for better (for me) or worse (for her).

I got a taste of a wide range of music over next four years in
England. Five following years in Libya were a cultural desert.
My wife, two daughters and I settled in North America nine
years after the first Das Lied and we renewed our association
with the concert scene. At this stage, the works of Beethoven
and Mozart were the staple and our small record collection
consisting mostly of their symphonies and piano concertos
with Mahler songs and symphonies being somewhat on the
periphery.

It was around this time, in 1981, I read the essay "Late
Night Thoughts on Listening to Mahler's Ninth Symphony by
Lewis Thomas, a New York physician. The connect between the
sad situation of the human race and the coda of Mahler's Ninth
Symphony and the memory of my introduction to the Western

classical music induced me to spend an evening listening to the ninety minute work which was composed around the same time as Das Lied in the last years of composer's life. I was intrigued by it. I decided that to appreciate what the composer was telling me, the listener, I had to become familiar with his other compositions. Thus I began the journey which is nowhere near its end thirty years later.

My first discovery was that Mahler's symphonies, including Das Lied sometimes numbered 8½, form one long book. Each individual symphony is a chapter and a movement is a section. In each chapter the composer asks the question, "Why am I on this Earth?" He provides a provisional answer in the last movement and then revisits it in the next work. Although there is continuity musically, each chapter is philosophically different reflecting the circumstances and the maturity of Mahler at that stage of life. The first symphony often called 'Titan' suggests heroic deeds while the second ends with all living creatures participating in the glory of the Heavenly Father. Third is about love – love of nature, love of life, love of God in an ascending order. Fourth further expands on the theme but in a humorous way. Fifth is the joyful homage to love, love of another human being, which creates a range of emotions from the tragedy of loveless life in first two movements to the excitement of love in the third to peace and harmony of the fourth movement and finally the great joy and brilliant climax – sexual in its intensity – of the last movement. It is as if the composer has found a reason for living in the love of a woman.

The pendulum turns the other way in the sixth symphony,

originally titled Tragic. The beauty and joy is snuffed out by brute force and life is snuffed out by three strokes of a sledge hammer. The joy is ephemeral in this long work and the last movement, as long as most symphonies, is a litany of misfortunes which lead to doom with no redemption. Perhaps as a reaction to the undiluted joy of the Fifth and unmitigated disaster of Sixth, the Seventh is a 'purely musical' creation: three haunting nachtmusic movements, albeit one termed scherzo, sandwiched between two joyous sunshine ones. It is as if the composer is telling us that joy and sorrow were fleeting emotions and Art was his reason for living. The Eighth is a Song Symphony dedicated to Love in all its forms. It integrates Latin hymn "Come Creator Spirit" in Part 1 with Goethe's Redemption of Faust in Part 2. Eros, God of Love, is the creator of all things material and spiritual and the symphony ends in a wonderful crescendo "Eternal womanhead, Leads us on high."

Das Lied, Ninth and the unfinished Tenth are different than previous works. These symphonies were written after Mahler had suffered three blows of misfortune and was living under constant fear of death. They are about coping with the finality of death and a deep melancholy hovers over the entire symphonies. While the ninth ends in a great coda of reconciliation described most aptly by Alex Ross as "a whisper of love at the edge of the grave", the tenth is, if it is at all possible, even more grief-stricken but it ends with "music of love" in Deryck Cooke's words.

~ 3 ~

Das lied is the first in the final phase of Mahler's composing career, the last three summers in the life of this 'summer composer'. I love all of them dearly and have traveled far to hear their performances. But Das Lied has been my favourite since that fateful day in Liverpool and any of 24 CDs of it that I own remain my first choice for listening pleasure. But my reaction to this work has changed over the years. The 'intellectual sympathy' of the first few years when only the strangers passed away started becoming tinged with emotion as the parents and then older friends started taking their leave. By my own late fifties "Farewell" was creating new emotional sensations; I began to feel as if I was taking leave of my world of a beautiful family, kind friends, and the glorious Mother Earth whose bounty I had the good fortune to enjoy in its many forms. But this was only an intermediate stage.

In my seventies I have gone beyond feeling emotional about my own death. During this year my granddaughters returned to live with us again because of their special needs. While helping their mother and grandmother in the recovery of the children's health, my concern increasingly became the headlong rush of humanity towards its destruction. Two major threats to the human survival are global warming and environmental pollution, both directly related to gluttonous consumption by human race. We destroy the forests to create farms, then destroy farms to build shopping centres and clusters of palaces which are left deserted a few years later to start the process somewhere else. We still live under the code devised two millennia ago in entirely different circumstances and ignore the permanent destruction due to an exponentially growing population. We create an economic system which threatens collapse if the economy does not grow day to day; leave alone shrink even for a few months. When handed a golden opportunity to lead the populace towards a system based on steadily reducing and eventually sustainable consumption, our leaders desperately try to reverse a miniscule slowdown in breakneck rush to consume and destroy while paying lip service to environmental protection. Already weak environmental regulations are being relaxed to encourage more production of unnecessary goods (bads!) all over the world. Alberta, my own province, is a particularly discouraging example where incentives are being offered to extract more oil from tar sands with cavalier disregard for extensive pollution of air, water and land; all in the name of protecting jobs. In order to promote our commercial interests we encourage increasing consumption among the middle classes in developing countries at the expense of the poor who have even less to eat and disregard the consequences in those lands of multiplying population, overcrowded cities, evermore polluted water and air. We are rushing to our inevitable end with our eyes shut with the exception of a few isolated voices who cry in the wilderness.

Given this scenario, I feel more and more disheartened with every passing hour. To me the third stroke in the sixth symphony is about to come and fell the human race and the deep melancholy of the coda of Das Lied is not a lament for an individual but for all of us. That is why I worry about my grandchildren's future and Das Lied echoes in my mind when these thoughts keep me awake at night.

Looking Back

~ *1* ~

I have been an atheist all my life. In my view, an atheist does not necessarily deny that the universe was created by a power. However, s/he believes that the creator, if still in existence, has not the slightest interest in the living beings, human or otherwise. An atheist believes that there is no afterlife; death is the final end of the chapter of life. In other words, there is no soul which transmigrates or is revived at some future date to enjoy the heavenly bliss or to roast in hell. That said, I speak only for myself in this essay, not for atheists in general. Atheists are very individualistic and have very personal opinions. They do not have any scriptures to quote as authority and to homogenize their opinions. In fact, dislike for authority figures, living or historical, is at the root of most atheistic beliefs.

People believe in an omnipotent God for one of the two reasons. Most often they were brought up in an environment where this belief was inculcated in them from their birth and they never saw any reason to think otherwise. In many cases, the person did not have any particular faith in a superpower impacting his/her life as long as s/he was able to cope with the events in life. When the disaster(s) of such magnitude struck that the person was not able to cope with the events, s/he found solace in the idea of the superpower to look after and pull him/her out of trouble. Along with superpower comes the paraphernalia of religion and human contacts which further soothe the troubled individual. This is a partial explanation of why religion is making a strong comeback of late. During most of the twentieth century, increasing prosperity coupled with conflict in science and religion made many people give up religion as the idea of superpower seemed superfluous to them. However, the pendulum seems to have swung and the stresses of life in these days of temporary jobs, gang warfare, terrorist activities, global warming, overpopulation, blatant consumerism are stressing people beyond their endurance and they are looking for solace in the virtual arms of a superpower. Churches are filling again and born again Christians, Hindus and Muslims are gaining political power. Even in communist China, religion appears to be making a come back.

There are days when I think that the only reason I am not a devout Believer is because no major calamity has befallen on me. On the other hand, I have had significant failures, family illness and conflicts to cope with. I have taken them in my stride just as I did with minor successes, family well-being and periods of harmony. Two observations help me keep my equanimity. First, I observed around me that good and bad in life even out over a period. Therefore, I did not go overboard with joy in good times or suffer depression in bad times expecting pendulum to swing before long. Second, I am by temperament a problem solver. When I see trouble my focus is on possible solution. I concentrate on minimizing the damage and coming out as whole as possible. This leaves me little time to panic, be sorry for myself, to feel helpless. I have been able to cope with my problems so far with my internal resources. However, I have no idea of what is to come except the belief that I will tackle whatever comes with whatever ability I will have at that time.

As I said, being an atheist I do not believe that a superpower is guiding my life. While a person does not need a guiding personality, he surely needs some principles to live by. Principles help in deciding what to do without having to think pros and cons every time. A religious person asks his God in prayer when he has a tough decision to make. An atheist falls back on his principles: what will be the right thing to do? A selfish person decides to act in his interest irrespective of how harmful it is to others. I suggest to you that many apparently religious people fall in this group. An unselfish person does things that help others, often at considerable inconvenience to her. I know many atheists who could be included in this group.

Before I discuss my principles, I will tell you about my childhood if only because the environment in which one grows up and the genes one is born with are the most vital factors in what the child is to be as an adult. I was born in a family with history of wealth but now surviving on the generosity of rich relatives. My father never earned a cent in his life and my mother, an only child, first used her dowry, then the handouts from her mother to keep the family together. She was not formally educated but was a voracious reader and a very proud woman as befits some one known as the princess in her childhood. She was determined that her four sons will do well and did everything possible to boost their confidence and develop their abilities. I was the third in chronological order and her favorite by far. My younger brother was ill most of his life and died at the age of twenty. My parents were deeply religious but they did not force religion on us. It did not bother them that their sons took different paths as long as they were "good" boys. My oldest brother was very religious. As long as I can remember he prayed twice a day although he never went to the temple. The other older brother was an agnostic but became a devout Hindu later on. As long as I can remember I have been an atheist. I followed my mother's lead and read anything I could lay my hands on and that included a number of religious books. From this reading, I gained a little insight into religion which convinced me that the enunciated principles were worth considering but the idea of God and soul were tools to force people into obeisance and not the foundation of life as they were made out to be. Further reading about other religions in later years confirmed this view.

The basic principle of my life is the common element in all religions: Do unto others what you wish them to do to you. When someone does me what I find unpleasant, I try not to retaliate and get out of their way. I am sure I do not often succeed, but my efforts are geared towards making the other person feel better, although may not be as good as they wish. All religions call vengeance a sin because the natural reaction is to do unto others what they do to you. I wish to avoid sins not because I believe in Heaven but because I have observed that what goes round comes around. And it doesn't wait for next life. If you think about it, every aspect of good behavior has the source in this principle. One is fair and honest because you want others to be fair and honest to you. You don't covet neighbor's wife because you don't want the neighbor to covet yours. I do not lie to my colleagues because I don't want to be lied to. I try to help a person in distress because I know I will be in distress one day and I will need help. The sages have differed through the ages about the degree one must sacrifice his interest for others. The founders of the religion of my parents, Jainism, believed in sacrificing all worldly comforts and going without clothes, shelter and all but absolutely necessary food so the other forms of life were not deprived of their needs. Other sages were not this extreme and many recommended minimum inconvenience for the convenience of others. However, no one ever recommended looking after the numero uno irrespective of other numerals. I do not need to believe in a God watching over me and ready to punish me for any infringements to follow this basic idea to a reasonable degree.

The people with faith swear to the power of prayer. Praying to almighty gives them strength and praying for the well-being of a suffering individual transmits the strength to the ailing. What does an atheist do to find this strength and does a non-believer benefit from the prayers of the well-wishers to the almighty? Speaking for myself alone, when a task appears to be beyond my capacity, I do not say, "God, give me strength" but "come on, you can do it." Some times I do it and other times I can't. But prayers do not achieve results many times either. While I do not feel the strength transmitted by prayers of my religious friends, I do feel the urge to do my best in a desperate situation because my family and friends need me among them. My best has proved to be better than many expected and I have no way of disproving that their prayers were instrumental in the success of my endeavour any more than they have of proving the power of prayer.

How does an atheist define the purpose of life on this planet? Religions are quite specific on this issue: we are here for the glory of God and if we let Him, He guides us to our salvation. I believe that my purpose in life is to discharge my responsibilities to the best of my ability, to serve my family, my community and the humanity at large and generally live a lifestyle where I contribute more to society than I take from it. Let me add that this is an idealistic statement, probably hypocritical. However, this is the ideal I strive towards, with what success is not for me to judge.

~ 2 ~

A week after my sixty-fourth birth day seven years ago, I had a traumatic experience which changed the way I looked at myself. I had worked single-mindedly to become a successful Explorationist and my family life was, for all appearances, happy with Monica who is a physician and three grown-up daughters. Yet, I felt empty inside, rather useless and often thought that it wouldn't matter much if I were to drop dead. Then, while prospecting for gold on a densely forested bear-infested ridge in British Columbia, I got separated from the party and spent three days in heavy rain without any food and two nights sleeping under dripping trees on wet ground before making my way out of the forest to the forestry road. It was close to midnight and pitch dark. I was totally exhausted and trying to summon up the last ounce of energy as I trudged up the steep hill to the camp. This was the state in which Monica and three daughters saw me standing by the side of the path to let their car pass. They were driving back to the hotel after giving up all hope of finding me alive and at first thought that they were seeing a ghost. The glorious family reunion in the forest changed the way I looked at life. The erstwhile emptiness was replaced by a keen desire to be useful to the family and the community.

The opportunities to help the family came thick and fast. While still recovering from the external and internal injuries of the adventure in the forest, I drove three times to Edmonton to help my youngest daughter get settled as a dentistry student. Then it was the extremely premature birth of the second daughter of the partner of our oldest daughter; the baby started her life weighing just 800 grams. We moved the family from California to live with us and every one joined in the Herculean effort needed to help the new-born grow into a normal baby, which she thankfully did. No sooner had we breathed a collective sigh of relief, our oldest daughter was discovered to have a huge tumor in her breast. After a year of intensive treatments of various kinds, she improved enough for the family to return home to California. To celebrate our good fortune, we had a dinner party in a restaurant with friends and professionals who had made it come to pass. Many guests expressed the view that the happy outcome was largely due to Monica's utter selflessness, enormous energy level and professional expertise.

As it turned out the celebration was premature. While reminiscing our last three years Monica felt a lump in her breast. She asked me to feel it. It felt like a misplaced bone. Her suspicion proved correct; after all she had diagnosed hundreds of such cases. It was breast cancer, negligently overlooked in the mammogram by the radiologist only a few months ago. Another round of surgery, chemotherapy and other treatments followed. It is four years since her diagnosis and she is only now regaining some of her old verve. But we are not ready for celebrations yet. The stresses of their lives took a heavy toll on the relationship of our daughter and her partner and they have separated. We are doing what we can to minimize its impact

PAGES FROM AN IMMIGRANT'S DIARY

on our two granddaughters.

When I look back over those years I often wonder what helped me keep my sanity. No doubt the closeness of the family played a vital role. But the most important factor is the impact of that moment at midnight in the forest. I am living to help the family and the community. I write thought-provoking letters to the local and national papers and short amusing tales for the enjoyment of our friends. I contribute to all volunteers who come to the door to raise money for good causes. I volunteer for the cancer society in their fund-raising drives and as a volunteer driver. In the latter role, I drive cancer patients who need a ride to the Baker Cancer Clinic for treatment. I pick them up from their homes, wait at the clinic when they receive radiation therapy and drive them home. It takes a couple of hours once or twice a week. The work brings me no recognition, except from the people in need. But it brings me what I need the most, the satisfaction of helping a stranger from whom I have no expectation of any return.

Being an atheist I do not credit a superpower for showing me the way on that dark night. But the event changed me and I feel much better for it. I am for ever thankful for that experience and even more to the individuals who give me the opportunity to feel good by serving them in my small way and thus replenish the spiritual energy drained by the events in my daily life.

~ 3 ~

I don't know whether it is a recent phenomenon or an age old human characteristic. I have noted that many of my friends believe deep in their hearts that all good things that happen to them are their due and that nothing harmful can happen to them. Serious injury, illness, financial misfortune or other calamities are for other less fortunate folks; they themselves are protected by a special star shining above their heads. They go out in inclement weather without adequate protection and supplies, drive when tired or even drunk and treat management of finances as something for those of more limited means. When they get lost on their hike for several days, an accident happens or sudden financial emergency arises, first instinct is to blame others for it. If they can't find someone else to shoulder the blame "why me" feeling takes over; every body does it and gets away; here they are – in a pickle for no fault of theirs. Why did it have to happen to them?

It is my observation that misfortunes happen much less often to safety conscious people. If they do occur, these "lucky" people deal with them before they become a disaster because they are prepared to handle them. On the other hand, new paths are found by people who take risks. Progress is made by those ready to strike out in unknown directions. Much of joy in living has inherent risk. You can not enjoy the sunrise from a mountain top without taking the risk of camping out in the wild, probably on a cold night or climbing a mountain in the dark. But the risk must be reduced as much as possible by taking appropriate measures – correct boots and other clothing, sufficient water and food, flashlight and first aid kit, maps and compass etc. Sir Edmund Hillary took risks in climbing the Everest but years of preparation went in before his party even got to the base camp. No amount of preparation will eliminate all risks; a number of very well prepared climbers have perished due to unforeseen conditions. But enough preparation is paramount to reduce risk to the level that maximizes the probability of enjoying the reward and minimizes that of a serious loss. To proceed on a venture without an intelligent assessment of risk reward ratio often leads to grief.

Why do so many intelligent persons disregard something so obvious in their daily lives? The other night I went out in spite of bad roads and severe cold weather to a show panned by the critic in our local newspaper. It is doubtful that I would have gone had I not bought the ticket already. For the price of a ticket I risked injury to myself and damage to my car if some vehicle had lost control and I became involved in an accident. Fortunately, the roads to the theatre were rather quiet. However, several people were lining up to buy tickets and the hall was full to capacity. Many of these people must have known of the weather warning but they disregarded it. They took the risk they considered worthwhile to watch a show that had received a poor review. I believe they did so because they "knew" that accident won't happen to them. Indeed, so far as I know no one was involved in any accident and their belief in their invincibility was confirmed. However, this does not prove that they did not take undue risk. By definition, risk means that there is a probability, not certainty, of failure. On slippery roads there is a greater probability of accident and in cold weather greater probability of mechanical failure and bigger inconvenience as a result. Risk in travel becomes greater as the distance to destination increases. Nothing would have persuaded me last night to travel to Banff 100 kilometers away for any show but driving 5 kilometers on well lit and well traveled roads in the city seemed worthwhile. Let me explain why. Statistically, every one on the road has the same probability of accident; let us say one in ten thousands for each kilometer traveled on bad roads in inclement weather compared to one in a million of being hit by a drunk driver. Therefore, the probability of an accident is one in a thousand for a ten kilometer two-way journey in poor conditions, In other words, if I made the same journey in the same conditions one thousand times, I would have one accident. Or one person out of one thousand traveling on similar roads will have an accident. Probability of one in a thousand is acceptable but one in fifty for two-way journey of 200 kilometers to Banff is not; except in a dire emergency. Incidentally, my risk is no less because I had an accident recently; probability theory does not consider the past. Now suppose, for argument's sake that on my way to the theatre my car had skidded on an icy patch, struck another vehicle and seriously injured somebody. "Poor me" would have happened to be the one chosen by gods of probability and other 999 drivers could carry on being invincible. But in the long run, gods catch up with them too and eventually their accident rate is higher than that of those faint of hearts who heed the weather warnings.

~ 4 ~

As I grow older I become more introspective. I analyze more and more why I do certain things, express certain thoughts and indulge in certain behavior. It is very clear that there is an underlying consistent pattern which hasn't changed much since my earliest memory; I was born to be the person that I became; my life has been controlled by my genes. I was born and mostly educated in India in a traditional Hindu family. I have been changed in some ways by eight years of post-secondary science education, 45 years of living as a research scientist in the Western culture and by being happily married to a Western woman. But I contend that the changes are superficial. By superficial I mean that my considered reactions are probably different than they may have been if I had a different life but my instinctive responses are not much different. For instance, I am basically an impatient person, quick to get annoyed, egoistic and self-centered. However, I have learnt to suppress these characteristics somewhat. Most people will probably agree that I now come across as a fairly decent person. I doubt that they will think so if I let my first reactions take expression.

I find confirmation in my opinion in my three adult children. It will be tempting to take credit for their success in their chosen endeavours. But their basic qualities were predictable when they were babies. They developed these with and without assistance from their parents as they grew up. It would be erroneous to suggest that nurturing created their qualities; at best nurturing helped in their flowering. My two young grandchildren already demonstrate qualities they were born with which they will retain whatever their parents and teachers do.

There is more. I can connect behavior patterns of the kids to my parents or grandparents quite clearly. For example, no random process could make one of my daughters so similar to my maternal grandmother. The similarity has to be transferred through the genes, exactly how is not for this layman to say. What I could say, though, is that if my grandmother were living today, she would be more like my daughter than like any one else I know. If I were a believer in ancient Hindu scriptures, I would say that my daughter is the reincarnation of my grandmother; the soul of my long dead grandmother is alive and well in my daughter. You may define soul the way Hindu philosophers did; the life element that lives in the heart and escapes at the death and moves into another body. Or it may be the particular pattern of DNA which got transmitted to my daughter through two generations and defines her the way it defined my grandmother. In other words, what Hindu philosophers called soul is functionally the same as what geneticists call DNA. Irrespective of Kipling's century old observation, twains do meet although in most unexpected spheres.

~ 5 ~

Gravitational force exerted by one mass on the other is inversely proportional to the square of distance. It follows that you must be close if you want to have an impact on someone. Closer you are more effective you will be. Stay distant and kiss the relationship goodbye.

Gravity works both ways. Closer you are to some one, more impact they will have on you. If you resist their impact, the distance will grow. It is fine if you wish this to happen. However, resistance is often due to pride and distance grows in spite of the desire, even need, of a loving relationship. Conversely, if you do not resist, the distance gradually shrinks and the growth cycle takes over.

Law of gravity demands that you open your heart and mind to one you love. Open heart and open mind means that when you hear words, you also hear the feelings behind those words; you sense the ideas trying to find expression in them. If you are not able to go beyond words, look within yourself. Why is the heart shut tight? Why does the brain disconnect with the ear?

If one person will not open to the other, other person will start closing as well, i.e. start becoming distant. Before long the relationship will cease to exist. It may be what the parties want. But if it is not, they have to look deep into their selves and then open up to the other if they genuinely want to love the other. Do not expect reciprocation straight away. It will come in due course. The incontrovertible law of Physics demands it.

Opening yourself to someone does not mean accepting every wart in their personality and absorbing it. It means you face up to it, find the cause behind it, and bring your impact on him to modify it. Remember, gravity works both ways. If the close friend is an addict, you can help her if you listen with empathy; establish what drove him into that hell, work at the cause and cure of addiction simultaneously. If you are unsympathetic, your behavior towards the addict will increase the distance and reduce your impact.

If you are not able to open your heart and mind, you are distant. You can stay distant but do not expect the other person to feel greater attraction than the distance permits. If you want them to love you, you must reduce the distance; you must open yourself to them. You must express your true feelings. Not in anger, but directly and honestly. Similarly, you absorb their feelings and react to them with empathy. This is the most vital step towards the goal of total relationship. In an ultimate relationship the effective distance is zero. Both know and feel at the same time irrespective of the physical distance between them because an unseen delicate communication line connects two bodies that have spiritually united into one.

~ 6 ~

I was brought up by my devout Hindu parents to believe that Atma, the soul, is what separates living beings from inanimate objects; living beings possess it and inanimate objects don't. Atma, a long lost part of Paramatma - Prime soul, finds temporary shelter in a body at its creation and gives it life. The body becomes lifeless when soul leaves it and moves on to reside in another body, much like we change our clothes at the end of the day. Karma, the sum of actions of the body in this incarnation, determines whether the soul will move to a higher or lower life form in the next cycle. Therefore, I was taught to devote my life to the selfless service of others so that my soul can move higher in the following life, ultimately achieving Nirvana - the reunion with Prime Soul. My Christian friends, on the other hand, believe that the physical body is resurrected on the day of the judgment. Soul is a part of the body and presumably stays with the body after death. I discovered that according to all major religions, noble thoughts spring from the soul because soul is in close contact with the Creator. Many modern psychologists proposed that soul, or subconscious, is the depository of the experience of past generations and an individual needs to pay attention to the directives from the soul, rather than the ego or outside sources.

As an atheist, I do have difficulty believing in the existence of soul. It is not a part of the body that can be observed. All

SUDHIR JAIN

my physical and mental activity can be explained as a function
of organs. My thought processes originate in the brain and are
controlled to a large extent by my experiences stored in my
memory. I have observed that some of my, and my children's,
basic characteristics were passed to us from older generations
through DNA and others were acquired through training during
the childhood and experiences during the lifetime. This leads
me to believe in two aspects of human personality; an inner
self and an outer self. Inner self is what I truly am. Whether
I consider the inner self as the wisdom of the ages passed on
to me through my DNA, my deep subconscious, the voice of
God or my soul is immaterial. The important issue is that it
originates from deep within me and is nearest to my real wish.
I think it is noble because it is the call of my noble self. Outer
self is what physical convenience and worldly considerations
force me to be and what I present to others. Two selves must be
in close harmony for me to be happy and relaxed. Conversely,
wider the gulf between the inner and the outer self, more
stressed and unhappy I will be. Two real life cases illustrate
my point. A homemaker friend really wanted to serve a larger
community rather than just her family. But she spent all her
time and energies focused on the family. Stressed and unhappy,
she developed various short- and long-term illnesses. Medical
prescriptions cured the symptoms but stresses did not go away
till she trained and joined a public service profession for part
of her day. Similarly, a highly successful executive friend was
stressed beyond endurance because he really wanted to paint.
He blamed his difficult job and responsibilities for the stresses
he was under and sought professional help when his work
started to suffer. On his analyst's advice, he took up painting

as a hobby. His stress level reduced significantly and his job performance reached a new level.

I learnt to suppress my inner self from early childhood. It was important to please my parents who were not happy when I did my own thing contrary to their wishes. I learnt later that discipline is often confused by adults and children alike with suppression of one's wishes in order to please others, rather than to focus on what one really wants and disregard temptation to seek short term pleasure. I have observed that happy and truly successful people learn to listen to the inner self and act in harmony with it. Doing the convenient thing is not for them. Because they are happy, they please others while being themselves and not by acting against their basic principles.

How do I find my real inner self? I have spent all my life covering the inner self layer by layer as I suppress it to please my family, teachers, neighbors and friends by doing what they expected of me rather than what I wished of myself. I can not strip off all the layers at once. It has to be done in small steps. I am now determined to listen to the whispers from within and be deaf to the clamor from outside As I pay attention to this soft inner voice, interpret its message and put it in practice, I hope to begin discovering the source of the message, the stage of my development the message is from. And each time I do this, I will strip off a layer and get closer to true me. If I live long enough, one day I will reach my true inner self and live in ultimate harmony. Then, I would have achieved the blessed stage sages called Nirvana.

~ 7 ~

There is an old proverb — the flutter of a butterfly wing may be the source of a thunderstorm somewhere far away. A surgeon in Toronto moving a few hundred kilometers to another country set me thinking here in Calgary three thousand kilometers away. The thoughts set strange reverberations in me with great potential to change my life for the better.

Globe and Mail reported recently that yet another surgeon was leaving Canada. According to the report, a two years long waiting list was the main spur for the decision to relocate and the multifold salary increase was barely mentioned. Brain drain to more prosperous countries is a familiar story. I myself have moved countries four times, telling friends each time that it was the working conditions that prompted the move. The locals were wonderful, I told them in all sincerity, as were the country and the living conditions. The jump in salary was only incidental. But I knew, and they knew too, that salary was the main motivation and protestations were a way of reducing the underlying feeling of guilt. I had used their hospitality and the resources of the country and moved on when it suited me.

Large-scale emigration of medical specialists has resulted in patients having to wait longer for all except the most critical ailments. Delays in treatment, particularly operations like hip replacement, are stressful and the situation needs to be improved. The privatization of health care would make the waiting lists shorter for those who can afford it. Alternatively, the publicity regarding the surgeon's move may prompt the governments to work on improving the medical system and attract more young people into the profession. In the meantime, Canada can continue to attract professionals from the developing countries and deprive them of most of their home grown professionals. The plight of third world citizens going without medical care strikes a chord with me because of my experience as a young man in India. My younger brother was a brilliant student and a stellar career was his for the taking. But this was not to be. He had a complex heart condition which could not be treated locally. Doctors who could have performed the necessary operation had moved to bigger cities and many of them to the West. Our family did not have the means to move to Delhi for an extended period and my brother passed away at the tender age of 20. I left India for good a few months later. My father died of broken heart within a year.

A normal person would feel sorry for not having done more for his brother. But I felt relief rather than sorrow at his death as it helped relieve the dire financial straits of the family. I could now accept a scholarship to go to England rather than stay home to support the family. Realization of selfish side of my personality a few months later gave me a feeling of guilt which I tried to assuage by sending money to my mother even though I was quite hard up during the student years. However, the feeling would not go away.

SUDHIR JAIN

This experience may have had a profound impact on my personality. As a young man I felt hurt easily. For example, when I was eleven, an uncle told me off for going around the house barefoot. This made me cry for hours and stay away from him for weeks. However, I assumed an insensitive persona in adulthood, nothing bothered me. I could work my way out of almost impossible situations without emotional involvement. It had its pluses in business but in personal life it has been a disaster. Monica and daughters need a husband and a father who feels their joys and pains and reacts accordingly. I, on the other hand, coldly looked at events and pointed out the folly of their feelings. I was often right in analysis of the situation but the cold rationalistic approach moved me further and further out from the emotional core of their beings. I realized this during a long lonely walk in a forest and now I desperately want to get close to their hearts. To do that, I must change myself and to do that I must identify and defeat the demons hidden in my subconscious. I have exposed one, let me mention another. When I was thirteen and my family was going through a particularly rough patch, I was awarded some money for a scholastic achievement. My mother suggested that the purchase of a sewing machine would be a big help to her and the family. But I bought a bike. It may seem trivial, a typical childish act, but the helplessness of a mother in face of the selfishness of the son for whom she was sacrificing her total self, has haunted me ever since and no doubt added to my insensitivity in later years. I do not know if it has made me less selfish.

Thinking of childhood in a socially upscale but financially

threadbare family, I discovered the source of my feeling of insecurity. One aspect of this insecurity is my absolute need to provide for the family, come hell or high water. Another is the great care I exercise in my financial dealings in spite of inherent entrepreneurial spirit. The other side of the coin is that this insecurity may have contributed to my inability to share genuine feelings with others. This failing keeps me at a distance from friends. Therefore, I have few close friends and do not miss them. Several instances of my insensitive behavior have made worse this sense of insecurity and driven me more into my shell. This has stopped me from achieving my full potential professionally. On a lighter note, it made me a compulsive eater. I eat food not for nourishment or taste but because it is there and fitting in the suit is a constant struggle.

Will these reverberations become a thunderstorm that moves me to find and defeat my demons and get me emotionally closer to my loved ones? I am working on it.

~ 8 ~

It is a fine winter morning. Clear blue sky, squirrels running about happily in the yard, sun making its way into our world. While contemplating my day before I get out of bed, it strikes me that it is the birth day of my younger brother Ramu. He would have been sixty five if he were alive. And my life would have been very different. On a stormy afternoon forty five summers ago he moved on to a better world. He was sick, had been for a long time. I was the main breadwinner in the family and my parents depended on my income to support themselves and their dying son. After his untimely but expected passing at the age of twenty, I was free to accept a scholarship to go to England for graduate studies. I married an English girl who grew into a wonderful mother and wife as well as an admired member of her profession. Life couldn't be any better except....

After I reduced my work load as a geophysicist in the oil patch, I started writing. I wrote short letters to the newspapers and the magazines at first and then essays and short stories as well. As the files containing published letters bulged, others containing unpublished stories were bursting at the seams. On Monica's suggestion, I collected the better ones and sent them to a publisher friend of a friend. I also sent individual stories to various magazines, from local community papers to the New

Yorker. The only replies, if there were any, were courteous rejections. I did get two essays published in our national newspaper which were well received. Overall, the response of the editors to my stories was discouraging, to say the least.

On this fine morning I did something I never do before my morning regimen of long workout and hurried breakfast. I went to the computer and checked the email messages. Lo and behold! The friend of the friend wants to publish the book and wants it out in three months. Great news but there was no one to share it with. Monica was away visiting the daughters in Vancouver. It was too early to phone her and I couldn't tell any one else before she knew it. I did call her three hours later and sent messages to the family gloating on my success. It would only be the second book authored by someone in our otherwise highly educated family; following our professor daughter's book published last year.

What is the connection in my long gone brother's birthday and the most flattering news I had received for a while? I have had many pieces of good news of late; my family members recovering their health after critical illness being the most important. There were pieces of bad news too but none of these reached us on any notable day. In any event, these were progression of events culminating in the finale, happy or tragic. The acceptance by the publisher, on the other hand, was a distinct event that occurred on a specific day quite out of the dark screen. And that was the day when Ramu was on my mind. More than Ramu, I was thinking of my own reaction when he passed away: Relief, rather than grief at a young life lost. After relief, there was the joy of anticipation – life in the West which turned out to be even better than I could have dreamed. Of course our parents were shattered. One son was gone and the other would be moving away. My father could not cope with it and joined his son a few months later. Our mother mourned her losses for rest of her life.

However much I try, I can not put away the feeling of guilt deep in my heart, the guilt due to my selfishness, inconsideration towards the grief of parents who had done their best for me, insensitivity towards a dying brother. The feeling was dormant for nearly forty years when I was occupied in building a career and providing for the family, raising its head only rarely only to be brutally suppressed by excuses which now seem hollow. The sentiment is stronger when something good happens to me. It is as if I do not deserve the compliments being showered on me; they properly belong to the one who gave away his life to enable the healthier brother to succeed.

One way to assuage the guilt would be to dedicate the book to Ramu. However, this dedication raises two issues. First, my two grandchildren started my writing career by providing suitable subjects for stories and Monica encouraged me in the endeavour, edited the material and made invaluable suggestions. Their claims are substantial because their contributions were direct and concrete. Second, the dedication has to be brief and it should not raise questions in a reader's mind which need a lengthy explanation to resolve.

After much consideration I have decided that the book will be dedicated to my granddaughters and Monica in public but also to my brother in the privacy of my heart. No dedication will recompense the debt that I owe Ramu. If he is watching from his abode, perhaps he will understand.

~ 9 ~

Looking after the sick is a job for some, duty for others and privilege for a few. When it is a job, you do it to make a living. The money is an important, though not the only, concern. This is how it should be. A professional has student loans from the past, bills in the present and contribution to pension funds and various insurance schemes for the future. An independent practitioner has payroll, rent, operating and other business expenses. A businessman disregards the cash inflow at his peril.

If a family member is sick, taking care of him or her is a duty. Many do it because that is expected of them. There is another motivation as well. I look after him when he is sick, he will reciprocate when I need to be cared for. While there may be a sense of accomplishment in discharging one's duty, there is not much joy in it. If it lasts long, the duty tends to become increasingly bothersome and eventually a burden.

Caring for someone you love is a privilege. The pain of the loved one, be it the spouse, the parent, the child or an intimate friend, is my pain, her relief is my relief from my pain. There is no joy for one whose loved one is in distress except in the relief and in being the agent of the relief. One does the caring because one must. Not being able to care for the beloved when he needs it is much more than a disappointment; it is a wound one carries in her heart for as long as she lives. The greater the unattended need of the beloved, deeper the wound.

When a critical illness of a family member is discovered, every member suffers a shock. Of course, the biggest shock is felt by the ill person himself. Others quickly recover, at least superficially, and take over roles to handle the new situation. When our daughter's cancer was discovered, her partner and mother took over the caregiver roles. My role was a back stop, doing the cleaning up behind them. When Monica's cancer was discovered a year later, I was the only family member within one thousand kilometers. In both cases caregivers felt the grief of the sick and did all they could to improve her situation. Being a caregiver was a privilege although no one would have expressed it that way. During our daughter's illness many of her friends and her youngest sister visited most weekends and stayed with us. Although these visits increased the workload on us considerably, they were most welcome because our daughter felt better in their company. During Monica's illness, the circumstances of our daughters changed and their visits were few and far between. I became the primary care giver and there was no back stop. Fortunately, in a family of two there is much less to do than in a family of six with two toddlers.

I have learnt a few things from these experiences of caring for the critically sick. One important lesson is that one can be so occupied in caring that the concern becomes a little overpowering. It took me a long time to learn to hold back so that the caring did not suffocate the loved one. Sick still have their personal needs and wishes which sometimes conflict with those of the caregiver. While caring is a privilege, the caregiver must realize that the needs and wishes of the sick have the priority. After all, it is the sick whose morale is low and needs building up. More serious the illness, more important is this consideration.

I did not realize until it was almost too late that it is normal for an otherwise active person to feel depressed when suffering from a long disability. There is anger too at the suffering and the dependence on others. Much to my regret, I was a cause of this anger on a number of occasions. Anger and/or depression can take many forms. Whatever the mode of expression, these tend to be focused on the primary caregiver. She is the closest and responsible for almost every act. She is the one whose errors make the impact and she is the one who becomes the focus of anger. It is at times like these when the care giver needs patience and understanding howsoever difficult it may be. I miserably failed in this respect as in many other ways. Care giver can not forget that sick person is the weak and the helpless; he is the one who is less able to be patient and to understand. Caregiver must not fight back; the patient needs to be soothed, not put in his place.

Let us face it; the care giver is a human, not a machine. She needs rest and recuperation. In fact, the care giver needs to care for herself almost as much as the patient. There is a tendency to postpone the rest because there are so many things to do. But *recreation* can not be delayed for ever. There comes a point when the energy level drops below the critical level and the caregiver begins to feel that she is being taken advantage of or the patient is exercising undue control on her or the patient is not pulling her weight. A physically and/or mentally tired person also becomes less efficient. The patient may begin to feel neglected and protest. This is a danger point and many a relationships have hit the rocks because it was not appropriately dealt with. Once again the onus is on the caregiver. She must realize when she has to have a break and arrange to have it. Young parent can lean on the parents, older spouse on adult children, friends or on social services. Caregiver must appreciate that she is the one who is in charge – not only of the patient but herself as well. She must do all that is necessary to maintain physical and mental strength to keep control of the situation. If she fails to do so, the consequences could be dire indeed.

If the caregiver has most of the responsibility and all the work, what about the patient? Patient has the tougher job of the two, overcoming the disease. Fighting the disease must be the primary focus of the patient. This does not preclude the patient from helping or even working on his job but *only when he is feeling up to it*. At other times the caregiver has to be indulgent and work extra hard to minimize the stresses on the patient. In my case, the patient carried on with a number of responsibilities, both professional and at home which added greatly to the stress level. Then there were events beyond our control which contributed to major upsets. Unfortunately, each such incident took away vital energy from fighting the demon and may have prolonged the illness. The patient does not want to be upset but is sometimes unable to cope with the total volume of external and internal stresses caused by the illness and misunderstandings with or misdeeds of the caregiver. It needs great compassion, quick thinking and considerable tact on the part of the caregiver to deal with some situations. Unfortunately, caregiver is also under some stress, particularly if illness has lasted a while and she may not be able to muster these qualities. In our case I never had them in abundance any way. Monica was wise to seek the advice of appropriate professionals and it helped us both overcome our stresses.

A life threatening illness has an impact that can last long after the patient has recovered. Caregiver can not relax and the patient must not be rushed to assume full charge of life as it was before the illness. Return to normalcy is a step by step process, the size of step depending on the particular case. Hopefully, with mutual love and open hearts each difficulty will be overcome and the couple will look back at the time of their trial with satisfaction one feels after a difficult job has been done particularly well.

10

The pastor of my wife's church chooses exotic topics for his sermons. Last week he planned to talk about food and its relationship to God. To drive the point home he organized a pot luck "appetizer feast" after the service. My wife contributed our favorite snack for the occasion. I have loved food ever since my mother heartlessly pulled me away from breast almost seventy years ago. A combination of the best samosas in town and the delectable dishes to be contributed by other members of the congregation was too much to resist and this self-proclaimed atheist accompanied his wife to church. I have met the clergy and several members of the congregation on social occasions. The thought of renewing their acquaintance was also an incentive.

After some jazzy devotional songs by a youth group, the assistant pastor read her selection from the Bible. She chose the piece about sin and how the sinners are redeemed by their belief in an all forgiving God. Sin is generally defined as an act of offense against other life forms and I am well aware of countless such acts in my life. The quotes chosen by the speaker emphasized that there was no prospect of sins of non-believers like me being forgiven. At this point I started to recount to myself the varieties of sins that I have indulged in. There are sins of commission – unkind acts, let us be merciful and not count thoughts, towards family, friends and foes. Disregarding the oft expressed wishes of wife and children, criticism of friends in their absence to their colleagues or friends, attempting to get 'enemies' fired from their jobs are some of the examples. These sins may not appear to be as bad as physical abuse of family members, seducing the neighbor's wife or murdering a competitor but they are sins regardless and there is no way of knowing how much harm they inflicted on the victims.

Sins of omission are countless. Not defending wife's professional reputation when the opportunity demanded it, not establishing an emotional bond with the daughters, not helping friends when they needed it, being insensitive to the needs of colleagues, – the list goes on. I commit many of these every day without even noticing. I know that many people are doing similar acts, and some worse. But does this knowledge absolve me of my sins? It may console me but at the end of the day I have not helped when I should have and this realization leaves a bitter taste.

There is another kind of sin which is not often recognized. A close friend tells me of a slight she suffered. Rather than share her feeling of hurt I hypothesize about the reasons behind the slight. Whether my hypothesis is right or wrong, my action is a sin, albeit committed with the best of intention. Rather than offer her empathy I have tried to justify the person that hurt her thus compounding the original slight. One can call this a Sin of Ignorance. It can be more devastating and harder to forgive than any other sin. It so happens that due to my gross insensitivity I specialize in such responses.

When I was younger hurting others did not bother me.

It was part of living; you had to do what you had to do. But lately the thought of being a conscious and/or subconscious sinner has begun to upset me. I can not bring myself to believe in redemption of my sins by an outside agency. On the other hand, I do not relish the thought of punishment although I think I have endured it in the past with reasonable grace and will endure whatever form it takes for the rest of my life. But I do want to stop sinning. One could argue that if I am sincere in my wish I can accomplish this easily. All I need to do is to be deliberate in my verbal and physical responses, think from all angles before any action and then act in a way that will be, to use what has now become a cliché, a win-win for all involved.

Most of the joy of living originates in spontaneous activity. Deliberation is an enemy of spontaneity. I know people who are spontaneous, enjoy life to the full and manage to do so without hurting any one. These are the people with proverbial "heart of gold." They are like a natural spring where generations of all life forms have gone to quench their thirst and will do for generations to come. I have to face it. I am not a natural spring. I am like a fissure through which natural gas escapes. The gas can be useful if it can be harnessed or dangerous if it is allowed to poison the atmosphere. Irrespective of what I have been and how much poison I have spewed out, I must decide what direction I want to take. It is going to be difficult; after all I have grown accustomed to shooting from the hip. But only way for me is to control my emissions if I want to feel good in myself. This atheist owes it not only to himself but to all who have given him sustenance through his long life. This can be his only redemption.

~ *11* ~

It was a beautiful afternoon on August 14, 1965 when Monica and I exchanged our vows in a church in Selhurst, a suburb of London, England. After moving internationally three times, drastic career changes, three children, several near fatal experiences in the family any one of which would have destroyed many relationships, we are still together in our sunset years.

Our marriage, solemnized in presence of immediate family of Monica and some close friends, was not generally expected to last. Her parents thought Monica was too young at 21 and our six year age difference was too much. Her friends expected her to give up on a dictatorial Indian husband sooner or later. My friends thought I will find the family a hindrance in the achievement of my career goals. They were right with their basic assumptions but wrong in the conclusion.

I am not gloating that we proved them wrong; just thankful that, in spite of their fears, we received from them full support when we needed it. 45 years is a long time to go through without trials and tribulations. We certainly had our share of these. Several events that appeared catastrophic then, look laughable in the hindsight now. Irritations of life in the Third World like receiving notice to evacuate the villa after the overthrow of the king in Libya, anxiety about work visas when preparing to move to the U.S. and Canada, coping with our first sand storm in Tripoli or the first winter in Calgary and many other such occurrences caused stresses at the time but nothing compared to major events: birth of our oldest daughter in England when Monica felt desperately lonely and physically and emotionally exhausted having been evacuated from Libya with expatriate wives and children during the six-day war in June 1967; the decision to leave Philadelphia soon after we had finished renovation of our new home; the period of Monica's excruciating migraines which lasted several years, her decision to go to medical school soon after our third daughter was born, discovering that two of our daughters were gay, extreme premature birth of our second granddaughter, serious illness of our daughter and Monica immediately following one another, developmental and behavioral problems of our older granddaughter and lately drastic reduction in our retirement funds by stock market meltdown were each major stress points. Just the survival of the relationship through them all is a testament to its inherent strength.

Monica and I share some characteristics which are crucial to a stable relationship. We believe firmly in the sanctity of marriage and family is the most important element in our lives. We are glad to do what we can for each other or any of the progeny. Thus, when our granddaughter was born premature, or our daughter had a serious illness, or our daughter-in-law needed to stay with us for an extended period, we both welcomed them with open arms. When I was lost in the forest, Monica and the three daughters left whatever they were doing and rushed thousands of kilometers to help with the search.

When Monica was ill, I did all I could to help her recover. In good times, Monica helped me integrate in the Western societies in England, United States and Canada and helped me in my business; I helped her in preparation for med school and in management of her practice and we helped our girls earn seven university degrees between them without significant student loans. We have taken pride in achievements of the other as if they were our own and have rejoiced in those of our children.

Needless to say there were times of serious strain in the relationship some of which I have mentioned already. We handle our stresses differently. Monica expresses her feelings strongly and I am left in no doubt as to the level of her stress. For a long time I fruitlessly suggested corrective measures for her problem and learnt only recently that what she needed was an expression of empathy; the solution could come later. On the other hand, I bear my stress silently and work my way out of the wood on my own. It works for us because we make allowances for our differences. Important point is to understand the source of stress and help the partner handle it. We learnt early that taking other's problem lightly can have serious long term consequences.

Although we have very different professions there is a unity of purpose to our lives provided by our concern for other's well-being and family's general welfare coupled with shared interests in classical music, opera and literature. We belong to different faiths but are guided by essentially similar principles in our daily actions. Therefore, our major conflicts are resolved without serious emotional injury. We have not built a large catalogue of past hurts and, even though the slate is not as clean as one would wish, it has plenty of space for fresh designs in our sunset years.

If there is a lesson to be derived from our relationship it could be expressed in one word: Consideration. What partner feels, thinks, says and does is at least as important as what you feel, think, say and do and deserves equal consideration on your part. It does not matter what others think, or how it is rewarded. What matters is that someone more important to you than any one else in the world will not be happy if his/her emotions, ideas, words or actions are not valued by someone who is more important to him/her than any one else in the world. If one partner is not happy, the other can not be happy. This is the essence of a good and durable relationship.

~ 12 ~

My family history is strange, even for someone born and brought up in India when it was the jewel of British Empire. My mother was born in a landowning family. Although the only child, she was deprived of her inheritance because of her gender. My father, the son of a well-to-do civil servant, focused on sports and fun as a teenager and did not finish grade school. He was a debonair young man who won the heart of his fourteen year old cousin by uncle's marriage who resisted all sane advice and insisted on marrying him. My mother loved him to her dying day although he never earned a rupee, never helped with the chores and left it to her to fend for the family. She did this by first selling her jewellery and silk saris that came with her dowry, and when these ran out, begging from her mother and rich aunt at whose mansion she had met my father. I never heard a word of complaint from her mouth about my father's inability to provide for the family. Her only comment was "at least he doesn't drink or gamble." She had a grade two education but loved to read whatever was available. A proud woman, she inculcated a desire to do well in her three sons. We worshipped her and spent our childhood years disregarding our father.

The motto of my life, even after he was long dead, was "not to be like my father." He was a poor student, I worked hard to be the top in the class; he was a good sportsman, I avoided sports; he could spend the whole day apparently doing nothing, I had to be busy every second I was awake; he was religious, I became an atheist; he did not provide for his family, I worked long hours to make sure my wife and daughters got everything they needed to develop their talents, whether to become an Olympian or the respected professionals. Unlike my mother, I never had a good word for my father and never understood what she saw in him. It took a long discussion with a psychologist friend on my childhood for me to start seeing him and his relationship with my mother in a new light. "He does not have any bad habits" meant that he respected my mother and never had a harsh word for her. It meant he was proud of her and their children and never uttered an unpleasant word about them outside the home. It also meant that he said his piece but left it to us to decide its worth. If I were to be honest, I could not claim any of the above.

During my visit to India last year I had several discussions about him with my brothers. One of them pointed out that social customs of the day prevented our father from doing menial jobs which would have reduced the 'standing' of the family in society, making it harder for the children to grow up to be successful. Similarly, my mother could not work as a maid or a cook without her sons ending up in menial jobs too. In any event, such jobs would not have provided the means family needed for anything but the most basic necessities. My uneducated mother understood these implications and wanted more, much more, for her sons than mere survival. She wanted them to grow up into adults others looked up to, not looked down upon as her rich cousins tended to do. Strange though it may seem, I chose to disregard this aspect till recently. It is now obvious to me that the dye was cast for my father in his teenage and for my mother at birth. Thanks to his upbringing by an alcoholic mother my father, who was a decade younger than his siblings, did not develop the confidence needed to run a business nor the personality to supervise people. My mother was of the wrong gender to inherit the wealth and status due to her but she retained a burning ambition to acquire it through her progeny. It has taken me most of my years to appreciate what should have been clear long ago: It is to the immense credit of *both* my parents that they were able to hold the family together and maintain a respectable social status, whatever the emotional cost, for the sake of the future of their children. "Children is all we had" my mother said to me the last time we met before she passed away. I now realize that my father's love for my mother - which she reciprocated fully - kept the family together and enabled us brothers to make the best of the genes we inherited. I owe a huge debt, not only to my mother which I always acknowledged, but also to my father who struggled with his inner demons in silence all his life. I so regret that it is now too late to tell him this realization in person.

~ *13* ~

Monica and I are professionals who have worked hard and, we like to think, won respect of our colleagues. We have been married for forty five years and have three daughters. They are successful career women and we are justifiably proud of their achievements. Although spread out over three cities and two countries, ours is a close knit family. I have lived and worked in five countries on four continents and we have been fortunate in being able to travel to interesting destinations on business as well as for pleasure. We had our ups and downs, emotionally and physically, but overall gods of fortune were kind to us.

It so happens that Monica and I were on a cruise to Alaska when I crossed into my eighth decade. I did not feel any different on the day I turned seventy than on the day I was sixty nine - or sixty one if you asked me then. We had spent last few years in helping our adult kids get over their physical and emotional crises. Even in normal circumstances it was our practice on visits to our daughters that Monica took over the cooking, I did the dishes and both helped with other household chores and gardening. When kids visited us we took time off from work and looked after the grandchildren in addition to preparing meals, cleaning, washing, even making their beds while they renewed their old friendships. But what difference does a year make! Something vital changed when I stepped into seventies and approached the average life expectancy of a Canadian male. First, the short term memory departed, perhaps for good. Then, appearances to the contrary, my energy level dropped. I do not seem to have much get up and go even when I can remember what to get up for. Taking over the households on visits to younger generation is no longer an option just as the extra workload when they visit us is hard to handle. To state the truth bluntly, *we are in a transition from caretakers of our progeny to the car taken by them.*

Monica is working hard to implement the transition. There are two important considerations in this process. First is the eventual move on some unforeseen but not too distant date to a smaller accommodation and second, the uncomplicated state of our affairs when we have taken our final leave. To get the ball rolling, Monica is reducing the 'possessions' cluttering our home which now shelters just two instead of the five it once did. Acquaintances are carting away for a pittance what they can use, charities are offered whatever they can take and the recyclables are transported to appropriate depots. The rest, a fully functional refrigerator, solid cupboards, a set of office furniture and miscellaneous household items are being sent to the Refuse Resource Station, commonly called The Dump, at the cost of several hundred dollars. Old appliances are gradually being replaced by new fool proof wonders of latest technology which will see us through our years of growing feebleness of body and mind without the expense and the hassle of waiting for repairmen to do what I would have happily done when my muscles were taut and limbs strong. Trusty ten year old Subaru Outback is being replaced by a new one that will serve us trouble free for our remaining period of independence - years before our driving license is taken away by a worried daughter if not by the province. We are considering the resumption of the delivery of the local paper so that we can check the obituary columns and make sure we do not miss any memorial service we should attend. After all if we do not go to our friends' final adieu who will come to ours.

On the positive note, we are reviewing our priorities for the remaining good years, not taking any specific number for granted. Having only recently settled, albeit provisionally, the unpleasant matters like wills and the funeral arrangements, we are focusing on what we wish to accomplish. This includes Monica working on complete recovery from her recent illness, finding a publisher for the novel I have just completed, volunteer activities to help the needy, travels to distant lands we have always wanted to visit but somehow never did and the timing and the best ways to fold our businesses. However, the most important aspect of this situation is not what we do or plan to do but how we feel within ourselves and towards each other. To this end, we renew in our hearts our forty five year old oath - to love and cherish the other; for better or worse - meaning that the better off will ungrudgingly look after the worse off whoever it happens to be at a particular time. Last but not the least, every night before closing our eyes we thank each other for the kindnesses during the day and exchange "I love you" just in case we do not open them again.

CPSIA information can be obtained at www.ICGtesting.com
Printed in the USA
BVOW071857181112

305828BV00001B/1/P